Dudley Bernard Egerton Pope was [...] ancient Cornish seafaring family. He [...] Navy at the age of sixteen and spent [...] sea. He was torpedoed during the Sec[...] resulting spinal injuries plagued him [...] Towards the end of the war he turned to journalism becoming the Naval and Defence Correspondent for the London *Evening News*. Encouraged by Hornblower creator C S Forester, he began writing fiction using his own experiences in the Navy and his extensive historical research as a basis.

In 1965 he wrote *Ramage*, the first of his highly successful series of novels following the exploits of the heroic Lord Nicholas Ramage during the Napoleonic Wars. He continued to live aboard boats whenever possible and this was where he wrote the majority of his novels. Dudley Pope died in 1997 aged seventy-one.

RAMAGE
AT TRAFALGAR

DUDLEY POPE

**HOUSE OF
STRATUS**

This edition published in 2001 by House of Stratus, an imprint of Stratus Books Ltd., Lisandra House, Fore Street, Looe, Cornwall, PL13 1AD, U.K.

www.houseofstratus.com

Typeset, printed and bound by House of Stratus.

A catalogue record for this book is available from the British Library and the Library of Congress.

ISBN 1-84232-475-6

For the Glass family,

- with memories of Italy.

AUTHOR'S NOTE

In this novel culminating at Trafalgar, all the facts concerning Nelson and the Battle are true: only the events surrounding Ramage are fiction. Of all the ships in the Battle only the *Victory* remains.

Dudley Pope
Yacht *Ramage*
French Antilles

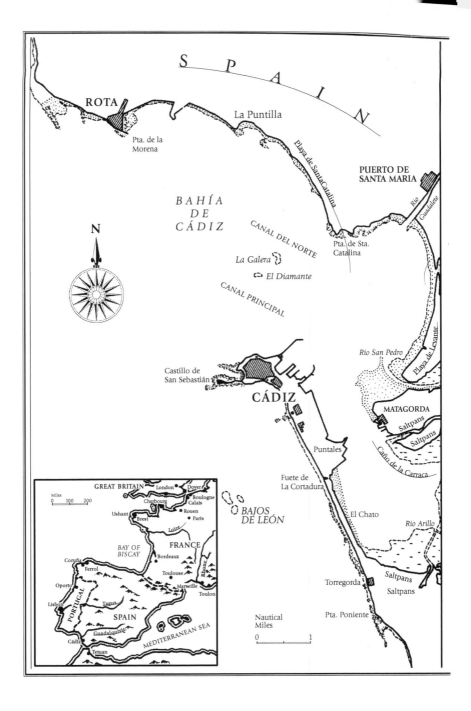

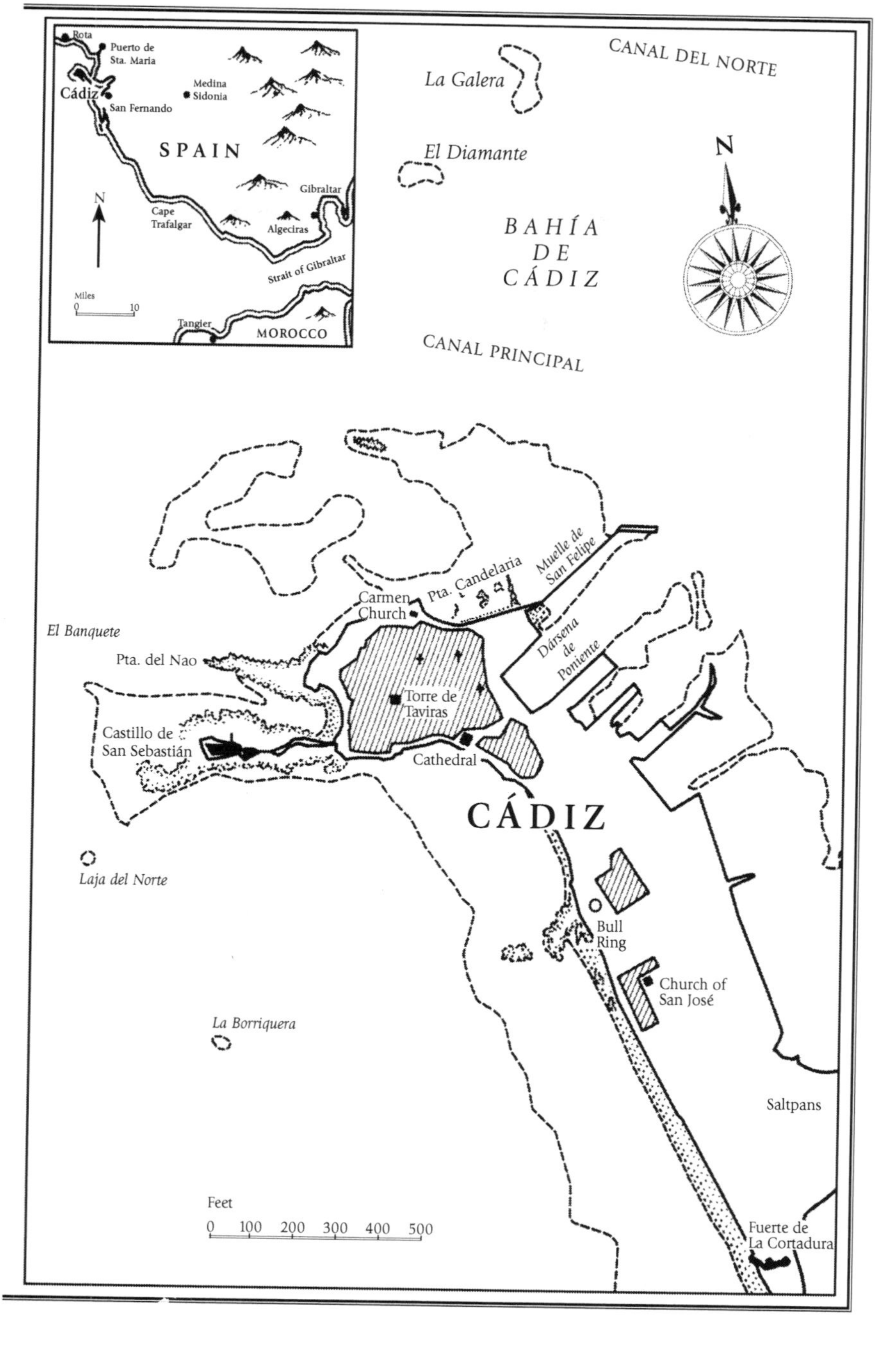

Rota
Puerto de Sta. Maria
Cádiz
San Fernando
Medina Sidonia
SPAIN
N
Gibraltar
Cape Trafalgar
Algeciras
Strait of Gibraltar
Miles
0
10
Tangier
MOROCCO
CANAL DEL NORTE
La Galera
El Diamante
N
BAHÍA DE CÁDIZ
CANAL PRINCIPAL
Muelle de San Felipe
Pta. Candelaria
Carmen Church
El Banquete
Pta. del Nao
Dársena de Poniente
Torre de Taviras
Castillo de San Sebastián
Cathedral
CÁDIZ
Laja del Norte
Bull Ring
Church of San José
La Borriquera
Saltpans
Feet
0 100 200 300 400 500
Fuerte de La Cortadura

CHAPTER ONE

The lawyer took the parchment from his worn leather case, carefully smoothed it out flat on the table and perched a pair of spectacles on his bulbous nose. "Your uncle's will is quite straightforward, My Lord," he assured Ramage. "In fact I drew it up for him myself after his wife – your aunt, of course – died so unexpectedly last winter."

Ramage nodded and glanced across the table at Sarah. The lawyer was a chubby little man with a red face, a redness caused by sun and wind rather than too much port, yet his air of being a prosperous farmer was curiously at odds with his irritatingly precise manner. He had placed the will squarely in front of him on the dining room table, which was serving as a desk, and taken great care to make sure the lower edge of the page was lying parallel with the side of the table. There is no way of hurrying this man, Ramage was trying to tell Sarah.

There was a curious air of unreality about the whole affair. The last time Ramage had sat at this table his uncle, Rufus Treffry, had been alive and well: alert and brisk of manner, he had seemed good for another twenty years. His aunt (his father's sister) seemed if anything younger.

Now both were lying side by side in the Treffry family vault at Saltwood Church, a few miles away, and the new owner of Treffry Hall and the several hundred acres belonging to it was Captain Lord Ramage of the Royal Navy...

1

"May I ask, My Lord, if you have made up your mind what you are going to do with the property?"

Property? A lawyer's word for what all his life he had thought of and referred to as "Uncle Rufus' place": an imposing, four-square brick house on the high land at Aldington overlooking the great flat sweep of Romney Marsh, with the Channel a blue line in the distance sweeping round to Dungeness, the point of land marking the south-eastern corner of Kent (and, for that matter, England too).

"I haven't thought about it," Ramage said. "I don't know the details of the bequest," he pointed out, nodding at the parchment. "I don't know whether or not my uncle made any provision for the servants, but they are certainly my responsibility now."

Uncle Rufus' butler, for instance. Raven was a sinister-looking man because of a long, wide scar across his left cheek, the result (as the man had explained to Ramage years earlier) of a misunderstanding with a Revenue officer – a polite way of admitting that he had been caught smuggling. But Raven, the perfect servant in the dining room yet equally able to make sure that the horse brought to the front door was glistening of coat and shiny of harness, had been an important part of Ramage's childhood (some of which had been spent in Italy). Staying with Uncle Rufus had meant exciting hours spent along the banks of sunken lanes with Raven, handling (and being nipped by) his ferrets, pegging nets over rabbit holes, or quietly skirting the edge of one of the woods, being taught how to stalk pheasant holding one of Uncle Rufus' second-best fowling pieces (were all those splendid guns included in the will?). And learning to ride – Raven had all the standards and sharp language of an Army riding master, and the fact that Ramage was now a good rider (though not an enthusiastic horseman) was entirely due to Raven.

Ferreting and rabbiting, shooting rocketing pheasants, riding a horse over the Downs or leaping the dykes and ditches that laced the Marsh, brushing horses' coats and polishing harness, hearing stories of Marsh smugglers and tales of strings of packhorses making their way in the moonlight from the sandy beaches off Romney and Camber and "the Ness" slung with barrels of smuggled brandy for the squire and lace for his lady...that was Raven. What *were* Raven's links with the smugglers? Ramage's concern was only curiosity; like most of the people living along the coasts of Kent and Sussex, he saw smugglers and smuggling as a part of life. Sensible folk looked the other way, and only a fool paid customs duty and excise on his liquor.

"Ah, yes," the lawyer said, "the staff are mentioned in the will."

"We would be interested in the details," Sarah said unexpectedly and the lawyer, unused to women (even the daughter of the Marquis of Rockley) taking an active role, looked startled.

"Yes, indeed, My Lady. Should I begin reading?"

"Unless you would like more tea?" She gestured towards the large silver urn that Raven had left at the end of the table. "Or perhaps something stronger?"

"Oh My Lady, no thank-you: never before noon, and rarely even then. My wife, you see. A very strong-minded woman, and if she smells liquor on my breath too early in the day, she thinks I will be damned."

"You will, too," Sarah said and then looked despairingly at her husband when she saw the little lawyer had taken her remark seriously. But at least he was now holding up the will with one hand and adjusting his spectacles with the other.

The man coughed twice, as though it was part of a ritual before reading a will, and then put the will down again. He looked up at Ramage.

"A copy of the relevant parts of the will was sent to your father to await your return to England, My Lord."

Ramage almost sighed aloud. How to explain to a lawyer that copies of documents mattered less than actions? That people owning large estates which had passed from father to son for generations took much for granted, so that a brief remark could describe as much as two pages of a lawyer's writings? Ramage had never seen the copy of the will sent to his father; when he had returned from this last affair in the Mediterranean his father had said simply that Rufus had died "and of course the property goes to you".

The "of course" took notice that Rufus had no children and that Ramage was his only nephew; it took in what they had all known for years, that Treffry Hall would go to Ramage – who else? But all that was mixed up with things like *noblesse oblige* and family affairs that lawyers never really understood because they could not be written down in their curiously stilted legal language. Stilted and legal, Ramage realized, because their phrases had stood the test of probate law and litigation and there was no mistaking the meaning, but nevertheless it always sounded stilted to ears that rejoiced in the rich flow of Shakespeare.

"Yes, so my father told me," Ramage said, "but circumstances prevented me from reading it. So please proceed…"

Again a deep breath, again a twitch at the spectacles, again two coughs, and the lawyer launched into the will. "I, Rufus Charles Aldington Treffry, being of sound mind…"

Aldington? Ramage thought as the lawyer droned through the preliminary phrases, I didn't know that was one of his names. Ramage knew the family was one of the oldest in Kent, and that Treffry Hall had a history almost as old as the county, but he had not realized that the Treffrys went so far back. One of the habits of belonging to such an old family as the Ramages was that you tended to regard almost everyone else as a *parvenu*! Although come to think of it, it was not part of family history that there had been any fuss when Admiral the Earl of Blazey's young sister had become engaged to and then wed a Kentish landowner.

Ramage was startled by a double cough and looked up to see the lawyer, spectacles now in his hand, looking at him. "We now come to the sections concerning you, My Lord," he said apologetically, clearly having noticed that Ramage's attention had wandered.

"Oh, indeed. Please continue," Ramage said, aware that Sarah was looking at him with an expression combining love and exasperation.

First came the bequests to the staff. A tidy lump sum for Raven, another for the housekeeper, and three more to the cook, gamekeeper and head gardener, "All of whom," the lawyer said as though an explanation was necessary, "had been in Mr Treffry's service for many years."

"And all of whom have been paid regularly since then by my father until I could get back to England and take over the management of the estate," said Ramage, irritated by the lawyer's almost patronizing manner.

"Oh, indeed, My Lord, and in any case I could have arranged a loan on their bequests, using the terms of the will as collateral."

Why is it, Ramage wondered, that just as I begin to think you are not a bad fellow after all, you make some crass remark like that?

The man resumed reading. Treffry Hall and all its furnishings and appurtenances, outbuildings, livestock and contents, and the land comprising the estate, was left to his nephew but (so Uncle Rufus was a realist, since Nicholas Ramage was a serving officer who had nearly been killed several times already) should that nephew predecease him, Rufus Treffry then indicated who should inherit.

Sarah went white, and for a moment Ramage thought she would faint. "But – but...he met me only once, at our wedding," she gasped. "To leave me all this if I was widowed!"

Ramage laughed to lighten the moment. "I shall make a point of staying alive to cheat you out of your inheritance!"

The lawyer, missing completely the lightness of Ramage's tone and not noticing Sarah's shock (after all, Ramage realized, the man had drawn up the will and the terms were no surprise to him), said: "Well, My Lady, I expect it will all come to you anyway if anything happens to His Lordship."

Sarah, knowing just how many times she had already just missed being widowed since her marriage, and how many times Nicholas had nearly lost his life since she first met him, nodded politely. "I'm sure it will," she said, trying to keep the chill from her voice. "Pray continue."

The lawyer was near the end of the will. Rufus Treffry had obviously been very proud of his collection of armour, and also his sporting guns, and he expressed the hope "though creating no trust in the matter" that his legatee would continue to maintain all the pieces in good condition. "In fact the butler, Raven, has looked after them for many years," the lawyer explained, oblivious to the fact that as a boy Nicholas Ramage had delighted in helping Raven.

Finally the lawyer took another document from his case. "The deeds to the property, My Lord." He searched for another sheet and then handed it over. "That is just a note delineating the boundaries of your land, My Lord. You may wish to ride round the boundaries. I am sure that Raven knows them well."

No better than I, Ramage thought. As a boy, when he was allowed to borrow one of Uncle Rufus' fowling pieces, it was curious how the best game always seemed to be roaming the neighbours' fields. To a lawyer (and to an Uncle Rufus if Ramage was caught) it was poaching, but to a young boy it had been a great adventure. And now Treffry Hall and its estate was all his. His and Sarah's. And at Chatham Dockyard his frigate was being refitted after a long period in the Mediterranean.

Ramage was lounging in an armchair watching Sarah embroidering a cushion cover the following afternoon when Raven tapped on the door and came in with a silver salver, which he offered to Ramage.

Ramage looked at the packet resting in the middle of the salver. It was too thick to be just a newsy letter from his father. He recognized the griffin seal and the handwriting, but it was obviously a packet which also contained other letters.

"This has just arrived, sir," Raven said, and when Ramage had taken the packet he turned to Sarah. "Is there anything your ladyship requires?"

Sarah smiled and held up the embroidery. "I'm almost out of silks," she said.

Raven nodded understandingly. "I'll talk to my friends, madam. A selection of colours?"

Sarah frowned, looking at her work, and then nodded.

"A day or two, milady," Raven said.

By then Ramage had broken the seal of the packet and found that it contained a brief letter from his father and another letter whose cover was closed by a large seal showing a slim woman wearing a crown and standing with an anchor at her feet.

"Who on earth is that from?" Sarah asked as Raven left the room as silently as he had arrived.

"The gentlemen at Lloyd's, from the look of it," Ramage said, breaking the seal. "Don't say some damned shipowner is complaining about that convoy I brought home from Barbados... No, the Committee of Lloyd's would have written to Their Lordships, and then the Admiralty would write to me…"

"Open it!" Sarah urged. "Why speculate when you're holding the answer in your hand?"

How did he explain? "You've no idea how peaceful it is just sitting here in front of the fire, watching you sewing, and knowing no first lieutenant or master is going to come to me with a problem. And knowing that there are no orders from Their Lordships in the top drawer of my desk which I have to carry out or "answer to the contrary at my peril". You want some smuggled silks, Raven wants to take the bay mare down to the farrier, cows have knocked down about four yards of a spile fence on the south side of the beechwood meadow, and the housekeeper wants to know if she should tell Raven to bring up another case of sherry from the cellar. That's all. No strange sail on the horizon, no ship's company to send to general quarters just before dawn, no orders in the drawer…"

"And a loving wife to share your bed," Sarah said unexpectedly.

"Especially that," Ramage said, breaking the seal of the letter and then deliberately putting it to one side while he read the letter from his father.

"Father and mother send their love…Hanson spilled soup over Lady Cardington's dress…oh yes, and the dear lady was so enraged that father sacked Hanson on the spot and re-engaged him as soon as Her Ladyship had left!"

"It sounds to me as though Hanson and your father have an arrangement!"

"Oh, they have," Ramage said. "He's been with us about forty years, and you know how his spectacles keep sliding down his nose? Well, without the spectacles he can't see a thing, and probably as he served the soup his spectacles slipped, so while one hand reached up for the spectacles, the other tilted the soup tureen! Means Lady Cardington never gets invited to dinner again!"

Sarah looked puzzled until Ramage explained. "If she came and found Hanson still in the house, she'd be most upset. As far as father is concerned, Hanson is worth any dozen guests like Lady Cardington!"

"Isn't she the woman with a very deep voice, married to that extraordinary fat Welshman?"

"Yes – he was created about five years ago and she has never got over suddenly becoming a lady without any effort on her part. A bass voice and a falsetto brain – my mother's opinion!"

"And Lloyd's?" Sarah asked as Ramage put down his father's letter. "I think you're scared of it!"

"No, just savouring it. After all, one doesn't want to eat the tastiest thing first."

"I always do," Sarah said firmly "I can't bear the suspense."

Ramage put the letter down, stood up and walked over to select a thick log before putting it on the fire.

"You've never seen me in a temper yet," Sarah said, "but when I let myself go…"

Ramage glanced at her and stared at an ankle showing below the hem of her dress. "I'll wager ten guineas to an empty bottle you stamp your foot!"

"Oh, you are a beast! *Read the letter!*"

"I know what it says, so there's no hurry."

"*What* does it say, then?"

"The Master and Committee of Lloyd's request the pleasure of our company at a dinner being given to some visiting bashaw, and we are not going all the way to London for that!"

He sat down and picked up the letter. A couple of minutes later, after he was obviously beginning to read it a third time, Sarah said ominously: "Well?"

"Well, it's not for some bashaw after all." Ramage said lamely. "It's a dinner, though."

"For whom?"

"Me, actually," Ramage said, his voice a mixture of puzzlement and modesty.

"Nicholas!" Sarah, now completely intrigued, was also impatient and on the verge of losing her temper. "Nicholas, what's it all about?"

"I'll read it out, darling. It's addressed from the 'Merchant Seaman's Office' and is dated the beginning of last week – the same day we left London to come down here. A Monday, wasn't it?"

"Darling, what does it matter?" Sarah demanded.

"It was Tuesday, actually, but as you say, it doesn't matter. Well, it's headed, 'At a meeting of the Committee for Encouraging the Capture of French privateers, armed vessels & c, Rawson Aislabie esquire in the Chair'... Then there's a break and a sort of heading before it goes on with the point of it all."

"You're teasing me," Sarah said crossly. "You wait until tonight; I'll pay you back!"

"No," Ramage protested, "it's damned difficult reading this sort of thing; it's not a continuous paragraph. Anyway, 'Resolved' – that's the Committee resolving, you realize – "

"Oh, I thought it would be the French privateer captains: oh, do go *on*, Nicholas!"

"Yes, well, they resolved 'That Captain the Lord Ramage of His Majesty's ship *Calypso* be requested by this Committee to accept a sword, value one hundred guineas, in acknowledgement of his very gallant behaviour in the destruction of two French frigates and the capture of two more, along with seven merchant ships, in the action off Diamond Rock; and in testimony of the high sense this Committee entertains of the protection he has thereby afforded to the commerce of Great Britain.'

"There's a covering letter explaining about the resolution and asking me to suggest a date," he added. "And it says I can also bring any of my officers present at the action as my guests."

Sarah was puzzled. She accepted the reference to the sword as though her husband deserved a dozen, but when had it happened?

"That was before – why, before you came down to Isla Trinidade and we first met. *Two* French frigates taken? And you destroyed two more? Is that when you captured the *Calypso*?"

A bewildered Ramage nodded. "Southwick and the rest of them usually refer to it as 'The Diamond Rock Affair'. It's taken Lloyd's long enough to make up their minds!"

"You're hardly ever in England," Sarah pointed out. "No sooner are you home than you sail again. Then you spent that brief peace marrying me and honeymooning. Then we were captured and you escaped and went to Devil's Island when war broke out again... Then you went off to the Mediterranean, and we've only just returned from there, with all those unlikely people you rescued, including me so the Committee of Lloyd's haven't had much time..."

She stared at the log on the fire which was now beginning to sizzle and flare. "You'll wear uniform. I have that white dress. I wonder if your mother would lend me the pearls?"

Ramage laughed. "And the tiara too! She hates wearing it."

Sarah suddenly looked embarrassed. "I forgot! Of course, she'll want to wear the pearls. I'll wear my emeralds."

"What about me?" Ramage grumbled. "I have an enormous problem, and all you think of is pearls and tiaras."

Sarah, distressed, said quickly: "What problem, darling? What's the matter?"

"Do I wear a sword to the dinner? – it is correct uniform. But what do I do with the old sword while they present me with the new one, 'Value one hundred guineas'? I can't stand up there wearing one sword and holding another in my hand: I'll look like a sword cutler plying for business!"

"Your father will know," Sarah said. "Anyway, I can always hold your regular one while you march up to collect the new one."

"It's all such a fuss," Ramage grumbled. "Pity I can't ask them to send me a hundred guineas, and I'll use it to buy you some new jewellery!"

"Clothes perhaps," Sarah said laughing, "but not jewellery. I inherit a quantity from my mother and I expect your mother will…"

"So in a few years' time you'll be tottering under the weight of Rockley and Ramage jewellery. Me? I'll just have a hundred guinea sword to hang on the wall…"

"At least you won't have to spend your prize money buying me shiny baubles. You'll be able to pay a cutler to keep your sword sharp! Anyway, you must write and tell the Committee when you can go to London. And your officers," she reminded him. "Southwick will enjoy this as much as you. He thinks of you as a son."

"Grandson," Ramage corrected. "but in fact if anyone deserves a sword from Lloyd's, it's Southwick."

"I seem to remember he has a sword of his own the size of an oar. It's big enough for Father Time to use as a scythe!"

"And that's just how he uses it. He whirls it round his head, bellows like a bull, and charges along a French ship's deck. The bellow paralyses 'em with fear and the blade slices 'em in half."

Sarah shuddered and then said: "Yet he always puts me in mind of an old bishop: the kindly round face and all that flowing white hair."

"Like a mop drying in the wind!"

"Yes, but it looks very distinguished. Think of his sword as a crozier, and he has a very rich voice: I can just imagine him in a pulpit preaching to his flock."

"Tell that to Paolo Orsini! The poor boy still makes silly mistakes working out sights, and Southwick still hollers at him. I'm sure Paolo would reckon that by comparison a bull's bellow would sound like music!"

"Apart from Southwick, which of your present officers were with you at Diamond Rock?"

Ramage's brow furrowed. Diamond Rock...so much had happened since. Sarah, for instance. Diamond Rock was long before they had met and were married. Yet already he found it hard to remember a time when he was not married to this tawny-haired woman whose body made those Greek statues seem clumsy, whose sense of humour kept them both laughing, and who understood his moods almost better than he did himself.

"There's Southwick, and young Paolo," she reminded him.

"Yes, and Aitken. Wagstaffe was there, but he's gone to another ship. Rennick, of course: one can't forget the Marines! And Bowen, the surgeon. Two of the lieutenants were Baker and Lacy: good youngsters, but neither with me now."

Sarah was keeping a check as Ramage did little more than reminisce. "So you must write to Aitken, Southwick, Rennick and Bowen and Orsini. Well, I know all of them well enough. Any others?"

Ramage shook his head. "No, my present three other lieutenants all joined the *Calypso* long after the Diamond business..."

"Very well, that's five of them you have to write to. And the Committee of Lloyd's. And your parents – they'll be excited. Do you think I could bring my parents? They'd be so proud."

"Proud? I'm sure the Committee of Lloyd's would be proud to have the Marquis of Rockley and his wife present at their dinner. He must be one of the most powerful men in Parliament, and I'm sure Lloyd's always likes to have friends there!"

"Well, they're getting good value with your father," Sarah pointed out. "He may not have the Admiralty in his pocket, but the new First Lord listens very attentively when he speaks, and that would be a help to Lloyd's."

"The Committee of Lloyd's are only concerned with getting even more frigates to escort even more convoys," Ramage commented. "Still, a hint over a glass of sherry often does more than an official letter."

"Your officers and your parents and my parents – so much for the guests. Do we post up to London? Which is the post road?" Sarah asked.

"From memory that starts at Folkestone, and you get fresh horses at Hythe, Ashford – where we'd join – and then Lenham, Maidstone, West Malling, Wrotham Heath (you need fresh horses as well as an extra pair to climb that dam' long hill), and then Farningham, Swanley and after that I get mixed up. The most important thing, according to Raven is that there are no turnpikes on that road! There are plenty on the Dover, Canterbury, Faversham, Sittingbourne, Rochester and Gravesend road, though."

"I hope that doesn't mean the Ashford road will be in poor condition. We haven't had much rain lately. Does that mean we breathe dust the whole way?"

"My dear, don't think that turnpike tolls mean good roads! The people who own the land and establish the toll gates put that story about." He thought for a minute or two staring at the flames dancing in the fireplace. "You know, Raven hasn't been to London for a long time – Uncle Rufus hated cities – and I don't like having to borrow father's carriage every time we want to go out. And we both hate posting…"

"So why don't we take Raven and our own carriage?" Sarah finished the sentence for him. "Yes, and let's not hurry. I don't know Kent, so why don't we take a week or two, staying at whatever inn takes our fancy?"

"You've had one honeymoon, you know," Ramage said teasingly.

"Yes, I vaguely recall it, but that was in France and, if you remember, it started the war going again…"

CHAPTER **TWO**

The long and jolting journey to London by carriage in the lee of the Downs was enjoyable only because of the sunny weather, and because each night a brisk shower just before dawn laid the dust, although the two horses still kicked up enough at times to set them all coughing and make a cursing Raven slow down from a trot to a walk.

Day by day they skirted the North Downs, the great ridge lying on their right hand and deeply scarred with the white of the chalk showing through grass closely cropped by flocks of sheep. Once past West Malling the Downs began to curve round to the south-west across their path, and just as their road met the steep hill Raven reined in at Wrotham Heath.

"Better hire a couple of extra horses here than wait till we get to Wrotham village," he explained. "Often as not they've none left, or they want an extra couple of guineas for 'the last pair in the stable'. "

The ride up the hill was spectacular: in climbing the side of the North Downs, with Raven stopping frequently to rest the horses, Ramage and Sarah would get out and look back over the rest of Kent spread out to the east and south of them, a green table with church towers and steeples sticking up like stubby pegs on a lawn, each surrounded by a huddle of houses and barns.

But Sarah seemed preoccupied, and when Ramage pressed her admitted she was saddened by the tablet they had seen at the foot of the hill back in Wrotham village. "Near this place," it said, "fell Lieut. Colonel Shadwell, who was shot to the heart by a deserter on the morning of the first day of June 1799." Four lines carved below in italic added cryptically: "The Assassin with another deserter his companion were immediately secured and brought to justice."

"Three men dead," Sarah said. "They all intended to fight the French – well, obviously the deserter and his companion changed their minds – but all three have ended up in graves here at the foot of the Downs. Colonel Shadwell – was he a young man eager to fight the French? Or did he buy his commission to get away from a nagging wife?"

"Was he serving in one of the regular regiments of foot, or simply a wealthy landowner here, soldiering on Sunday mornings in the local yeomanry?" Ramage murmured.

"Oh, darling, you are spoiling the whole thing. Here I am thinking of a young colonel with a brilliant future ahead of him – "

"And belonging to one of the fashionable regiments!"

" – and you conjure up a portly farmer..."

"Your imagination is running wild. Why did the soldier desert? Where did he get the pistol to fire a fatal shot – or was it a musket? Who was his mysterious companion – another soldier, or a trollop he'd picked up? Was it at night? Did the colonel call upon him to halt? Or was the colonel leading a column of men?"

"If it wasn't such a steep hill, I'd insist we go back to Wrotham and ask some local people," Sarah said. "It happened only a few years ago, so they'll remember the details."

"We'll inquire on the way back," Ramage promised. "Come along – Raven is sitting on his box, so the horses are rested enough."

As they approached the city the road gradually became busier. After reaching Farningham they went on to Swanley (by which time they were looking for an inn to spend the night), and carts, carriages and coaches were passing each way, either on their way to the coast or bound for London. Everyone, Ramage noted, seemed to be in a hurry; Raven's leisurely progress, he realized, would probably be the only time until the war ended that Ramage would ever travel this road so slowly: every time he had previously left London for Dover, or had travelled the parallel road to the Medway towns to join a ship at Chatham, the horses had always been in a lather.

Raven still remembered where the house was, having brought his late master there a few times, and, as he pulled up with a clatter and a loud "Whoa, there!" intended to warn the earl's butler, Sarah sighed.

"How nice to be back in Palace Street. I think I prefer travelling by ship, though: you don't have to keep on packing and unpacking at post inns!"

"We must persuade father to get a house on the Thames side at Greenwich, and we'll sell Treffry Hall and buy a place near Dover. Then we can sail round when we want to see them!"

"We've come to see the gentlemen at Lloyd's," Sarah pointed out as a grinning Hanson let down the steps with a crash, opened the door of the carriage and, pushing his spectacles back up again, blinked and welcomed them. "Your father is just coming, sir. Leave the luggage to Raven and me."

Admiral the Earl of Blazey, hook-nosed and white-haired came to the front door just as Sarah reached it. In his usual courtly fashion he kissed her hand before giving her a fatherly hug.

"We guessed you'd be here today: your father and mother are calling this evening." He shook hands with his son. "Your mother is busy with her dressmaker but she'll be ready as soon as you've washed off the grime of London. We could do with a shower of rain to lay the dust," he grumbled, looking up at the clear blue sky.

Ramage followed Sarah up to their rooms on the second floor. These two rooms had been his since he was a child and father had bought the Palace Street house: a bedroom and what had first been a nursery, then a playroom and finally a study. Finally, that is, until Sarah arrived: now with a third change of furniture it was their dressing room.

Undressing room, he reflected. In three or four minutes Sarah would be standing there naked, washing herself with a grace and ease of movement that always left him breathless. How often, in boyhood and bachelor days, he had spent hours lying on his bed, his head a whirl of wild fantasies and furious longings.

She walked across the room, undoing the ribbon of her bonnet and running a hand through her long, tawny hair. She checked that the jug on the marble washstand was full of water and that there was soap in the black alabaster container that Ramage recognized as one of the half-dozen his mother had bought at Volterra many years ago when they had lived in Italy.

There was a knock at the door and Hanson's wife called: "Two jugs of hot water: I'll leave them outside the door, ma'am."

While Ramage collected them and used the contents of one to fill the basin, Sarah undid the silver clip at the neck of her pearl-grey travelling cloak, took it off and hung it in one of the two large wardrobes.

"Oh, I feel grimy," she said. "Help me unbutton this, or that water will be cool before I'm ready."

Undressing her was still one of the most erotic sensations he had experienced and, noticing it, Sarah smiled. "What will I do when you no longer enjoy helping me undress?"

"Refuse to push my wheelchair," Ramage said cheerfully, lifting off her dress and then beginning to unlace her drawers. "Do you begrudge me a look at those bosoms?" He cupped one in his hand and kissed the nipple.

She pushed him away. "Stop it, you're making me think of other things – " she gestured towards the dark-blue curtains of the four-poster bed which could be seen through the door, " – while that water is getting cold."

As she began washing, he stripped off his clothes. How comfortable it was, not to be wearing uniform. The stock round his neck was tied lower and less tightly than demanded with uniform; his waistcoat had shrunk compared with the bulky fashion of ten years ago and did not nick up under his coat. And, despite the protests of his tailor, the breeches were cut with a comfortable fullness, so he could sit down without the feeling that he was cutting off his legs at the knees and, more important, take them off without assistance.

Tailors are more conservative than North Briton farmers and they have a more nose-in-the-air attitude than the wife of the most recently knighted nabob. A much shorter waistcoat, more comfortable breeches, less padding in his coat...the damned tailor would have continued protesting if he had not been afraid of losing the custom of the son and heir of the Earl of Blazey who was, in his own right, not unknown as a frigate captain.

"My back," Sarah said, turning towards him and offering soap and flannel. "My, you look so fierce!"

"Pure lust," Ramage said. "No, I was having an imaginary argument with my tailor."

As Sarah turned slightly when he took the soap and flannel, she gave a slight sniff and Ramage chuckled, guessing what she would say. "Darling, one doesn't *argue* with one's tailor."

" 'Argue' wasn't the right word, but I've heard you and your dressmaker bickering over where to put a plaquet or a pleat or a couple of buttons. And as for hats..."

"That's enough," Sarah said, holding his hand. "That's not my back. Now please rinse off the soap and dry me."

While Sarah and Hanson's wife unpacked their trunks, shook the creases out of clothes and hung them in the wardrobes, Ramage went down to the sitting room and found his father reading the *Morning Post*, having finished *The Times*.

"It seems odd, having you back *and* a married man," the earl said. "This Lloyd's business is long overdue. You should have had half a dozen presentation swords by now!"

"One is quite enough," Ramage said. "Imagine all this presentation business...it was so peaceful down in Aldington!"

"Ah yes, how did you get on with that lawyer? Did Rufus leave everything in good order?"

Ramage nodded. "Yes, and with handsome bequests to his staff, whom I'm keeping on anyway."

"That fellow Raven," the earl said. "He's a good chap but mixed up with the Marsh smugglers, you know. Rufus told me."

"He helped me get to France that time – you remember? I don't think anyone knows the Marsh better."

The earl laughed dryly and said: "Who better than a poacher to guard the pheasants!"

The old admiral thought a moment and then said gruffly: "This probably isn't the right time to mention it, but now you're married I've got to make another will to take care of Sarah – the family jewels and that sort of thing quite apart from when you start a family – so I have to ask you this: how are you treating Treffry Hall?"

Ramage looked puzzled. "How do you mean, father?"

"Well, you know you inherit the St Kew estate. That's a dam' big house and fifteen thousand acres of Cornwall. It's not the lush land you have in Kent, though: more rocks than blades of grass. But when I've gone over the standing part of the foresheet, will you keep open both places – and this house here?"

Ramage shrugged, not because of indifference but because he did not want to contemplate his father dying. "It won't arise for a long time! You look as if you'll weather a good many more years yet!"

"Don't be squeamish," the admiral said impatiently. "I've got to go sometime – although the way you get yourself into scrapes, I may well outlast you. But I've got to draw up a new will which allows for me outlasting you and you outlasting me – and covers Sarah."

"Backing the horse to win and lose!" Ramage said lightly.

"Exactly. If you don't, lawyers get rich, and there's no better goldmine for lawyers than the probate court: give them a disputed will and they dig away until there's nothing left of the estate."

"I see your point," Ramage said. "What exactly do you want to know?"

"Well, obviously the earldom comes to you the moment I die. St Kew Hall – the house itself – is entailed to the eldest son. So that comes to you as well and goes on to your eldest son and grandson. But the land itself *isn't* entailed. I've bought up a few farms (to help out the owners) and doubled the acreage since I inherited the house from your grandfather. Fifteen thousand acres is a lot of land. Now you have Rufus' place, do you want all that land in Cornwall? If you carry on farming, I'll tell you right now you'll make a lot more profit from Treffry Hall than

St Kew: Rufus had some of the richest land in the country, let alone county. Do you want an estate at one end of the country and a second at the other? With Palace Street inbetween?"

The question was a sensible one, but how the devil did one answer? Ramage knew he could not compare St Kew and Treffry Hall. For a start you could lose Treffry Hall in the St Kew house, and if you dropped the Kentish acres among the Cornish ones it would take a day's riding to find them.

But places were memories, the bits and pieces that made up a life. Part of his childhood had been spent in Italy with his mother, part at St Kew, and there had been many happy holidays at "Uncle Rufus' place", much of the time spent out on the Marsh with Raven.

Palace Street came into a different category. It was within walking distance of Parliament and the Admiralty, and of Downing Street, and the rest of the ministers'offices come to that, so when he inherited the earldom and had to attend Parliament regularly (when he retired from the Navy, in other words) he would need Palace Street: it was the perfect town house: not too big but ideally placed, close to Parliament but far enough away from the drawing rooms of Grosvenor and Berkeley Squares.

But did he have to choose between St Kew and Treffry Hall? Was that what his father meant? Hellfire and damnation, what would Sarah want? He sensed that Sarah had fallen in love with Treffry Hall: the rolling and rich green countryside of Kent, the North Downs rising on one side and the flat plain of Romney Marsh to the south and meeting the sea intrigued her: no matter what the weather, the clouds ensured an ever-changing view whichever way one looked.

Sarah. Yes, sons and daughters. There would be some, though at the moment he did not welcome the idea. Where would Sarah want them to grow up? He knew instinctively that she would choose Aldington: it was wonderful riding country – he pictured children graduating from ponies to hunters – and there were plenty of oaks and beeches to climb, and Treffry Hall's orchards meant scraped knees and fun, scrumping apples and cherries, and hurling sticks up at the chestnut trees to bring down the prickly cases. Finding horse chestnuts and playing conkers, and cheating by gently roasting them or pickling them in vinegar... "Mine's a twicer." "Go on, hold it up: mine's a twelver..." Yes, they'd need at least two sons.

Treffry Hall for when the children were young: that was certain, and certainly for Sarah if she was widowed. But St Kew went with the earldom, and the Ramage family had roots in the St Kew countryside going back many generations. Centuries, in fact, and one did not cast them away lightly. For fifty miles around St Kew, the Earl of Blazey represented everything to the people: the man they went to for help when they had money troubles; the man they appealed to for justice; the man who could (if it was at all possible) get things done in far-off London. This was where *noblesse oblige* gave a hefty tug: yes, the Ramage family owned a vast estate, but living in the village on that estate were scores of people who considered the earl (whatever century it was) to be their guardian: a sort of father who saw they were protected against everything from highwaymen to unjust eviction, and who made sure the rent collector called with extra food and a bottle of wine when there was illness in the house, and put a special tick against their names in the "Paid" column of the rent book and far from taking a penny made sure on the earl's behalf that there was enough money in the house.

Treffry Hall or St Kew...what a choice to have to make!

"Do I have to choose now?" he asked his father.

"You don't have to choose at all," the admiral said. "It's not a case of one or the other, although I'd like to know something about the St Kew land. But don't forget the marquis... It's all right while you are alive and living in England, but supposing I've gone and something happens to you and then the marquis passes on. Sarah will inherit from you and from him. She's the only child – and God knows how many square miles *he* owns! Three estates, Rockley, St Kew and Treffry Hall. Going it a bit strong, even if you're still alive, retired from the Navy and rumbling away in the Lords demanding new laws against poachers! Especially if this fellow Pitt brings in any more of his fancy taxes."

"I'd forgotten the Marquis of Rockley," Ramage admitted, "but it's difficult talking to Sarah about what happens when her father dies…"

"And that's how lawyers grow rich and so many judges sit on the probate bench. Face up to death when you're young, my lad; it doesn't have such a frightening face as when you're my age," the admiral said. "Anyway, talk it over with Sarah, and plan for a big family, but let me know what you've decided before you leave: I really must get this new will settled: your mother is particularly fussed about all the Ramage jewellery – she wants to make sure Sarah gets it without lawyers scrapping."

"Very well," Ramage said, "but Sarah's not going to like it: the prospect of father- and mother-in-law, husband and father and mother all dying on her!"

"I'm sure none of us is in any hurry to go," the earl said, "but while you are at Lloyd's, just inquire if any underwriter will insure your life while you're serving at sea commanding one of the King's ships. You're not a good risk!"

"Let's change the subject. Who will be at this damned Lloyd's Patriotic Fund presentation?"

"You're going to be surprised. First the usual Lloyd's people – the Master and Committee, and various folk from the City. I hear the Lord Mayor is attending and that's quite an honour.

You're the famous young frigate captain. You with the little ships, Nelson with the big fleets!"

"Sarah's father and mother are coming." Ramage said, adding with a laugh: "Between you, the fathers will probably bring along a quarter of the House of Lords."

"All those whose opinions matter, anyway," the earl growled contentedly. "For years your *Gazette* letters were the only good news they had to read. Anyway, I hear the Admiralty will be well represented."

That was a surprise: the Admiralty's attitude towards the Patriotic Fund swords of honour presented by Lloyd's was hard to understand. It acted as though jealous because it had nothing of its own to present to deserving officers, but at the same time its view was that officers were only doing their duty and therefore needed no presentation swords. However, despite this dog-in-the-manger attitude they could not afford to offend the Committee of Lloyd's which, apart from anything else, organized the sailings of all convoys.

"Who can we expect from the Admiralty? Is Mr Secretary Marsden taking a day off from attending to the Board's affairs?"

"He might be; I don't know. But I met the new First Lord, Barham, in the House yesterday and he said he'd never met you but would be there – curious, I think. Having Lord St Vincent applauding should also satisfy you: he told me he hoped to come. Probably the only sign of praise you'll ever get from him," the earl added. "And Lord Nelson's just arrived in Town and tells me he will be there – with Lady Hamilton, I fear."

"So he's back in England after that long chase... Well, don't be too critical of the lady," Ramage said. "If she inspired him at the Nile and then Copenhagen, I don't care if she has two heads and three legs...after all, but for him Sir John Jervis would have had a miserable defeat at Cape St Vincent, not a victory, so he wouldn't have received an earldom and a name to go with it…"

"I know, I know," the earl said, "and St Vincent knows it, too. He's tried to pay off that debt by pushing Nelson: command for the Nile, then Copenhagen…"

"Copenhagen?" Ramage said sarcastically, an eyebrow raised. "Surely My Lord St Vincent guarded himself by putting that nincompoop Hyde Parker in command – and Parker's nervousness and limp hand nearly lost the day!"

"Be fair, be fair," the earl chided. "I know you have no very high opinion of Lord St Vincent after the battle which gained him the earldom, but at Copenhagen he knew Nelson as second-in-command would twist Hyde Parker round his little finger, if necessary – as indeed he did, and won a fantastic victory."

"Then why not have the courage to put Nelson in complete command from the start? Hyde Parker wasted days fiddling about off Elsinore when he should have been down to the south at Copenhagen. After all those luxurious years of West Indian sun and blue seas, the dark nights and cold green seas of the Cattegat frightened him."

The old admiral laughed and started to fill his pipe. "You're not going to get me into that argument again. Anyway, now St Vincent is out and Middleton is in as First Lord, created Lord Barham for the purpose, perhaps things will be different. I've known him for most of my life as Charles Middleton, and it's difficult to remember he was recently ennobled."

"What sort of man is he?"

The earl shrugged. "About fourteenth on the list of admirals of the white, just below Duncan and just above St Vincent. In his eighties now, but a very good organizer and clear-headed: apparently he has shaken up the Admiralty Office – it needed it. Everyone's precise task is now written down; clerks have to be at their desks by ten o'clock; even sea lords arrive earlier. Barham himself is usually at work by daybreak."

"Sounds a welcome change," Ramage commented. "Those clerks for the most part are a crowd of insolent time-servers – sons of creditors, tailors' nephews, friends of cousins, and so on."

"Ah, Lord Nelson," the earl exclaimed, "I nearly forgot. He's in town from Merton for only three or four days, staying at Lady Hamilton's place in Clarges Street, and he asks that you call on him. Seeing him at Clarges Street will save you from going all the way down to Merton."

"Did he give you any idea what he wants to see me about?" Ramage asked cautiously. "From what the newspapers say, I should think that now he's back everyone in London wants to shake his hand and give him dinner…"

"That's exactly why, if I were you, I'd send Raven round to Clarges Street at once to suggest a day and time."

Sarah came into the room at that moment. "Who lives in Clarges Street?" she asked. "Oh yes, that wretched man Charles James Fox, if I remember rightly. I went to his house one day with father and mother, And doesn't Lord Nelson's friend have a house at the other end?"

"It's all right, you can say Lady Hamilton's name out loud – father is very broad-minded," Ramage said teasingly.

"Who are we going to see, then, Fox or the famous lady?"

"I don't know that 'we' are going to see anyone," Ramage said. "Apparently Lord Nelson has asked me to call on him. Told me, through father," Ramage corrected himself.

"Then it's 'we'," Sarah said blithely. "I've always wanted to meet His Lordship, and who can resist meeting the famous lady? I wonder if their child is with them. Horatia."

"She is usually referred to as His Lordship's god-daughter," Ramage said stiffly.

Sarah waved a hand airly. "Unless you're a servant, legitimacy only matters if you're inheriting property or a title. If Lady Hamilton inspires Nelson – and clearly she does – then hurrah for England if she has a dozen such children, particularly if it produces a dozen great victories. We need a few more at this moment!"

The earl sighed and was about to chide Sarah when she sat down on a sofa and wagged a finger at him. "Before you start disapproving of Lady Hamilton (who after all is a widow now, although admittedly she wasn't when Horatia was born), let me tell you this. If Nicholas had been unhappily married when we first met, then *you* might have had a Nichola in *your* family, with people gossiping about 'the notorious Lady Sarah'!"

The earl sighed again, and then smiled. "Yes, I believe you, and Nichola would have been just as welcome in the family," he admitted, "as 'the notorious Lady Sarah'."

"That's easy enough to say now," Sarah said reflectively, "but supposing…"

The earl looked at her squarely. "You forget Gianna, my dear. Nicholas couldn't have married her because she is a Catholic – or, to be more exact, she wouldn't have married him because he is a Protestant, and anyway she could never return to rule Volterra with a Protestant husband. But believe me, the countess and I were quite prepared for an eventuality such as you mention!"

A startled Ramage blurted: "*Were* you, father?"

"Of course! For the first two or three years, anyway; then we realized that your feelings for her were changing."

"I should hope so," Sarah said mildly, and then asked curiously: "But you really were quite ready for a grandchild born the wrong side of the blanket?"

"Quite ready? Well, to be perfectly honest the countess was readier than I: Nicholas can do no wrong in her eyes. But had

Gianna had such child, yes, I would have accepted it. We were very fond of her, you know. *Are* fond of her," he corrected himself, and all of them thought of the young Marchesa di Volterra, the lively and lovely Gianna, whose fate was still a mystery: had she been assassinated by Napoleon's men, or imprisoned?

"Well, you've no grandchildren yet," Ramage said hastily, "and I must write a note to Lord Nelson. How long has he been back in London?"

"Only a few days. We were all very worried when he seemed to vanish."

Ramage nodded. "Yes, he took a risk making for the West Indies after leaving the Mediterranean, instead of coming north – but he was right! Villeneuve *had* fled across the Atlantic, not made for Brest or Coruña."

The earl lit his pipe, and as soon as it was drawing satisfactorily, asked Ramage: "Would *you* have risked it?"

"I might. After all, once he sailed through the Strait from the Mediterranean, Villeneuve could only go north, to join the Spanish in Cadiz or Coruña, or to Brest, where he'd risk being blockaded, or to the West Indies. What a prize Jamaica would have been, and all those convoys captured...Bonaparte would have kissed him on both cheeks!"

"Well, I was talking to Radnor in the House the other day, and his son is a midshipman in Nelson's flagship. That doesn't make the lad an authority on the chase across the Atlantic and back, but he knew Nelson's feelings on board the *Victory* and reported them to his father, the earl."

"And so the Earl of Radnor approves?" Sarah asked.

"He does now, though he was pretty windy at the time. As we all were."

"Nelson's young, outspoken, just a parson's son, and he wants Society to accept his mistress. The fact is none of you are comfortable with him; you don't really trust him," Ramage commented bitterly. "Had that old fool Hyde Parker been in command of that fleet, you'd have all said: 'Well, Hyde Parker knows what he is doing: he spent four years in Jamaica.' But all he learned in those four years was how to get rich from prize money: Copenhagen showed that a young man with an agile mind was needed for the fighting part."

"You seem particularly vindictive towards the worthy Sir Hyde," the earl protested.

"I should think so!" Ramage exclaimed. "He started off badly at Copenhagen. Given command, he stays abed with his new young wife in Great Yarmouth instead of sailing at once for Denmark with the fleet. When he gets there, he hovers off Elsinore, giving the Danes all that time to prepare the defences of Copenhagen...how many hundreds of seamen's lives – British and Danish – did those two delays cost?"

"You favour young admirals with young mistresses, then," the earl observed teasingly.

"Young admirals, yes. If such a man can only have the woman he loves by defying convention and making her his mistress, well and good. Then there's a hope that when it comes to fighting battles he'll defy convention and throw those dam' Fighting Instructions overboard. As Nelson did at the Nile! Parker would never have dared to do what Nelson did at Aboukir Bay. Nor would Parker dare do at Copenhagen what Nelson did, even though it was for all intents and purposes a repeat of Nelson's tactics at the Nile. So give me a man who defies convention when necessary: he's more likely to win the battle."

"Do *you* defy convention?" the earl inquired mischievously and then almost immediately waved his pipe to dismiss the remark. "No, that's unfair: no conventions so far have governed the sort of things you've done; you – " he grinned, " – favour the bizarre rather than the unconventional!"

"Which heading do I come under – bizarre or unconventional?" Sarah inquired sweetly.

"Oh, bizarre; definitely bizarre. After all, didn't Nicholas find you in mysterious circumstances off some island near Brazil?"

"At least my father-in-law is more unconventional than Nicholas'; I'm afraid my father is rectitude personified."

"We need a stable marquis in the family," the earl said, eyes twinkling. "It adds respectability to what would otherwise be a rout."

CHAPTER THREE

As Raven drove the carriage along Piccadilly, Sarah turned to Ramage and said: "I haven't felt so nervous for a long time!"

Ramage looked at her pale-blue dress, bonnet of slightly darker blue, and her face, which still had some Mediterranean sun-tan. He reached across and put a wisp of the tawny hair back in place. "I don't know why you worry. I'll be very jealous if Lord Nelson looks at you for more than five seconds at a time!"

"I'm not worrying about His Lordship," Sarah said, "it's Lady Hamilton. I haven't the faintest idea how to talk to her!"

Ramage thought for a moment, watching coaches clatter along in the opposite direction. "Think of her as the widow of Sir William Hamilton. She was a good deal younger than Sir William when they married, but he became a good friend of Lord Nelson's and the – er, well, the relationship developed from there."

"The fact is," she admitted with a smile, "I haven't much experience dealing with famous men's mistresses!"

"You'd have been one if I'd been married – you told father that yesterday," Ramage said, smiling. "I like thinking of you as my mistress: much more stimulating than regarding you as my wife."

Sarah pouted at the left-handed compliment. "I'll never hear the last of that. Anyway, you're not as famous as Nelson yet."

"Give me time – he has fifteen years or so advantage on me! Ah, this is Clarges Street."

Just then, Raven stopped the carriage, asked a passer-by for directions, and called to Ramage: "We're almost there, sir. The house is this end."

The houses were small but well proportioned. As he reached for his hat and gloves and hitched at his sword, Ramage tried to recall the last time he had seen the admiral. He had been only a commodore then. Yes, Bastia, in Corsica, when Commodore Nelson had given him his first command, the *Kathleen* cutter. After that he had seen him only in the distance, striding his quarterdeck (a minuscule figure recognizable in the telescope lens only because of his stance) in the brief minutes at the battle of Cape St Vincent before the *Kathleen* cutter was sunk by a Spanish three-decker.

That battle had brought Nelson a baronetcy. It had also brought Sir John Jervis the earldom (of St Vincent) that he did not deserve but, as father had said, St Vincent had done his best to make it up to Nelson ever since.

The carriage came to a stop. Ramage heard Raven pulling on the brake; then the folding steps clattered down, the door was flung open and a grinning Raven stood waiting to help Sarah down. Grinning, Ramage knew, because Raven, long accustomed to rural life and more used to setting snares than opening carriage doors, was enjoying the sudden change (quite apart from being proud of his new livery of dark blue edged with gold) and delighting in the gold griffin now painted on the door of the carriage Ramage had also inherited from his uncle.

Ramage followed Sarah, then took her arm and led her to the front door, which was suddenly and unexpectedly opened by a small figure in plain uniform, one empty sleeve pinned across his breast, a green shade over his left eye.

"Welcome, Ramages! I heard the carriage and guessed it was you," he explained to Sarah, taking her parasol and putting it in the stand just inside the door. "Follow me, I am the major domo and butler. Lady Hamilton is waiting upstairs with Horatia."

It was the same rather high-pitched and nasal voice with the flat Norfolk accent: the curly hair was greyer. The face was tanned and thinner, too – no doubt about that, but it only emphasized the strong bone structure. The single good eye sharp, the small body (he was shorter than Sarah) as erect as ever, the single hand gesticulating. In a moment, in a brief phrase, he had both welcomed them and set the tone of the meeting with Lady Hamilton and his young daughter: now there would be no uncomfortable pauses, searching for the right word or phrase: here was the same Nelson he had met years ago: a coiled spring. One knew it was under control, but at the same time had no doubts about its latent power.

The drawing room upstairs was large, high-ceilinged and furnished with considerable taste. Sarah, at first not seeing Lady Hamilton, paused at the doorway, intrigued by a pair of urns – urns? No, they were amphorae, and surely that was coral growing on them? Recovered from the sea?

Nelson stopped when he noticed her interest. "Some of the late Sir William's treasures, which he left to me. We have the finest ones down at Merton: perhaps we can lure you and your husband there one day and show them off. Ah, there is Lady Hamilton!"

Sarah saw a small, beautiful and graceful woman rising from a chair in an alcove. Brown and curling hair, a body perhaps now a little plump, a friendly face also now plump, but with the fullness of happiness and contentment.

Nelson introduced them and she said with unfeigned pleasure: "At last, Captain Ramage! Horatio did not tell me you were so handsome. And you have a lovely wife!"

Before Ramage could answer, Lady Hamilton looked down. A vivacious little girl was tugging shyly at her skirt. "Yes, yes. This is the Captain Ramage who wrote all those exciting letters in the *Gazette*, and this lady is his beautiful wife. May I introduce Horatia?"

It was all done so naturally that Sarah took an instant liking to the woman. Warm, doting on Nelson and their child, well informed apparently, taking an interest in everything that went on round her and – if this room was anything to go by, and it *was* her house – a woman of refined tastes.

Oh yes, there were stories about Emma Hart (passed on to Sir William by his nephew) who became Nelson's mistress, but Sarah could understand and forgive Nelson's infatuation.

Sarah had twice met his wife, Lady Nelson, and the former Mrs Nesbit (widowed in the West Indies when her Army major husband died of one of those vile tropical diseases) was by comparison a cold and shrivelled person: Sarah could imagine that the warm and spontaneous Nelson would find her chilly, not unresponsive but instead – well, just plain and dull.

He should never have married her, Sarah thought; but from what Nicholas said the young Nelson had fallen in love with a married woman in Antigua – wife of the commissioner at English Harbour, she remembered – and when the couple were sent back to England, a broken-hearted Nelson had then met the young widow Fanny Nesbit on one of the nearby islands. Wasn't she staying with her uncle, who owned a large plantation on Nevis? Sarah had a picture of interfering female cousins plotting to marry Fanny off to the young frigate captain…and this was how it all ended up.

Nelson made her comfortable in a chair close to Lady Hamilton, and Sarah found herself talking to an excited Horatia, anxious to display her new pink dress and shoes. Nelson waited until Horatia stopped for a moment (she was explaining that she now had piano lessons and was nearly five years old) and then said apologetically to Sarah: "I am taking your husband to the next room for a few minutes' chat: once we've got that out of the way we can enjoy ourselves!"

What *had* Nicholas done? Yet the admiral seemed friendly enough. Nicholas had not served under Nelson for several years. She shrugged and then was embarrassed to find that Lady Hamilton had noticed. Would she misinterpret it?

As Ramage turned to follow Nelson from the room, Lady Hamilton said: "The life I lead! My late husband Sir William, when we were at the Embassy in Naples, was forever breaking up conversations by taking away husbands for discreet talks... His Lordship, by the way, thinks highly of your husband."

"I'm very glad," Sarah said, "but Nicholas has not served with him for several years."

"Ah, no, but His Lordship has read all the *Gazette* letters: he has them among his papers. In fact he was reading the one about how your husband rescued all the hostages – and *you*! – in Italy, and concluded by reading it aloud to Horatia and me. It was enthralling! Fancy finding you, when he thought you were dead! Dead," she repeated, the word obviously reminding her of some incident. "I worry about His Lordship. Do you know, he has been wounded more than twenty times? He lost the arm at Tenerife, the eye in Corsica. At the Nile a splinter nearly knocked his head off and cut his forehead. I think that last battle, Copenhagen, was a miracle: all those dead, and Horatio for once not even scratched!"

Nelson had taken Ramage to the next room, which he obviously used as a study. He gestured to Ramage to sit in a leather-covered armchair beside the unlit fire, and sat in the opposite one. He adjusted his eyeshade – Ramage noticed he had chosen the chair with its back to the window, so that he did not face the light – and said: "Well, you've had a busy few years since I last saw you!"

"And you, sir," Ramage said with a grin. "I am jealous that I was not with you at Aboukir Bay and Copenhagen."

"Ah yes, interesting actions. Hard pounding, against the Danes. It was touch and go. The Danes and the Dutch – we need parity when we fight 'em, unless we use better tactics."

"Tell me, sir," Ramage asked, "did the success of your tactics at the Nile influence you at Copenhagen?"

Nelson laughed and slapped his knee. "You know, young Ramage, it's a strange thing: few people have ever noticed that. The Danes had their ships drawn up outside their capital city just as the French had their fleet anchored in Aboukir Bay – so close to the shore they were sure no ship could get inside them. But the French were wrong, so I won.

"Still, I was sure the Danes would have studied that battle, so when I saw their ships drawn up in a long line outside Copenhagen, I wondered. Had they, I asked myself, really anchored so there was no room between them and the shore or – and this was my sharpest worry – had they found some answer, in case I did intend to use similar tactics, and had set a trap for me?"

"But," Ramage said, "the Danes didn't seem to have learned any lessons from the Battle of the Nile!"

"No. I talked later to the Danish Crown Prince and to their admiral, Olfert Fischer, and I had the impression they regarded the Nile as a far distant place… They didn't seem to understand that tactics apply anywhere, from the Equator to the Arctic. Still, I am more interested in you. That must have been a pleasant shock when you found you had rescued your wife! Tell me, did you think she was already dead?"

Ramage paused, briefly, reliving those long months of not knowing whether the ship taking Sarah to England had been sunk in a storm or captured by French privateers – or even a French national ship. "Yes, sir, I must admit that secretly I thought she was dead. I don't believe in miracles, and it seemed only a miracle could have kept her alive..."

Nelson nodded understandingly. "It's the not knowing... but anyway, she is safe. And a beautiful woman. You're a lucky fellow. And I hear from your father you've just inherited a fine estate down in Kent. What more can you want, eh?"

"Oh, nothing sir. I have everything."

Nelson smiled knowingly. "Except, of course, that the *Calypso* frigate is always at the back of your mind, and you wonder what action you are missing at sea..."

This man can see through a thick plank, Ramage thought. "Well, yes sir, in a way. I'm happy enough at the moment, but I know the feeling will creep in."

"Like mist rising at the foot of those chalky Kentish Downs, eh? Well now, what's wrong with the *Calypso*?"

"Oh, nothing actually wrong with her, sir: too many months' service in the West Indies and the Mediterranean without shipwrights having a chance to set a few things to rights. Anyway, now she's at Chatham and they are busy with her."

"Doing what exactly?"

"Replacing a sprung bowsprit and jib-boom, two topsail yards and all three topgallants; putting in new wood at the taffrail – they found some rot. Some new deck planking in way of the guns – where it had been badly scored by the trucks. New copper sheeting in the hanging magazine; replacing some woodwork in the bread-room... Replacing all the copper sheathing forward of the foremast – you know how it becomes paper-thin along the waterline at the stem..."

That's about all, sir. New sails, and replacing some of the guns..."

Nelson examined the nails of his left hand. "When will she be ready for sea?"

"The last I heard (the day before yesterday), in about two weeks, sir."

"You've still got that same master? What was his name, Southwell, South – ah yes, Southwick?"

"Yes, sir. He"ll be flattered that you remember his name."

"Ah, he's a good man. Master of the *Kathleen* cutter when I put you in command, I remember. I see you make a point of always mentioning him in your *Gazette* letters. He must be one of the most famous frigate masters in the Service. One of the richest, too," Nelson added. "You've done well with prize money. Have you kept mostly the same ship's company?"

"When Ramage nodded, the admiral commented: "They will be wealthy men. Some of your ordinary seamen could probably buy me out," he said without malice. "I haven't had much luck with prize money."

And here we are talking about prize money and I'm almost faint with wondering why you asked me to call, Ramage thought. It wasn't to yarn about old times nor discuss the tactics at Copenhagen, nor display your remarkable memory of men.

Did Nelson sense Ramage's train of thought? He looked up at Ramage and grinned. A boyish grin, one which stripped fifteen years from his lined face. "You wonder why I asked your father to tell you to call on me, eh? Isn't it enough that you meet Lady Hamilton and Horatia?"

"Yes, sir," Ramage said, and added shrewdly, "but they're in the drawing room and we are here!"

"And you, my dear Ramage, have had independent commands for too long. If you had served any time in a fleet, you'd know it's more important to please the admiral than handle your ship well."

"Not in your fleet," Ramage said bluntly, the words spilling out before he could stop them.

Nelson grinned again. "I take that as a compliment. How would you like to serve with me?"

Ramage looked so startled that Nelson laughed. "The idea doesn't seem to appeal to you."

"It isn't that, sir..." Ramage stammered.

"Had you been serving with me, you might at this moment be tacking back and forth in front of a French or Spanish port, keeping an eye on the Combined Fleets of France and Spain. You find that idea daunting?"

Hell-fire and damnation, Ramage thought: if in a dream (the only circumstances in which it could happen) Lord Barham had asked Ramage what appointment he would like, he would have asked to be sent to join Lord Nelson. Now here was Lord Nelson himself (and Ramage knew he was not dreaming) offering him just that job, and his mouth suddenly filled with sand and feet, and the right words disappeared up the chimney.

He grabbed at Nelson's earlier remark. "I'm not used to dealing with admirals, sir: I'm short on tact!"

"You're the son of one of the greatest admirals this Navy's ever had, and if gossip tells stories correctly, you've ignored the orders of most admirals you've ever served under. But, so have I," he admitted with a spontaneous grin. "Well, time is getting short – I expect I'll have to rejoin my fleet within a few days, and I'm a great believer in 'better one volunteer than three pressed men'."

"Me – I'm a volunteer, sir," Ramage said quickly, afraid he had offended Nelson by implying tardiness. "You took me by surprise because my name is near the bottom of the Post List and – "

"And it's not often that an admiral commanding a fleet offers a junior post-captain a chance to join him, eh?"

"Exactly, sir," Ramage took a deep breath. "If we can join you, sir – I mean, if you and the Admiralty approve – we'll have the ship ready for sea in a week and as soon as we can get up to Black Stakes and take on our powder, the *Calypso* could join you."

"Well spoken," Nelson said quietly. "You'll receive your orders from the Admiralty in a few days. In the meantime, if you can pass the word to your man Southwick, and your first lieutenant, of course, that might speed things up. Southwick knows most of the dockyard tricks. Replacing that copper sheathing is the most urgent job. Just the sort of time they run short of sheathing nails."

Ramage looked carefully at Nelson and then decided to chance it. The admiral had chased the French fleet across the Atlantic and back, and he had seen it evade him and join up with the Spaniards. The Combined Fleet must number thirty-five or more ships of the line, and some of those Spaniards carried more than a hundred guns. Nelson must have fewer than twenty ships, though Lord Barham was rushing out every available 74.

"Is there a chance they'll come out and fight, sir?"

Nelson shrugged, a curiously awkward movement which tugged at the empty sleeve. "The French – well, this fellow Villeneuve is no coward, but there's no telling what orders he gets from Bonaparte, who is a great soldier when fighting land battles but doesn't understand the sea. The Spanish? I don't think their hearts are in it. The French can rouse themselves with all this revolutionary nonsense (quite apart from Villeneuve knowing he'll be punished if he loses an action), but the Spanish...they seem to be trying to catch hold of Bonaparte's coat-tails, and that won't turn any captain into a fighting demon."

Nelson readjusted his eyeshade and the movement seemed to signal a change in the topic. "Well I shall see you at the Royal Exchange tomorrow, when you receive your sword. As I told the Master of Lloyd's Coffee House last week, you ought to have had a dozen swords by now. Let's rejoin the ladies."

As the carriage clattered back along Clarges Street and then swung right into Piccadilly on its way to Palace Street, Sarah said: "I'm proud of you, darling. Lord Nelson thinks you are one of the best frigate captains in the Service, and Lady Hamilton says you are certainly the most handsome!"

Ramage grinned and took Sarah's hand. "That makes you the luckiest wife in London – or in Clarges Street, anyway! What did you think of His Lordship?"

"The biggest contradiction I've ever met!"

Ramage's forehead wrinkled. "How so?"

"Well, he has an irritating nasal voice, he's obsessed with his health, he's obsessed with Lady Hamilton and wants everyone to accept her, he's so confident of himself he seems a braggart, he has a quick tongue and isn't afraid to use it, he's physically insignificant…"

"Yet…"

"Exactly, yet! He's also one of the most fascinating men I've ever met. He can't help his voice and one forgets it because of what he has to say. Yes, he's obsessed with his health, but he's been wounded so many times, and losing his right arm and being almost blind in one eye must give him a sense of frustration – in a lesser man it could almost destroy him.

"Lady Hamilton? Well, she's obsessed with him too, but she's thoughtful, understanding, and I for one don't care that she was once Emma Hart, Sir William's nephew's mistress: I'd be pleased to have her among my friends, and clearly she is His Lordship's inspiration.

"He has enormous confidence in himself because he knows what he wants and how to do it – that makes him unique among our admirals at the moment. Your father is about the only other one I can think of. Look what a mess Howe made at the Glorious First of June, and that indecisive fool Mann, and as for Lord St Vincent at *his* (I mean yours and Lord Nelson's) battle…

"What else was there? Oh, yes – the quick tongue. That must upset a lot of the slow-witted and tongue-tied admirals, but I've noticed one thing: a quick tongue usually goes with a quick wit, and a quick wit with a quick brain. Which means that for once we've got the right man commanding the fleet which may have to fight the Combined Fleets of France and Spain. Just think, it might have been St Vincent, or Lord Howe, or – it terrifies me to think of it."

"You must be one of the few wives who could sit with the full Board of Admiralty and make them sit up and listen!"

"Lady Hamilton says more or less the same thing as me."

"Yes, but she says it out of a blind faith in Lord Nelson," Ramage said. "You at least have worked it all out for yourself."

"The devil take logic," Sarah said unexpectedly, "at a time like this, when Bonaparte – his fleet, anyway – could defeat this country in an afternoon, I trust to what I feel in my heart. The Board of Admiralty would laugh at that, and with their crystal clear logic they almost invariably pick the wrong man. Sir Hyde Parker for command at Copenhagen, for example."

Ramage leaned over and kissed her. "I agree with every word. Anyway, St Vincent, not the Board, chose Parker. And remember, I'm not a member of the Board!"

"You will be one day, so remember what I've just said."

CHAPTER FOUR

The sword from the Lloyd's Patriotic Fund, presented to him on its behalf by Sir Josiah Hobart, the Lord Mayor (hot and perspiring in his splendid but heavy robes of office), was a superb example of the sword cutler's art. Back in Palace Street after the presentation, when his father and Sarah examined it with him, they were amused to find that it was made by Mr Prater, of Charing Cross, who always made their swords.

"The first sword I ever bought you – your midshipman's dirk, rather," the earl said, "cost twenty-five guineas, and the first real sword forty guineas. Soon after that I stopped buying you new swords because you made a habit of losing them on the decks of French ships!"

"Yes, so now I use an ordinary cutlass if we have to board," Ramage said. "But I must admit my present dress sword looks shabby; the brasswork on the scabbard corrodes. This will look smarter when I call on admirals – you can't beat gold fittings!"

Sarah lifted the heavy curved blade, decorated in blue and gold, holding the white ivory grip and gilt hilt. "What is this?" she asked, pointing out the stub sticking out at right-angles opposite the knuckle-guard.

"That's called the guillon. You can see it's designed as a Roman fasces."

"And this?" she indicated the hilt running upwards from the guillon.

"That's the backpiece. It represents the skin and head of a lion, as you can see."

"And this?"

"The knuckle-guard – stops the other fellow's sword sliding down the blade and lopping off your hand. It's shaped like Hercules' club, with a snake twisted round it."

She gave the sword back to Ramage. "It's magnificent," she commented and then sighed. "You know, I sat through that enormous dinner and was polite to Lord Barham on one side and Lord St Vincent on the other, but I still don't really know what Lloyd's Patriotic Fund is or who Lloyd's are. Neither the past nor the present First Lord seemed to know much about them, either."

"Well, I do know," the earl said, "so I'll tell you. In James IIs time a worthy fellow called Edward Lloyd opened a coffee house in Lombard Street, and there men of business connected with ships and the sea tended to congregate. They met in Lloyd's place to gossip and exchange information. Edward Lloyd always knew which ships had arrived, which ships were for sale, and so on. And if you own a ship or propose shipping a cargo somewhere, you need insurance, so it wasn't long before shipowners, shippers and insurance brokers were congregating there, arranging voyages.

"The original Edward Lloyd died but the coffee house remained the centre for shipping folk, and of course one of the most important things they wanted – whether they were owners, shippers or underwriters – was news: news of whether their ships and cargoes had arrived safely in the West Indies, sailed from Gravesend, or been wrecked off Dungeness. A shipowner was also interested in how much a rival sold a ship for, while shippers needed to know the latest price for carrying a hundred tons of molasses from Jamaica or a hundred pipes of port from the Peninsula. And the underwriters, of course, were involved in providing insurance cover for all of it.

"So in 1743 the coffee house started publishing a newspaper – little more than a broadsheet, really – which it called *Lloyd's List*, giving just the sort of news its customers wanted. Eventually – bearing in mind the need to guard against shipping fraud and the necessity of accurate news – a committee was formed to run the place, and a few years later the whole thing moved to the Royal Exchange, where it still is. The Committee chose the subscribers (whom it now called 'members', for reasons best known to itself) and when the war started it began co-operating with the Admiralty and shipowners in arranging convoys, and that sort of thing.

"When a ship's captain misbehaves in a convoy – " the earl looked at his son and smiled, " – not an unknown occurrence, as you know, my dear Sarah, the Board complains to the Committee of Lloyd's who, in theory, chide the owner of the ship, who disciplines his captain. The Board suspects, though, that the Committee tears up the letters."

"Swords," Sarah reminded him. "Who pays for the swords?"

"Ah yes. A couple of years ago Lloyd's set up a Patriotic Fund intended to help the Navy's wounded and reward the brave. It was an immediate success, I remember: the East India Company and the Bank of England each gave £5,000, while the City of London came up with £2,500. Several of the theatres gave gala performances, with the night's takings going to the Fund."

"I wonder where the hundred guineas came from that paid for Nicholas' sword?" Sarah said.

"The profits from shipping spices from the Indies or a spicy play at a theatre, eh?" Ramage said mischievously. "Lieutenants and masters get the fifty guinea swords, and mates and midshipmen rate thirty guineas."

The earl said: "I saw you had a word with Southwick and your first lieutenant, Aitken. Your news made their day, I shouldn't wonder!"

"Yes, both of them were all for posting straight back to Chatham to get young Martin to chase his father!"

The earl looked puzzled and Ramage reminded him. "You've forgotten that Martin's father is the Master Shipwright in the dockyard. A private word with him can be worth ten urgent letters from the Navy Board!"

"Hmm, you'd better check up and see whether the master shipwrights at Portsmouth and Plymouth have sons who want to ship as midshipmen, then you'll be set up round the South Coast."

"You'll never believe me, but when young Martin joined the *Calypso* I had no idea who his father was."

"More fool you. It'll be thanks to him if you get down to Cadiz in time. By the way," he said heavily. "Don't forget that frigates are just an admiral's scouts and means of signalling: they *don't* stand in line of battle. That's why," he added sarcastically, "64-gun ships and larger are called 'line-of-battle' ships. And no admiral today likes to put even a 64 in the line; he wants 74s and larger."

"Yes, father," Ramage said dutifully and, bearing in mind that he had lost the *Kathleen* in a successful attempt to prevent a Spanish three-decker from escaping at Cape St Vincent, added with a grin: "I'll remember: frigates stand at the back of the crowd and cheer."

"You were lucky with the *Kathleen*," the earl said, reading his thoughts, "and Lord Nelson is now repaying that debt. But anyone who relies too much on luck is a fool and – " he said jocularly, but intending Ramage should take notice, "Sarah is too young to be a widow."

He sighed and then grumbled, "I might just as well talk to myself." He turned towards Sarah. "Tell me about Lady Hamilton's daughter, my dear. Is she Lord Nelson's child?"

"Oh, there's no doubt about that, when you see them together, and for all the polite talk of 'godfather' he is just a normal doting father. And why not?" she said unexpectedly. "This war goes on year after year, and Nelson has nearly been killed so many times. Why shouldn't he seize what happiness he can? Anyway, if he goes on as he has in the past, he'll be lucky to be alive for Horatia's fifth birthday..."

"Now, now," the earl chided, "you fly to His Lordship's defence at the mere mention of his name!"

"I should think so!" Sarah said crossly. "You didn't have to listen to those wives at the Royal Exchange today! Why, they even made comments to me, thinking I would agree with them."

"But you didn't, so what answer did you make?" the earl asked, curious.

"I said that Lady Hamilton was a particular friend of mine," Sarah said defiantly, "and because I'm my father's daughter and my husband's wife, the hypocritical wretches had the grace to blush."

"Good for you," murmured the earl. "I'll follow your example with the husbands!"

Next morning Hanson, flustered at being interrupted while polishing the silver, bustled into the drawing room where Ramage was reading the *Morning Post* and reported that there was an Admiralty messenger at the door with a letter for Captain Lord Ramage which, Hanson added heavily, he would not hand over to anyone else.

"He's got a receipt book that needs signing, too," Hanson commented gloomily, as if this was proof that the man was not a messenger but a lurking thief after the silver.

Ramage went to the door, signed for the letter and carried it back to the drawing room, picking up a paper-knife on his way.

As he weighed the bulky packet in one hand, looking at the fouled anchor Admiralty seal, he savoured the moment. Yes – when he was a small boy up an apple tree and finally managed to reach the largest and ripest fruit…that moment with Raven when a rabbit shot out of its hole and landed with a thump in the net, to be followed by the beady-eyed ferret looking left and right as though the daylight dazzled him after the darkness of the warren…the moment when the masthead lookout hailed that he had sighted a sail which could only be French. And opening fresh Admiralty orders. All were preceded by excitement and anticipation – and a tincture of apprehension too, just enough to add spice.

He slid the paper-knife under the seal and unfolded the single page of thick paper. There was the usual address and introduction, and then William Marsden, who had recently succeeded Evan Nepean as Secretary to the Board, had written:

"Whereas my Lords Commissioners of the Admiralty are given to understand that His Majesty's frigate *Calypso* now at Chatham will soon be ready for sea, you are hereby directed and required to put to sea in His Majesty's frigate under your command as soon as maybe and use your best endeavours to join the fleet under the command of Vice Admiral the Lord Nelson, agreeable to the enclosed rendezvous, placing yourself under His Lordship's command for your further proceedings."

And that was that: a few lines of copperplate, neatly written by the Chief Clerk or one of the "Senior Clerks on the Establishment", and then signed by Marsden before being sent round to Palace Street by (if Ramage's memory served him) the Admiralty's only messenger, John Fetter, who for £40 a year delivered Their Lordships' letters and orders within five miles of Whitehall.

"As soon as maybe", according to Aitken and Southwick yesterday, would be about five days: most of the sheets of new sheathing had been nailed like fish scales round the *Calypso's* bow, and the tarred paper was already in place ready for the last of it, so rain would not cause delays. The new guns were already swayed on board and all the ropework spliced and, where necessary, rove through blocks.

Then the dry dock in which the frigate was sitting would be flooded at high water and the *Calypso* floated out. After the usual dockyard receipts and vouchers had been signed and Ramage formally resumed responsibility for the ship, taking over from the master attendant of the dockyard, the *Calypso* would run down the mud-lined Medway (unless the wind decided to be capricious and blow from the east). Then into the Thames (almost certainly in a foul wind and tide) for the beat up to Black Stakes, to lie alongside the powder hoys and load the *Calypso's* magazine and powder-room. It was a dangerous nuisance having to unload powder into the hoys before going into the dockyard and take it on board again afterwards, the risk of stray grains keeping the pumps sluicing the decks, but nothing compared with the danger of a ship in the dockyard catching fire with her magazine full and exploding to destroy half of Chatham.

Ramage often wondered about the men on the hoys who lived their lives on top of enough powder to blow them all to eternity and with only the mud flats along the Thames to look at. Low water, high water and the stink of mud governed their days. Did they sneak a smoke knowing that they lived within inches of a few hundred tons of gunpowder? Who commanded them? Probably some benighted lieutenant, leg shot off in distant action or disgraced by something that did not quite merit a court martial?

Sarah came into the room and saw the letter he was holding. "Your orders?"

He nodded. "I'll have to leave for Chatham in a day or two."

"I was hoping we'd have another couple of weeks together at Aldington," she said, obviously making an effort to keep her voice even.

"Will you go down there when I've left?"

"Yes. Once I knew you – " she paused, managing to swallow to be sure her voice would not falter, " – once I knew you would be sailing soon, I asked mother and father to come down for a few weeks. They'd like to see the house and father will enjoy the riding. Oh Nicholas!"

He stood up and held her tightly as she burst into tears. This was the first time he had seen her breakdown and he felt particularly helpless. Somehow she seemed to grow remote in her grief. But he knew it was because he felt guilty at leaving her.

"I shan't be away long," he murmured. "Just off Cadiz. It's not as if I'm going to the West Indies or the East Indies. Or to the Isla Trinidade," he added, hoping to make her smile.

She stopped weeping and tried to laugh. "Look what happened to you when you went *there!*"

"Just a pleasant cruise, or so I thought. Little did I know that a scheming woman was waiting for me in an East India Company ship…"

"But now you've married her, you're deserting her!"

Sarah was getting control of herself but he *was* deserting her, in a way, and the dreadful thing was that he was excited at the prospect of getting to sea again in the *Calypso*. That pleasure was all mixed up with his feeling of guilt at leaving her, and now he knew what many married officers went through. Now Lord St Vincent's stern comment that "an officer who marries is lost to the Service" seemed more reasonable, though harsh.

There was no reason why serving in the Navy should condemn a man to a monkish existence, yet how else could the Navy be run? More generous leave, perhaps – but every ship that could swim was needed at sea, which meant she spent as little time in port as possible, just long enough for provisioning and any necessary repairs. The regulations, strictly kept, said that a captain must always sleep in his ship in port unless he had Admiralty permission to remain on shore...

"You'll go riding with your father?" he asked, realizing as soon as he spoke what a damned silly question it was, but it served its purpose: Sarah stood back, wiped her eyes, gave a faint hiccup and said: "Thank goodness we have some decent horses. And Raven will be pleased to see us use the harness he polishes with so much love."

"I'll soon be back," Ramage said, and could have bitten off his tongue the moment later: it was a particularly stupid remark to make to Sarah, of all people.

"If only I could be sure you'd remember what your father said about frigates not being line-of-battle ships, and if I didn't know that Lord Nelson's fleet is about half the size of the French and Spanish, I'd smile and say 'Of course you will, darling' like any other dutiful wife, but one of the disadvantages of marrying a Ramage and being the Marquis of Rockley's daughter is that I know far too much to take comfort from such platitudes. It's going to be a desperate business, darling; it always is where you or Lord Nelson are concerned."

He held her tightly and kissed her. Words simply brought more trouble.

Ramage was again sitting in the drawing room reading the *Morning Post* and noting the obvious relief that the newspaper expressed that Nelson was back in England and, presumably, consulting with the ministers on the question of defeating the Combined Fleets of France and Spain and Bonaparte's plans for invading England. As if defeating the enemy was only a matter of consulting with ministers.

If anything, he thought, battles were won in spite of ministers – Mr Pitt seemed to listen to some strange companions, particularly that drunken scoundrel Henry Dundas, the recently created Viscount Melville, reckoned to be as corrupt as he was impetuous. Certainly Dundas' advice when Secretary of State at the War Department had led to thousands of soldiers and sailors dying of vile diseases while garrisoning or guarding the wretchedly useless spice islands of the West Indies. Dundas must be getting some hefty bribes from the West India Committee – unless he himself owned some big plantations out there.

Still, Ramage was content. Upstairs were his orders for the *Calypso*: in another couple of days he would leave for Chatham… He gave a start as Hanson tapped on the door and interrupted his musings: at that moment he realized he had heard a carriage draw up outside. Who was expected? Probably one of mother's friends, calling to discuss something of no consequence and therefore, to her, of enormous importance.

"My lord, there's a Captain Backlog wanting to see you urgently…"

Backlog? Sailor or soldier? Ramage folded his newspaper. "Show him in."

Ramage stood up and reached the door just in time to meet a burly figure with curly hair and the ruddy complexion of a farmer, but an incongruous aquiline nose and sun-tanned features fitted well with the gold-trimmed uniform of a post-captain whose two epaulets showed he had more than three years' seniority.

Ramage did not know him but guessed who he was just as the man, hat tucked under his arm, said apologetically with the trace of a soft Irish accent: "Henry Blackwood. I'm sorry to intrude like this, but I've a message from His Lordship – from Lord Nelson, I mean."

Ramage noticed the badly creased uniform, grubby stock and red-rimmed eyes: Blackwood had been travelling in a post-chaise for hours and he had come from a sunny climate. And the thin white lines of salt in the creases of his high boots showed he had not had time to change since he was at sea.

Blackwood, Ramage then remembered (wasn't he said to be the son of an Irish peeress and an English baronet?), had served for a long time with Lord Nelson in the Mediterranean, and was commanding the *Penelope* frigate when he met a French ship of the line, the 86-gun *Guillaume Tell*, and set about her with his puny thirty-six guns with such spirit that he disabled her long enough for two of Nelson's ships of the line to come up and engage her. After fighting for several hours she surrendered – and it was discovered that she was bearing the flag of Rear-Admiral Decrès, now Bonaparte's Minister of Marine.

Now, if Ramage's memory served him, Blackwood was commanding the frigate *Euryalus*. And at that moment Ramage realized how weary the man must be.

"Do sit down. Have you eaten recently? A hot drink?"

Blackwood shook his head but sat down thankfully, obviously painfully stiff. "I'm a little weary, so forgive me if I don't make much sense: I arrived in Lymington village late last evening, after losing the wind at the back of the Wight and having to be rowed in. I managed to post up to Town – I kept those horses at a good gallop – and reached Lord Nelson at Merton at five o'clock this morning, and after giving him the news, posted on to the Admiralty to tell Lord Barham."

The man was almost asleep – certainly dazed with weariness. "What news?" Ramage asked gently.

"Sorry, I was thinking of Lord Nelson's message for you. What happened was, we understood the Combined Fleet was in Ferrol and Coruña – they'd bolted there when His Lordship chased 'em back across the Atlantic. But I was off Cape St Vincent with the *Euryalus* when I suddenly met them all at sea, steering south, either for Cadiz – most likely – or the Strait.

"I guessed they were making for Cadiz to join the rest of their brethren, so I chased them long enough to be sure. Then I steered for the Channel to raise the alarm. I met Rear-Admiral Calder with eighteen line-of-battle ships and warned him, and while he went south after the enemy I carried on for the Channel. Took me ten dam' days with contrary winds before I got up as far as the Isle of Wight and lost the wind altogether.

"I had myself rowed ashore in the dark – and a wretched muddy place Lymington creek is, I can assure you – and managed to hire a 'chaise to London: it's going to cost Their Lordships £15 9s. – if they agree to pay the charge."

He rubbed his eyes. "Shake me if I fall asleep on you: the drumming of the hoofs and the clatter of the wheels are still in my head. Anyway, I reached Merton and told His Lordship, and then went on to raise the alarm at the Admiralty. Lord Barham may be well over eighty years old, but he wakes up a deal faster than I do!

"Now we get to Lord Nelson's message (sorry, I had to tell you the rest so it makes sense). Before I left him at Merton – he decided to come up to the Admiralty in his own carriage with Lady Hamilton – he gave me your address and told me to call as soon as I'd finished at the Admiralty. The message is simply that His Lordship will be sailing in the *Victory* from St

Helens as soon as maybe, and you're to sail as quickly as possible, joining him at St Helens or, if he's managed to get away from the Isle of Wight, join the fleet off Cadiz and place yourself under my command.

"He said that he doesn't mind if you arrive short of a couple of new topsails and half a dozen guns, but he needs every frigate he can get. As he's giving me command of a sort of inshore squadron, I can bear that out: there'll be three or four frigates, once I get off Cadiz with the *Euryalus*, but for what His Lordship has in mind, ten wouldn't be enough. I tell you, Ramage, His Lordship is breathing fire: he won't be satisfied with less than the complete destruction of the Combined Fleet."

"How many ships have they?"

"About thirty or more," Blackwood said. "Depends how many were waiting for them in Cadiz."

"And His Lordship?"

Blackwood made a face and admitted in a soft burr: "Well, Lord Barham was counting them up while I was in his office and he waited for Lord Nelson, and with luck there'll be twenty. More, of course, if they can be got ready in time. But several ships of the line are in the dockyards, quite apart from frigates like your *Calypso*. I gather you've already had your orders from Lord Barham: it's just a question of chasing up the dockyard, and taking on powder at Black Stakes?"

Ramage nodded, thinking of Aldington, St Kew, his father's new will, and Sarah. Yes, it was different for a married naval officer. "Yes – with a decent wind I'll be at St Helens before His Lordship boards the *Victory*!"

CHAPTER FIVE

Farewells were over: Raven had carefully stowed his trunk on the post-chaise at London Bridge, where the Dover 'chaise started, and the Marsh man, before saying goodbye to Ramage and taking the carriage back to Palace Street, handed over a letter. "From Her Ladyship, sir. Said you was to read it on board your ship."

Then with shouts and the cracking of whips over the backs of the four horses, the post-chaise began its dash: the one other passenger was a bishop returning to his see of Dover, the usual plump and self-satisfied prelate who at first seemed put out at having to share the carriage with a Navy captain but who became almost servile the moment he heard Raven bidding farewell to "My Lord". Was His Lordship travelling far? the bishop inquired. No, Ramage said, not far. Perhaps His Lordship lived in Kent? Yes, Ramage said, at Aldington.

But...but this 'chaise doesn't go to Aldington: it goes through the Medway towns. For Aldington His Lordship needs the 'chaise that goes through Ashford.

"I'm not going to Aldington," Ramage said shortly, cursing that he had to start the day, let alone the journey (which would end at Cadiz!), with this dreary, cringing churchman whose pink complexion and bloated features labelled him a trencherman, as handy with a fork as a Biblical quotation.

"Oh, I thought you said..."

"You asked me where I lived. I also have an estate in Cornwall and a house in Town, but I'm not going to any of them," Ramage said coldly and was quickly ashamed of his exaggerations, but this wretched fellow refused to be snubbed.

"Ah, you're joining a ship; I can guess that."

Ramage looked out of the window. The carriage was just approaching the Bricklayer's Arms. "Yes," he said grudgingly, and suddenly felt a wish to boast that he was joining Lord Nelson, but to this bishop war, no doubt, was only an inconvenience since it did not interrupt meals.

"It must be an exciting moment."

"On the contrary; I've lived on board the same ship for the past few years and it will stink of fresh paint and men will be hammering away all day and night."

"Dear me, how unpleasant. You should send your deputy down, until everything is ready."

Was that how the Lord's work was done in the see of Dover? Ramage wondered.

The bishop lifted a large basket on to his lap and began folding back a napkin. The basket was full of food and the bishop began tearing the meat from a chicken leg. The chomping of his teeth kept time with the horses' hooves until he stopped to wrench the cork from a bottle of wine.

New Cross...they would change horses at Blackheath. How long would that basket of food keep the worthy bishop quiet? The 'chaise was soon passing the Isle of Dogs, over to the left, on the far side of the Thames as it snaked its way through London. In half an hour – less, perhaps – they would reach Shooter's Hill, passing the quiet beauty of Greenwich Palace on the left. Down there, within a few hundred yards of the Thames, Henry VIII and his two daughters, the great Elizabeth and the less favoured Mary, had all been born. Both the father Henry and the daughter Elizabeth had (almost alone among the monarchs!) understood the importance of a strong Navy due, perhaps, to childhood days spent watching the ships passing? Today the great palace was the Seamen's Hospital: men crippled in the King's service at sea now stumped about with crutches and wooden legs where once (three centuries earlier) a boyish Henry VIII had played.

The bishop chomped on, delving among the napkins to see what else he had to eat. Enough at the present rate to last him until the 'chaise got through Welling and stopped at the Golden Lion at Bexley Heath... Golf. The thought suddenly struck Ramage. Wasn't it somewhere round here – the common at Blackheath? – that James I first introduced the curious game to England? Ramage shrugged: he did not play himself, and the bishop looked as though he was already taking the only physical exercise he favoured.

Finally, the carriage swung into the courtyard of the Golden Lion and the two postboys leapt to the ground to drop the steps with the usual crash. The bishop groaned, though Ramage was not sure if it was the noise or the need to leave his food.

Ramage jumped down to be met by the innkeeper, anxious to serve sherry, cocoa, coffee, ale or whatever the gentleman fancied. The gentleman, stiff and bored, his thoughts suspended somewhere between Palace Street and the number three dock at Chatham, wanted to be left alone. The bishop called for "A cool mug of ale, my good man," and the ostlers led up the fresh horses.

Soon after the carriage had started again, the bishop belched contentedly as he dozed, and then wakened to assault the basket once more and continued eating until they had gone through Crayford and were pulling in at The Bull at Dartford to change the horses. Ramage walked round the carriage a few times and soon after they began moving again the bishop was snoring stertorously, lulled by more beer rather than the rough road.

Horns Cross (curious, he remembered a village of the same name in Devon), then Northfleet and Gravesend, the brown muddy Thames running alongside. The driver had barely started the horses pulling out of Gravesend when he had to stop at the first of the turnpikes, at Chalk Street. Like a thousand coachmen before him, he swore as he fished in his pocket for the coins to pay the toll-keeper.

Not far, not far, Ramage thought thankfully; the next village of any note is called Halfway House, though Ramage was puzzled by the name. It was certainly not half-way between London and Rochester. Perhaps between Gravesend and the Medway at Rochester?

The bishop woke up, grunted and made another foray into his basket, cursing a fly which was anxious to spend a few minutes on a crumb clinging to the bishop's chin. "Ha, soon be at Gad's Hill," he said, raising his head momentarily from the basket. "Damnably uncomfortable, these machines. I wonder they dare charge tenpence a mile. Ought to pay the travellers tenpence a mile to travel in 'em."

Ramage smiled politely at the only worthwhile comment the bishop had made so far. However, one does not have to attend his cathedral: imagine that voice droning on, warning the congregation against the sin of gluttony…

The horses seemed to find a second wind: perhaps they could sniff the Medway and knew they now had a good clear run down a gentle slope to Rochester, where they would be taken out and replaced by fresh horses to take the carriage on to Sittingbourne before being changed again.

Soon Ramage could see the 110-foot-high ruined keep of Rochester Castle, which had been guarding this crossing of the Medway since the twelfth century: yes, and there was the cathedral, one of the oldest in the county, if not the country.

Rochester was a fine old town with dignified buildings and, like all places built with a reason – to guard the crossing of the Medway – having its own purposeful air about it, even though it was now a distant memory.

Finally the 'chaise swung into the courtyard of the post inn at Chatham, and as soon as the boys had slammed down the steps, Ramage climbed down, every bone in his body aching, and the cobbles hard and unyielding underfoot. Make the most of it, he told himself; within the week you'll be tired of tramping the *Calypso*'s deck. And there'll be no changing horses at Cadiz...

The livery coach clattered through the gate and rounded up alongside the *Calypso* as she sat four-square in the dock, seeming twice as big out of the water, her masts towering so high it seemed they ought to scratch lines in the low cloud.

The steps slammed down and Ramage climbed out of the coach, thankful that he had left the bishop when he had changed from the 'chaise in Chatham town. But there was something odd about the *Calypso*. The new copper sheathing below the waterline was bright (but measled green where rain had started corrosion). A moment later he realized why it was different. Normally her hull was entirely black, with just a white strake the width of the portlids (which, painted red inside, made a chequerboard effect when the portlids were raised and the guns run out). But now there was a broad yellow strake along the side of the *Calypso* instead of the white. This was the way that Lord Nelson always painted his ship – the *Victory* had three rows, or strakes, of yellow – and many of his captains copied the style with their own ships, to show they were serving (or had served) with His Lordship. And now someone – Aitken, Southwick? – had added the yellow strake to the *Calypso* in anticipation.

Not only had whoever it was braved the captain's wrath (although it would take only a few hours to restore the white), but he must have paid for the paint himself, because the dockyard issued only black or white paint. Anyone wanting something different could paint his ship whatever colour he chose (Ramage could see a plum-coloured 74 in the next dock), but the captain paid for it out of his own pocket. A ship of the line painted a light colour showed that her captain had either a good independent income or had been lucky with prize money.

And there were Aitken and Southwick, both looking remarkably worried, hurrying towards him as two seamen ran up to lift off his trunk.

Aitken, as first lieutenant, saluted gravely and then, after briefly welcoming Ramage back, gestured at the *Calypso's* hull. "We thought, sir, as we are joining Lord Nelson's fleet, that..."

Ramage deliberately looked grave. Southwick, saluting, said quickly: "We thought we'd anticipate your orders, sir."

Ramage looked him up and down. "What makes you think I'd want to fling pots of yellow paint at my ship, eh?"

Both men looked so crestfallen, like guilty schoolboys, that Ramage laughed. "It looks very good, but I'll pay for it: give me the dockyard vouchers and I'll settle 'em. And we'll need a few gallons more to keep it looking bright."

Aitken sighed with relief, but Southwick chuckled. "I told him you'd be pleased, but he was *far* from sure. In fact yesterday he wanted to paint it out, so we'd be back to a white strake."

"How soon can we get afloat?" Ramage demanded, aware that the two seamen preparing to lift his trunk were deliberately dawdling so that they could hear what was being said.

"On the next tide, as long as the master attendant agrees," Aitken assured him.

"Very well, arrange that: Lord Nelson and the *Victory* – with yellow strakes – are waiting for us at St Helens, and the French and the Dons are waiting for both of us in Cadiz!"

Southwick grinned and said: "We'll get afloat even if we have to open the dock gates ourselves: the men will be happy enough to knock away the shores – they're fed up with life in dry dock!"

"Very well, get word to the master attendant and report to my cabin in fifteen minutes." With that he walked out along the gangplank and went on board. He stood on the quarterdeck before going down the companionway to his cabin. Yes, it was all here: the reek of paint, so strong that the smell ought to be visible as thick smoke, and somewhere there was the rapid metallic thud of hammers – the last of the sheathing nails being driven home? Probably. The noise echoed dully through the ship, as though the banging was on the outside of the hull.

His cabin smelled like a paint store, even though the skylights were wide open and the portlids for the 12-pounders were hoisted up, wide open on each side of the great cabin and in the bed place and couch. In half an hour he would have a splitting headache. But all three cabins sparkled: there was fresh white paint on the bulkheads and deckhead, reflecting the light, and the canvas on the soles of all three cabins had been repainted, the black and white squares freshened up so that it seemed he had new carpets. His bed swung from the heavy metal eyes bolted into the beams and there were no spots of paint on it – someone had, thank goodness, stowed it out of the way before the paint brushes were put to work. And Sarah had sewn new covers for him, and made sure they were packed in his trunk.

The letter from Sarah, given him by Raven as he boarded the 'chaise, nestled in the inside pocket of his frock coat, and after pitching his hat on to the settee he sat at the desk (the top freshly polished and still smelling of the bosun's special beeswax-and-turpentine mixture that the men had used) and took a paper-knife from the top drawer.

Pride, awe, delight...it was difficult to sort out the emotions, but the letter was addressed to him in Sarah's handwriting, and there was the griffin seal. A letter from Lady Ramage. The first he had ever received but, God willing, the first of many.

He was reluctant to break the seal for reasons he could not explain. Her handwriting and the Ramage seal seemed an entity: to open the letter would somehow spoil it. But leaving it sealed defeated the whole purpose...

He slid the knife under the wax and opened out the folded page. The letter was brief. She loved him and was disappointed that this time she was staying at home while he went to sea – he had to smile: it was typical of Sarah to dismiss the long months that she had been one of Bonaparte's prisoners in such a casual fashion. And, underlined, was a reference to his father's admonition that frigates did not stand in the line of battle. Her final sentence stirred up memories to which his loins responded.

He heard a stamping outside and noted that the captain now had his Marine sentry outside the door – either Aitken had passed the word or Rennick, the Marine lieutenant, had seen the carriage arrive. The sentry was probably rigged out in working dress ten minutes ago, painting or helping with the rigging, and had hurriedly changed into uniform, careful not to knock the pipeclay off the crossbelts.

Ramage was still holding Sarah's letter when he heard feet coming down the companion ladder and, a few moments later, the sentry's shout of: "The first lieutenant and the master, sir!"

Both men came into the cabin in answer to Ramage's call and he gestured for them to sit down. It was a ritual – the master with his flowing white hair and unadmitted rheumatism sat in the armchair beside the desk, while Aitken used the settee.

The two of them waited patiently for Ramage to begin. However, although Ramage had seen them less than a week ago at the Royal Exchange at the Lloyd's presentation, he wanted to hear first about the ship.

"Well, as I told you on the dock, sir, we're about ready," Aitken said. "The men are hammering in the nails on the last few sheets of sheathing, as you can hear, and every inch of running and a good half of the standing rigging has been renewed. The master sailmaker agreed to condemn all the topsails and t'gallants, so we have new ones. They've all been scrubbed to get the size out of 'em. We had three days without a breath of wind so we could hoist 'em, let fall, and check over the cut. They're all strong sails, sir, with the last row of reef points put in deep.

"All the cabins have been painted out. We've had your cabins open ever since but I'm sorry the stink is still here. Five 12-pounders have been changed. Two of the old ones were honeycombed, so I suppose we can count ourselves lucky they didn't blow up on us."

Aitken grinned at Ramage. "The master attendant wouldn't believe how many times we'd been in action with them."

"If a honeycombed gun is going to blow up, it's as likely to do it in practice as in action," Ramage pointed out.

"Aye," Aitken agreed, his Scots accent pronounced, "but the effect could be disastrous in action; in practice it'd be just an accident."

"Has everything else been checked?" Ramage asked. "Rudder, gudgeons and pintles, tiller ropes, wheel ropes... Capstan and voyol block...?"

"Everything," Southwick said with more than a hint of reproach in his voice. "Even the ensign halyard's been renewed, sir."

Ramage recognized the "why don't you give over?" tone of the "sir": Southwick had served with him since the day Lord (then just an unhonoured commodore) Nelson had given a very young lieutenant his first command. And that reminded him.

"By the way, Southwick, Lord Nelson was inquiring after you. You'll be flattered to hear that he remembered your name from the time he put me in command of the *Kathleen*, and seems to have noticed every time your name was mentioned in a *Gazette* letter."

The old master grinned with pleasure and then said, as a hint to Ramage to give some more news: "You mentioned in your letter yesterday His Lordship's plans."

"Yes, we called on him and Lady Hamilton, but I'm here now because of a message I received yesterday morning – after the Dover 'chaise had left, otherwise I'd have been here earlier."

He then told both men of the talk he had had with Nelson, followed by Captain Blackwood's unexpected visit the previous morning with the news of the Combined Fleet's concentration at Cadiz.

Southwick rubbed his hands together with the glee of a trencherman watching tender roast beef being carved. "St Helens, eh, and if the *Victory's* gone, we race her to Cadiz. Give us a bit o' luck with the winds in the Bay of Biscay, and we could beat her!"

"At least we have a clean bottom and a decent suit of sails," Aitken said.

"What about the ship's company?" Ramage asked suddenly, remembering he had caused several heads to shake in the dockyard when he gave permission for each watch to have ten days' leave, starting with the larboard watch.

The dockyard commissioner had wanted to countermand Ramage's order, declaring that a good half of the men would desert. "You're just turning 'em loose," he had said, "then you'll come whining to me that you haven't enough men to shift the ship out of the dock, let alone get under way." But Ramage had been adamant. It was a test of his own leadership: all the men had done very well from prize money (several of the senior petty officers were by their standards rich) and they served in a ship which was happy, frequently in action, and where sickness (thanks to the Surgeon Bowen and a sensible diet) was almost unknown. Ramage's feeling was that if any men took advantage of his trust to desert, he did not want those sort of men anyway.

"The ship's company, sir?" Aitken repeated, as though puzzled by the question. "Well, we are still a dozen or so short of complement, as before, but everyone's back from leave."

"All of them?"

"All," Aitken said. "In fact half a dozen came back early – spent all the money they'd drawn."

So much for the dockyard commissioner, Ramage thought. How did one let him know without offending a man who wielded great power within his dockyard walls?

"What's the earliest they can flood up?" Ramage asked.

"The master attendant reckons he can start in a couple of hours. But we'll have to wait for high water to get out over the sill of this dock, which is the smallest in the yard and used only for frigates, as you know, and by the time they've knocked away all the shores and fished them out so they don't tear the sheathing, we'll have an hour of ebb running..."

"Well, I'm not going down the dam' Medway on an ebb tide," Ramage said firmly. "Trying to save a few hours could cost us a couple of days stuck in the mud – and Medway mud is the deepest and stickiest known to man."

Southwick sighed thankfully. "I was going to suggest we waited for the first of the next flood, sir... We'll have a fair wind most if not all of the way to Sheerness, so it won't matter that we're butting the young flood. It'll be so near low water we'll be able to see the deep channel: this end of the river has more bends than a snake with colic."

Ramage glanced at Aitken. "I've no doubt you've lots of reports, accounts, and so on for me to sign before we sail...?"

Aitken lifted a folder which he had put beside him on the settee. "I have them here, sir."

"And the bill for that yellow paint?"

"That, too, sir, but Southwick and I had intended it to be a present."

CHAPTER SIX

The run down the Medway to Sheerness had been notable – as Bowen had commented – for its smell. Medway mud seemed to be a vile and viscous mixture of sewage, blue clay and brown glue, stretching out in a wide band on each side of the fairway as the river twisted from Chatham to Garrison Point at its mouth, where it passed between Grain Spit to larboard and Cheyney Spit to starboard and ran into the Thames at Great Nore.

"Look at those dam' sea birds," Bowen had exclaimed, pointing at a dozen or so waders. "By rights they should stick fast in the mess!"

Southwick was more concerned with two birds jinking across the river, uttering sharp cries. "Ah, if only I had a fowling piece I'd get one of those snipe!" he exclaimed.

"And who'd retrieve for you?" Aitken inquired sarcastically.

As the river widened at Kethole Reach and Saltpan Reach in the approaches to Sheerness, the flood stream – now strong, eddying and curling round the few buoys (marking the entrances on the starboard hand to Half Acre and Stangate Creeks and West Swale) and tilting them upstream – carried swans past them, proud-looking creatures which refused to hurry, moving in a stately fashion to give the *Calypso* just enough room to pass between them as she passed the mudflats, one of which had a curious name, Bishop Ooze.

"They remind me of three-deckers," commented Aitken, "but they tack and wear with less fuss."

Soon Sheerness was astern and Southwick took the frigate down the fairway clear of Sheerness Middle Sand to meet Sea Reach, turning to larboard at the Great Nore with the flood stream under her to go on a few miles and then turn to come alongside the powder hoys at Black Stakes.

This part of the Thames was grim: to larboard, the Yantlet Flats were flat fields of thick, stinking and bubbling mud with what were like ditches where scour had cut runways. To starboard, the names on the chart told a similar but less smelly story – West Knock and East Knock were the entrances to a deeper channel across Southend Flats, which merged into the Marsh End Sand, Leigh Sand and the long stretch of the Chapman Sands off Leigh.

As the hoys came into sight, Ramage cursed himself for a weakling; he had done nothing about the gunner. The man was a dodger: he evaded responsibility as other men tried to evade diseases. But changing him meant a long argument with the Army's Board of Ordnance, as well as the Navy Board. Both would want written evidence of his incompetence, and there was the rub: as a gunner the man was not incompetent; he looked after the *Calypso*'s guns and magazine; he – well, that was the trouble. He was just a man who dodged responsibility for anything, even boxes of slow match, although it was irritating for his fellow officers and his captain, it was not a crime.

Ramage could imagine arguments with both Boards – "I can't send him away in charge of expeditions" – "Give an example" – "Well, I haven't one because I daren't send him off" – "Then how do you know you can't trust him?" And so on.

Well, soon they would be alongside a hoy and taking on nearly ten tons of powder in 120-pound cases and 90-pound barrels. Ramage could be sure that both Aitken and Southwick would be watching every move, whether by seamen or the gunner, as the copper-hooped cases and barrels were hoisted on board, using the staytackle and a cargo net. And of course there would be boxes of portfires, signal rockets and quick match already cut into lengths and packed into boxes with sliding lids.

Gunpowder. Curious stuff, just an innocent-looking grey powder. Two sorts, naturally. Most of the powder hoisted on board would be coarse, used in the bore of the guns to fire 12-pounder roundshot. But some, in specially marked containers, would be the fine powder used for priming: put in the priming pans of the 12-pounders, carronades, muskets and pistols. "Mealed" powder, it used to be called, but the important thing was that it was so fine it took fire the instant the flintlock made a spark (unless the powder was damp or the spark particularly weak). Priming powder was, pound for pound, a good deal more powerful than the coarse sort: load a gun with priming powder instead of coarse and you risked it bursting.

Well, that was the gunner's responsibility: the coarse powder had to be used to fill the flannel cartridges, cloth tubes the diameter of the bore of the guns, and priming powder had to be put in the powder horns issued to gun captains as they went into action and to men armed with pistols or muskets.

One hour later the *Calypso* was secured alongside a hoy: bow, stern, breastropes and springs had been adjusted and the staytackle rigged, Aitken reported. Ramage had given orders to start loading the powder, after a second check had been made that the galley fire was out, that no men were smoking, that the fire engine had been hoisted up on deck and the cistern filled with seawater, and finally that the washdeck pumps were also rigged and the decks well wetted – running with water, in fact – in case any of the barrels or cases leaked powder while being slung on board.

Going into action? Ramage considered it was nothing compared to taking on powder. When going into action his mind was full of a dozen different problems, quite apart from giving orders and watching the enemy, but taking on powder – there was just the rattle and squeak of the blocks as the men hauled on the tackle to hoist the net on board, and he either paced the deck or sat in his cabin and thought of a tiny dribble of that grey powder falling on the deck, and something crushing it: just enough pressure to cause a detonation. No flame or spark needed. There would be a gigantic explosion and in the place of the *Calypso* and the hoy there would be a great circle of roiled water with planks and spars (and bodies) falling like solid rain... They'd hear the noise as far away as Chatham and Greenwich – and few would doubt what caused it.

With five tons of powder hoisted on board and carried below, Ramage decided he would inspect the magazine and powder-room. He had not been inside either since inspecting every inch of the ship when she was captured from the French. That was not quite true, since every Sunday he made his routine inspection of the ship, when he put his head round the door, but he did not enter because no one was allowed in unless he was barefoot or wearing felt shoes (and had been searched for any ferrous object: that could clink and make a spark).

He sat down on the settee in his cabin and took off his shoes. Silkin would not be very pleased to find his master had been walking round the ship in white silk stockings, but Silkin had an easy-going master, in Ramage's view; the captain's servant was a valet and many of them serving penurious captains had to spend much of their time mending stockings, shirts and stocks, so a little extra laundry would not overtax Silkin.

He padded out of the cabin, ignored the Marine sentry's startled gaze but returned his salute as usual, and went on deck calling for Aitken.

The first lieutenant joined him by the capstan and was careful to keep his eyes above shoulder level.

"Don't be so damned tactful," Ramage growled. "Go below and take your shoes off – we're going to give the magazine and powder-room a close inspection. Tell the gunner to stay on deck."

Aitken grinned happily: the gunner was the only man in the whole ship whose mere appearance could put him in a temper.

Ramage went below, waited for Aitken, and then led the way along the passage leading to the magazine and powder-room. The passage had the silent, cold feel of the entrance to a vault but, like the rest of the area, it was specially constructed.

To begin with, both the magazine and powder-room were called officially the "hanging magazine", because not only were both built below the waterline, but they were placed four feet lower than the deck level, like a large inset box, so that anyone entering had to go down several steps. More important, in an emergency it could be flooded with seawater and both magazine and powder-room would be submerged instantly, along with the powder, whether in case, barrel or flannel cartridges.

The passageway and both magazine and powder-room had the floors plastered with mortar, and over that had been laid a dry lining of narrow strips of deal planking, little more than lathes. Then all three had been lined with lead sheeting weighing five pounds to the square foot, Ramage recalled inconsequentially as he tapped with his knuckle, making sure that none of the sheeting had "crept", coming away from the lathes-and-mortar base.

At the end of the passage the magazine door (which was also the entrance to the powder-room) was hung with heavy brass hinges which were secured with copper screws. The big lock was made of solid copper, and the huge copper key (which always made your hand smell if you had to carry it) was normally kept by Aitken and issued to the gunner only on the captain's orders.

The only illumination came from the little light room, a wedge-shaped glass cupboard, accessible only from outside, in which stood a lantern which shone into the magazine with its flame separated from the powder by a thick glass window.

Ramage stood back to let four sailors pass him with cases of powder. The dim, yellow light of the lantern showed that the passageway was clean and none of the sheeting bulged on the sole, bulkheads or deckhead. Once the seamen had left the magazine, Ramage walked in. With its many shelves, which would soon be filled with flannel cartridges for the 12-pounders and the carronades, the magazine was completely lined with thin copper sheeting: a further precaution against sparks but, along with the lead, giving added protection against rats gnawing their way into the magazine and then chewing the flannel of the cartridges, allowing powder to spill.

The only reminder that from time to time an enemy could threaten the magazine was the rolls of thick felt, for the moment held up by tapes against the deckhead, out of the way of the men carrying powder, but in action the blankets of felt would be unrolled, to hang down, soaked with water, heavy curtains to prevent the flash from guns or an explosion from penetrating the magazine and blowing up the ship.

The last curtain had a small aperture cut in it: in action, each powder cartridge would be passed through it to a waiting powder monkey, who would hold up his wooden cartridge case and, with the flannel bag thrust in, push down the lid before hurrying back along the passageway past the wet felt curtains, and making his way back to the gundeck.

Ramage and Aitken, inside the magazine, inspected the copper. Several sheets near the doorway were a rich reddish-gold: they had been renewed in the past few days. The powder-room beyond – where both Ramage and Aitken had to back and fill so that their own shadows did not obscure what they were trying to inspect – also had some new sheeting.

When Ramage commented on it. Aitken said: "I took the opportunity when we had all the powder out. I asked the gunner if he had anything needing to be done down here, but he said no. So I made my own inspection. No sheet was actually worn through, but a dozen or more were paper-thin and would soon go..."

"That damned gunner," Ramage said. "I did nothing about him..."

The run down the Thames and out into the English Channel always excited Ramage, not because he enjoyed navigating between the sandbanks which littered the twisting channels, where being an instant late in tacking or wearing round a buoy or getting caught in stays (or even misjudging the strength of the current) could put the ship hard aground, but because of the names.

Start with the Yantlet, at the western end of Sea Reach. Very well, that took its name from the Yantlet Flats, over to starboard, miles of mud and ooze. But Yantlet? There was no village on the chart; simply a small creek of that name.

East and West Knock, off Shoeburyness. Knock – like knock, knock? Out to the Great Nore again and then steering south-east for the Four Fathom Channel, leaving the long tongue of Red Sand to larboard, to come into the Kentish Flats and then bear up to the north-east into the Queen's Channel to avoid two long stretches running parallel with the coast, Cliffend Sand (off Reculver) and Margate Sand.

And then the reach into Botany Bay, off Foreness Point, and a haul on the sheets to pass North Foreland, the eastern tip of the county of Kent. Botany Bay? The next to the west was called Palm Bay, but what could be botanical, backed by the wicked white cliffs that formed the Foreland itself?

Then Broadstairs Knoll, into the Old Cudd Channel and down the Gull Stream, to pass inside the Goodwin Sands and across the Downs, the comparatively sheltered anchorage favoured by ships of war and merchant ships waiting to go up to the port of London or the Medway.

Southwick was in his element in these waters: he knew the Thames and the Downs "like looking at my face in the morning"; he rarely glanced at the chart and, although the leadsman stood ready in the chains, rarely called for a cast of the lead.

The *Calypso* stretched down from the South Foreland, seeming to delight at being at sea again, her copper-sheathed bottom clean, the new topsails and topgallants stretching into shape, the wind flattening out the creases and pressing the canvas into fair curves.

The wind, Ramage noted thankfully, was beginning to veer as they rounded the South Foreland and hardened sheets to bring Dover into sight. By the time Shakespeare Cliff was on the quarter and Danger Rock on the beam, the wind had settled into the north-west.

"If it stays there," Southwick said jubilantly, pointing at the windvane stuck on the weather bulwark capping, a rod with lines at the top, each with a cork tied to it studded with feathers, "we'll be in St Helens a'fore His Lordship has time to sail in the *Victory!*"

"Don't count on that," Ramage cautioned. "His Lordship has the light of battle in his eyes: he wants a couple of dozen of the Combined Fleet destroyed. That'll give him wings, as well as teeth."

The *Calypso* was rising and falling easily to the crests, occasionally butting a large one into sheets of spray which flung up to darken the foot of the foresail and send streams of water over the planking, rivulets of water twisting and turning with the pitch and roll as they ran aft along the deck. Ramage could feel the salt spray tightening the skin of his face and once, when he incautiously rubbed his eyes, the dried salt made them sting.

Now for the long stretch across the shallow bay known to seamen as Hythe Flats, with Roar Bank and Swallow Bank just inshore of Dungeness Point at the southern end.

Half-way across Hythe Flat, Ramage looked at the chart. Yes, although it was not marked in, Aldington was now on the beam, four miles or so inshore of the long stretch of beach (with Martello towers like beer mugs every few hundred yards) in front of Dymchurch.

Were those towers any use? Would they be, rather, if Bonaparte tried to land his troops? The original Mortella Tower in Corsica, manned by thirty-three French soldiers, had held out against the British for weeks; the design was copied by the gentlemen at the Horse Guards (although for some reason the name was altered to Martello), with seventy-four of them built along the coast facing France. Father had inspected one, and he said they cost £7,000 each and had two storeys. The ground floor was the magazine and the upper accommodation, with a swivel gun or howitzer on the roof. With walls nine feet thick on the seaward side they must be proof against enemy gunfire but brutally cold for the garrisons in winter...

Now they were round "The Ness". He looked across the dead flat: Romney Marsh, where the smooth fields were occasionally punctuated by a church tower or steeple with a small cluster of the village round it, and saw where the land rose sharply at the back of the Marsh, like a long cliff. Somewhere there, if only he knew exactly where to look with the bring-'em-near, was Treffry Hall. Had Sarah come home yet, or was she still staying in Palace Street? Curiously he hoped she was still in Palace Street: it was depressing to think that she might be over there at home and this very minute looking out of one of the windows, across the Marsh and towards the Ness, not knowing that that tiny speck on the sea was the *Calypso*...

Now, almost a copy of Hythe Flats, Rye Bay curved inshore, with Broomhill Sands, Camber Sands and finally Winchelsea Beach before swinging out again at Fairlight, with another dozen miles to Beachy Head.

Names and history...just a few miles ahead of the *Calypso* the ships of the Norman King William had landed on the Sussex beaches, to meet Harold at what William later called Battle, and where he built an abbey to show his gratitude to the Almighty...that was almost 750 years ago. Over two hundred years ago the Spanish Armada had sailed up here, to anchor off Calais, some forty miles astern of the *Calypso*, and there Sir Francis Drake had set about them with fireships. That was the trouble with sailing up or down the Channel: one's thoughts kept foundering on reefs of history. There was an advantage in being someone like Southwick, to whom history was something that happened yesterday. What happened the day before yesterday (and earlier) was forgotten.

CHAPTER SEVEN

Up on the fo'c'sle the Italian seaman shivered and said to Jackson: "Is cold, this autumn. How long before we get into warmer weather?"

"That Italian blood 'o yours has been thinned out with too much wine," Jackson said unsympathetically. "Cadiz isn't very far south: won't be much warmer than here."

"*Al diavolo!*" Rossi swore. "We'll be there all winter blockading these *stronzi*. They don't intend to come out and fight. Why should they – safely anchored in Cadiz, yards sent down, sails stowed below for the rats to eat, whores waiting in the streets..."

"Rosey's getting bloodthirsty," Stafford commented.

"Your mother's cooking," Rossi said amiably.

"Yus, she fed our plump friend like he was a chicken bein' fattened for Christmas," Stafford said proudly, his Cockney accent sounding hard when compared with Rossi's deeper Genoese accent.

"I warned Rosey what would happen if he went home with you for his leave," Jackson said.

"We 'ad a good time, didn't we Rosey! Even had 'im admitting London ale was as good as wine. Mind you, by then 'e couldn't tell gin from 'oly water."

"I hope you've repented by now," Jackson said banteringly. "You're setting a bad example for the foreigners!"

"My oath!" Stafford exclaimed. "And where did *you* get to on your leave, my American friend? Bet you didn't set Louis, Auguste, Gilbert and Albert much of an example. Never could understand why four innocent Frenchmen should go on leave with you. Sin, that's what you was seeking."

"What about you and Rosey?"

"We weren't seeking it; it was seeking *us*," Stafford said quickly. "There's a difference."

"That's Beachy Head," Jackson said unexpectedly. "We'll be tacking soon, so's we can inspect the French coast."

"Where on the French coast?" asked Louis, his French accent revealed mostly by his trouble pronouncing "th", which usually emerged as "z".

Jackson glanced up at the clouds and then at the English coast. "The wind's nor'west and we'll point high with a nice clean bottom, so I reckon we'll have a sight of Barfleur Point a'fore we go about on to the larboard tack. After that I expect Mr Ramage'll want to get a good offing coming up to the equinoctials now, and he won't chance getting caught in a gale with Ushant too close under his lee. Not much chance of a sight o' your bit o' coast, Louis."

The Frenchman shrugged and shook his head. "I don't think of it as mine any more."

"Nowhere to call home, Louis?" Stafford said sympathetically. "Well, you're fighting on our side, so think o' England as home. Cornwall's the nearest to Brittany, and the Capting comes from there, so why doncher adopt Cornwall?"

Louis, who with the other three monarchists had helped Ramage and Sarah escape from Brest when war started again and then joined the Royal Navy, understood Stafford's concern and nodded politely. "Yes, there are close links between the two. Half the names are similar and in peacetime the fishermen use one or the other depending on the wind. But not to be worrying, Staff; this ship is my home. Yours, too, if you think."

Stafford's brow creased with the effort and then he admitted: "You're right, Louis. I was glad to be back on board at the end of that leave. Land people – they don't seem to understand. And someone like Jacko – " he turned to the American, " – well, I suppose the *Calypso* really *is* the only home you've got."

"Home?" Jackson exclaimed, "why, I nearly *own* her, along with the rest of the lads. Don't forget, we all captured her and have been here ever since we first boarded her."

"The Admiralty's paid you your prize money," Stafford said shrewdly, "so you're a sort of tenant."

"As long as they don't charge me rent!"

"*Senta*," Rossi said. "what about this Lord Nelson, eh? Is *simpatico*, eh?"

"He's all right," Jackson said firmly. "We first had truck with him in the Mediterranean, when he was a commodore and gave Mr Ramage his first command (which is where we first came alongside Mr Southwick: he was master of that ship, the *Kathleen* cutter). He's a fine admiral to serve under, but as far as the French and Spanish (and the Danes, too) are concerned, he's a killer."

"*All* admirals should be killers," Rossi pointed out.

"They're not, though, compared with His Lordship. The rest o' them reckon they've won the battle if they drive two or three of the enemy out of the line of battle, but Lord Nelson wants to destroy the lot! At the Nile he captured or destroyed eleven ships out of thirteen; at Copenhagen he captured or destroyed seventeen. Compare that with Lord Howe's six at the Glorious First of June or even Lord St Vincent at Cape St Vincent, when two of the four of those captured were taken by Lord Nelson (then only a commodore without any title) personally boarding them! He's not just a fighter," Jackson said sombrely, "he really hates the enemy!"

"That *Victory*," Stafford said, "she hasn't been docked, has she?"

"I don't think so," Jackson said "His Lordship only arrived back in England two or three weeks ago – so I understood from Mr Southwick – and we're off to join the *Victory* at St Helens, so there hasn't been time. Why are you asking?"

Stafford winked and tapped the side of his nose, a gesture he had copied from Rossi. "We've got a clean bottom and she'll be foul: weeks in the Mediterranean, crossing the Atlantic twice...just think of the barnacles and weed and torn and worn sheathing...in anything but a gale o' wind we should be able to show her our heels!"

"Don't bet on it," Jackson warned. "His Lordship's flag captain would be commanding a transport by now unless he was good, and the master has been with him for years."

"This woman from Naples..." Rossi said tentatively, but was immediately jumped on by Jackson.

"If you mean Lady Hamilton, she was the wife – now the widow – of the British ambassador to the Kingdom of the Two Sicilies, whose king and queen – as you well know – live in Naples – "

"*Accidente!*" Rossi exclaimed, "not criticalizing – "

"Criticizing," Jackson corrected.

"Is what I say, I don't criticalize Lord Nelson, I ask about the lady, is all I ask."

"All right, then," Jackson said. "She's His Lordship's friend, just as her husband was when he was alive. Good friends."

"Good friends!" Stafford exclaimed, "she's his mistress!"

"What's wrong with that?" Jackson demanded angrily. "Even when we were last in Antigua I heard stories about what a cold woman Lady Nelson was – the widow of a soldier, too," he added, the final condemnation. "After what he did at St

Vincent, the Nile and Copenhagen, I don't care if he has twenty mistresses; he deserves 'em!"

"And me not criticalizing His Lordship," Rossi said crossly, "I was only asking to make sure he has a mistress, I knowing about this wife..."

"Criticize an Englishman's horse," Gilbert said drily, "or even his wife, but be careful of his mistress: that much I learned while working in England as the Count of Rennes' servant. But," he added warningly, "if he is happily married it works differently: you can criticize his wife, but never criticize his horse."

"Just shows you mixed with different people," Stafford grumbled. "My lot have a wife or a horse or a mistress, and a wise man watches his tongue when talking about any o' them."

"Of course, the horse would be stolen, the wife regularly beaten, and the mistress paid with dud coins," Jackson commented to Gilbert. "Stafford's friends don't get taken up by the press because no receiving ship'd have 'em!"

"Sounds good comin' from the Jonathan," Stafford said, teasing Jackson with the name by which the Navy always referred to Americans. "Listen, Gilbert, whenever you stop a Jonathan ship and board to see if they're breakin' the blockade – 'specially in the West Indies – they're always carrying a cargo o' 'notions'. I arsk you, *notions*'!"

"What's wrong with that?" demanded Jackson. "Just means a mixed cargo. All sorts o' things. Needles and thread, pots and pans, clothes – all the things people need to live their lives."

" 'Notions'," Stafford repeated scornfully, "what a barmy word!"

At that moment, Aitken's hail from the quarterdeck rail stopped the talk: a reef point on the maincourse had somehow become entwined with the next one in the row and the pair of them, tightening up, would cause the sail to rip in a sudden puff. The mainsail had to be furled to clear the points, and the sailmaker would go aloft with the topmen to make sure the sail had not been damaged.

Jackson's estimate to Gilbert was correct: they could just make out Pointe de Barfleur at the western end of Seine Bay when the order came to go about. This gave the *Calypso* forty miles of sailing close-hauled on the larboard tack back towards England to reach the Nab off the Isle of Wight and close to St Helens, the fort, anchorage and village at the eastern end of the island, across the Solent from Portsmouth and Spithead. St Helens had the advantage that it was in the lee of the island and well protected from the prevailing west and south-westerly winds.

Ramage was by now certain the *Victory* would have sailed for Cadiz, but Southwick reckoned the *Calypso* would arrive in time. "My Lords Commissioners of the Admiralty will find some way of delaying him; you can be sure of that," Southwick said heavily, "and Mr Pitt will want to see him for discussions, and the Secretary of State for the Foreign Department: they'll all want to tell the tale in their drawing rooms, how they told the famous admiral how to fight his battle."

"You sound like me," Ramage said, laughing at Southwick's lugubrious voice. "But the only thing I can think of that might delay His Lordship is waiting for copies of Sir Home Popham's new telegraphic code. His Lordship told me he was determined to take out a copy for every ship in the fleet and he may have had to wait for enough to be printed and bound."

"What's so magical about this new telegraphic code that the admiral would let it delay him?"

Ramage gestured in a wide sweep across the horizon, indicating limitless distance. "With the present edition of the *Signal Book for Ships of War*, an admiral can only give – by flag signals – some four hundred-odd orders: in other words, only those that are printed in the *Signal Book*.

"But supposing he wants the fleet (or a particular ship) to do something else that *isn't* in the book? Well, he can't: if the evolution isn't in the *Signal Book*, it can't be ordered by signal. The admiral has his hands tied to the listed signals – and that doesn't suit Lord Nelson.

"Now, Home Popham has brought out his new 'telegraphic code', and from what I hear it means an admiral can as good as hail his fleet and tell them precisely what he wants done.

"Whereas the *Signal Book* gives a complete order for every signal number," Ramage explained, "Home Popham has chosen four thousand of the most important – the most active – *words* that an admiral might want to signal, and given them numbers, so that an admiral can make up a specific order, signalling each word. Home Popham has been quite clever, too: one word – one signal number – can have various shades of meaning: for example, 'Appear-ed-ing-ance', or 'Arm-ed-ing-ament' – "

"But that means signalling number 4,000 for the last word in the code," Southwick protested.

Ramage shook his head. "No, Home Popham has a much better way. He's also lumped 'I' and 'J' together and said there are twenty-five letters in the alphabet, and each letter represents a number – 'A' is one, 'B' two, 'F' six, 'P' fifteen, 'U' twenty and 'Z' twenty-five."

Southwick sniffed suspiciously, but Ramage ignored him. "One flag means units – 'G' would be seven, for example. With two flags, the upper one represents tens and the lower units – 'E' and 'F' would be fifty-six. Three flags are hundreds for the upper, tens for the middle and units for the lower. Thus 'A' 'B' 'C' would be signalled as 123."

Aitken, who had been listening to Ramage's explanation, said: "Once we get a copy, sir, I suggest we have a competition among the officers to see who can make up the most amusing signal using, say, six flags!"

"We'll do that," Ramage promised, "but His Lordship hasn't enough frigates, and if I know him, he'll be busy thumbing through Popham's code, finding detailed ways of keeping us busy!"

And, he thought to himself, thank goodness we've just left the dockyard with fresh sheathing, mostly new sails, and Aitken and Southwick having gone over every inch of masts, spars and rigging, both standing and running. If we have to get to windward in the teeth of a full gale, we won't have to worry about a mast going by the board...

He saw Aitken look at his watch and a moment later Martin, the young fourth lieutenant and son of the master shipwright at the Chatham yard, came up the quarterdeck ladder to take over as officer of the deck.

He was a lively youngster, known throughout the ship as "Blower" Martin because of his skill with a flute. Ramage had resigned himself to hearing only sea chanties and tunes popular with the seamen when, towards the end of the last voyage, he discovered that Martin himself preferred more serious music and was very familiar with the likes of Telemann and the flute concerti of Mozart and Haydn.

As soon as Aitken had passed on the *Calypso*'s course and details of the wind for the past hour and reported that there were no unexecuted orders, he went below, leaving Martin as officer of the deck, with the master and captain standing around, talking.

Soon Ramage said: "Well, Martin, I hope you've brought plenty of good sheet music with you."

"Yes, sir. I went up to London specially. I've been practising the newer items." He grinned. "I've discovered Mr Southwick doesn't share your enthusiasm for Mozart."

Ramage, pretending to be shocked, turned to the master. "Unmasked at last, eh Mr Southwick? I've always had my doubts about you."

"I don't exactly dislike him, sir, it's just that he's a foreigner and he doesn't put a tune together like our chaps do. To be honest, I prefer the tunes 'Blower' plays for the sailors."

"What about the other lieutenants and Orsini?" Ramage asked Martin.

"The Marchesa's nephew has been making my life a misery! He's so keen! When he was in London he bought me a lot of sheet music without realizing you can't play everything on a flute! Opera is his favourite, but there's not much you can do for opera with just a flute!"

There was a shout from aloft: the lookout at the foremasthead was hailing, and Martin snatched up the black japanned speaking trumpet.

"Foremast – deck here!"

Martin quickly reversed the cone-shaped metal tube so that it acted as an ear trumpet. He listened and, reversing it once again, shouted: "Very well, report every ten minutes."

"Two frigates on our larboard bow sir, apparently running up for Spithead."

Ramage nodded. "We'll be seeing several more of the King's ships before long: at the moment we seem to be in a particularly deserted stretch of the Channel. I imagine Lord Barham is calling in every possible frigate to provision and water and to make for Cadiz."

He thought for a few moments and then said to Martin, resuming the conversation interrupted by the lookout: "If we spend a few weeks blockading the Combined Fleet in Cadiz, you're going to wear out that flute of yours!"

"Ah," Martin said triumphantly, "I used some of my prize money to buy a *third* one, sir. So now I have one for the sailors, a good one for serious music, and a masterpiece for special occasions and as a reserve."

How often has prize money gone on a flute? Ramage wondered.

Ramage went down to his cabin and re-read the letter Sarah had written. Somehow rounding the Ness had put a great distance between them – a great *geographical* distance. If he went on shore at Portsmouth he could take a 'chaise and be with her in a few hours – a fanciful thought for the captain of one of the King's ships bound for Cadiz in wartime...

He brought his journal up to date, filling in courses, speeds and wind direction, read his orders again from Lord Barham, looked at the chart of Spithead and the east side of the Isle of Wight, and then just sat and stared round his cabin. It was going to be very different serving in the fleet: attention to salutes, always watching the flagship (and the senior frigate) for flag signals and repeating them as necessary, sending in weekly accounts to the flagship (something he had not done for years), accepting hospitality from other captains and entertaining them in return...all very nice for those captains who enjoyed a social life and slapped each other on the back; it was very unpleasant for a captain who had been lucky enough to spend several years with independent orders, his own master within the limits of the orders he had been given.

He woke up nearly two hours later, startled at having dozed at his desk, and was stiff-necked. There had not been much sleep for the past few nights – taking on powder at Black Stakes was a long, tedious and nerve-racking business, eating cold food because the galley fire could not be lit, and waiting for the crash of a barrel or case of powder slipping out of the cargo net and about to blow the ship apart.

He stared at his watch, calculating time: he had been in his cabin for three hours: by now the Isle of Wight should be close on the weather bow. He went through to the bed place and washed his face, using the jug of water and pewter basin kept in the special rack along with soap, razors and towel. Jamming his hat on his head and vaguely feeling guilty (although any captain was entitled to a nap), he went on deck.

And there it was: the massive bulk of the Isle of Wight on the larboard hand, stretching from St Catherine's Point in the south to the Foreland at the eastern end. And over there, fine on the starboard bow, the low land from Selsey Bill, with the Owers off the end, reefs of rocks waiting for the unwary, and stretching round to the westward and gently rising to the hills behind Portsmouth.

St Catherine's was almost obscured now behind the cliffs of Dunnose, and ahead the Foreland was hiding St Helens from view, although a ship drawing as much water as the *Victory* would have to anchor well out.

Southwick snapped his telescope shut.

"Is she there?" Ramage asked.

"Did we have a wager on it, sir?"

"No, we didn't. Can you see her?"

Southwick shook his head. "The anchorage is partly hidden by the Foreland," he said almost hopefully, but then admitted: "But I can see a couple of frigates and a brig anchored there, further out (I reckon) than a three-decker like the *Victory* would be..."

"So I was right – His Lordship wasted no time."

"Looks that way, sir," Southwick agreed reluctantly.

"We'll have to go right up through Spithead and look into Portsmouth," Ramage said. "She might have gone in to the dockyard for water or provisions. We'd look silly if we sailed for Cadiz, leaving the *Victory* behind..."

Southwick sniffed, and after years of experience Ramage understood Southwick's sniffs as other men understood speech. The master was indicating (without saying a word) that carrying on north to look into Portsmouth was wasting valuable time which could better be used trying to overhaul the *Victory*.

It was tempting: with this nor'west wind the *Calypso* could get out through the Chops of the Channel on one tack: a glorious fast stretch clearing Ushant by twenty miles, and (if the wind held) bearing away for an equally fast run across the Bay of Biscay to the Spanish Finisterre, almost in sight of Ferrol and Coruña, where the enemy fleet had been hiding until finally they made a bolt for Cadiz and were sighted by Blackwood in the *Euryalus*.

Damn, damn, damn...he had been doubtful that they could get round to St Helens before the *Victory* sailed but (quite absurdly, he admitted) he had hoped, regarding it as a challenge.

Now, stretching out of the Channel alone, at least there would be no question of keeping station on the *Victory*, forever watching for flag signals and busy taking vertical sextant angles of her mizenmast to make sure they were the precise distance off. Now – well, now they would be able to chase the wind, tacking as necessary without signal, noting the headlands and distances run...

A drunkard's life was measured out in tots of liquor, but a sailor's life in headlands, Ramage thought, particularly the last hundred miles before Land's End. There was Start Point at the western end of Lyme Bay, quickly followed by Prawle Point and Bolt Head if you were bound along the coast to Plymouth.

You left Plymouth and cleared Rame Head (with the next the Lizard if you were having to tack out of the Channel in a south-westerly); otherwise there was Gribben Head, showing the way into Fowey, and then the Dodman, just past Mevagissey, and some nasty overfalls, the Bellows, for any ship that kept in too close. Then St Anthony Head at the entrance to Falmouth (with more overfalls, the Bizzies, close by). You came out of Falmouth and cleared the next big headland, the Manacles, and after that the Lizard and the deep Mount's Bay ending with Penzance as it came round to Gwennap Head and Land's End.

And that, Ramage thought, is the story of any seaman who over the centuries has struggled up or down the Channel, trading, fighting, attempting to identify this headland or that shoal in daylight, fog or darkness, or driven by a storm and smashing into one of them.

Quite deliberately he had not thought of the Cornish coast: now he had his own estate at Aldington, the thought of St Kew was less pressing, but fifteen miles or so inland north of the Gribben was St Kew...

Do not, he warned himself, think of the French coast opposite where you honeymooned with Sarah and where the sudden renewal of war trapped us in Brest. He shuddered when he thought of the risks he had inflicted on Sarah. And finally, sent to England after the fleet had arrived, she had been captured by privateers...no, these waters held no happy memories.

CHAPTER EIGHT

By the time the *Calypso* was running across the Bay of Biscay, all sail set to the royals with a brisk north-westerly still blowing (the same wind that had taken them down-Channel, first to call in at Portsmouth and then along to the Lizard so that clear of Ushant they could bear away for the run to the Spanish coast), Ramage knew there was no chance of catching up with the *Victory*.

"This wind has been blowing for several days," Southwick declared crossly, as though somehow the *Victory* had been cheating. "She picked it up and was probably off the Lizard as we rounded Dungeness."

"Shows we were slow off the mark," Hill said. The tall and diffident third lieutenant delighted in teasing Southwick, who was old enough to be his grandfather.

"Slow off the mark be damned," Southwick exclaimed. "We were out of that dock and down the Medway like scalded cats."

"Ah, it was the navigation that let us down," Hill said sadly. "Wandering round the Thames Estuary like a befuddled curate at the wedding of the landlord's daughter; we lost the tide at the North Foreland and had to fight the current all the way through The Gull – I've never seen the Goodwins pass so slowly – and look how wide we passed Dungeness. I won't mention the stretch up to Spithead, and that leisurely amble along to the Lizard..."

"If you paid more regard to sail trimming, we'd get along a lot faster," Southwick said wrathfully. He pointed upwards. "Just look at those topsails...if the captain comes on deck..."

Hill stepped out quickly to look up first at the foretopsail and then at the maintopsail, ducking to see them properly. He came back to Southwick, puzzled. "What's wrong with the foretops'l?" he demanded. "It's drawing well. The maintops'l, too."

"Oh, are they?" Southwick said innocently. "I didn't say they weren't."

Hill grinned, acknowledging that Southwick was entitled to mild revenge. "Tell me," he said, "what's it going to be like as part of the fleet? I've never served with a large fleet."

"Very hard on lieutenants," Southwick said. "Signals, reports, station-keeping, sail-trimming...I've known lieutenants go mad with the strain and leap over the side, screaming."

Hill, realizing that Southwick could not miss such an opportunity to get his own back, and pretending to ignore it, said: "You've had a lot of fleet experience?"

"Yes, and I'll warn you right now, His Lordship's problem off Cadiz is going to be keeping the fleet supplied with provisions and water. He won't have enough transports, so we'll probably be used to go through the Gut to Tetuan and pick up bullocks... Very smelly, bullocks are."

"You're joking!" Hill exclaimed, but he sounded nervous.

"Am I? Look at it from the admiral's point of view. He's short of transports and he needs several hundred bullocks a week to feed the fleet, so they don't eat up their provisions, which they'll need in the winter if it's going to be a long blockade. He is trying to lure the Combined Fleet out of Cadiz to fight. Do you think he's going to send away ships of the line to collect bullocks?"

"Well, no, but a frigate can't carry many live bullocks."

"Who said anything about live ones? Kill 'em and salt 'em down, my lad. So along with the stink there's blood and salt everywhere. And flies: the sky'll be *black* with flies. Arab flies," he added darkly.

"I don't believe you," Hill said in a voice which was intended to be a flat denial but sounded more like a hopeful plea. "What about water – the fleet'll be just as short of water as meal."

"That's no problem, with Gibraltar down there. If it's not getting bullocks, it's water. Casks everywhere. Ship laden down, the very devil to handle because there's no way to trim her properly, and back and forth to Gibraltar. It'll be a flip of a coin whether we get water or bullocks. And God help us if we get a Levanter..."

"Ah, but who's keeping an eye on the enemy? That's where the admiral needs his frigates: his eyes, Southwick, his distant eyes, watching and instantly ready to signal over the horizon that the enemy is out. Using the new telegraphic code!"

"Have you been hoarding your tot?" Southwick inquired. "You sound to me like a hopeful drunk."

"But His Lordship *does* need frigates!"

"Oh yes," Southwick agreed. "We know that Captain Blackwood is already at Cadiz, commanding a small squadron of frigates: he told Mr Ramage that."

"There you are!" Hill said triumphantly.

"Ah," Southwick took off his hat, ran his hand through his hair and jammed the hat back on his head. "Ah yes, and do you think that Captain Blackwood, having his own little squadron of frigates who now know the job inside out – apart from the captains being friends of his – is going to send *his* frigates off, to salt down bullocks or hoist casks of water on board?"

Hill shrugged his shoulders. He admitted to himself that there seemed to be a lot of common sense in what Southwick was saying, and it did not bode well for lieutenants. He just had time to run his eye over all the sails as he saw the captain come up the companionway.

Hill waited for the captain to glance round the horizon before standing close by at the quarterdeck rail. He took a deep breath and ventured: "Southwick was just telling me about the bullocks, sir."

Ramage's eyebrows rose. "Was he, by Jove. And what are his views on bullocks?"

"Very smelly, he says, and salting them down is miserable work. So many flies."

"I imagine it is," Ramage said sympathetically. "Why, are you thinking of going into business as a supplier of salt tack to the Navy?"

"Oh no, sir. Southwick and I were just talking about what sort of work the *Calypso* will be doing when she joins the fleet."

Ramage glanced at Southwick and then said: "Ah, salt tack and fresh water, eh?"

"Yes, sir. Southwick explained the problem of supplying a blockading fleet, and said His Lordship would rely on bullocks from Tetuan and fresh water from Gibraltar."

Ramage looked at Southwick again and then said to Hill: "And you expect the *Calypso* will have to act as a transport – the fleet being very short of transports."

"Yes, that's what Southwick reckons."

"Did Mr Southwick give any idea how many bullocks, live or salted, the *Calypso* could carry, compared with a transport?"

"Well, no sir; he did make the point that His Lordship would not spare the line-of-battle ships to go down to water themselves."

Ramage gave a dry laugh. "Come, Mr Hill, in what sort of weather could the *Calypso* transfer casks of fresh water and salt beef (let alone live bullocks) to a ship of the line?"

"Well, it'd need to be pretty calm," Hill admitted.

"So His Lordship is going to chance the supplying of his fleet on the vagaries of the weather?"

Hill looked doubtfully at Southwick. "How else would he supply them, sir?"

Ramage shrugged his shoulders "We're only guessing that he's short of transports, but he's certainly desperately short of frigates. I can assure you, Hill, that there'll be frigates close up to Cadiz even if there are only half a dozen ships of the line waiting in ambush over the horizon. The enemy can *see* the frigates but they can only *guess* how many ships of the line are waiting out of sight – but within signalling range of the frigates. With respect to our reverend master, Mr Southwick, I suspect Lord Nelson will detach ships of the line, a few at a time, to make the dash to Gibraltar and Tetuan. He always wants his men to have as much fresh food as possible: they can use the fresh and keep the salt beef and pork in the casks."

Hill turned accusingly to Southwick, who grinned and said: "That'll teach you to question my navigation, laddy!"

On the tenth day out from Spithead, Southwick reckoned that they had passed the great rocky promontory of Cape St Vincent (so steep and riddled with caves that the booming of breaking seas could be heard for miles). The *Calypso* steered east-south-east with a good south-westerly breeze and good visibility. Cadiz was not far off.

"We have to keep a sharp lookout for three mountain ranges," he said. "Well, Orsini?"

The young midshipman looked blank and an irritated Ramage, standing within earshot, snapped: "I gave you a lesson about this coast the last time we were passing, on our way to the Mediterranean."

"I can remember about the Duke of Medina Sidonia, sir, who commanded the Spanish Armada and owned land nearby, but..."

"Tell him, Southwick..."

"You know the coast runs north and south, eh?" Southwick asked sarcastically.

A chastened Orsini nodded.

"Well, about forty-five miles north along the coast from Cadiz is a range of mountains called the Sierra de Ronda, with the Cabezo del Moro more than five thousand feet high. We should sight them first on this course, and the Cabezo is rounded.

"Then comes Pico de Aljibe, three and a half thousand feet high and just over thirty miles along the coast from Cadiz. It doesn't have a sign on it but its sides slope up gently.

"The third one, twenty miles along the coast from Cadiz, is the one that belonged to your friend the late Duke of Medina Sidonia. You remember of course that it's shaped like a sugar loaf, has a tower near the top, and the village of Medina Sidonia looks like a white patch on the west side..."

"Yes," Orsini exclaimed triumphantly, "all the houses in the village are painted white. And I can remember Cadiz and Rota, too, and the river running into the Bay of Cadiz is the San Pedro."

"Splendid," Southwick said and, turning to Ramage, commented: "You see, sir, midshipmen are better than performing bears: they can talk."

Ramage nodded and told Aitken: "Hail the lookouts, tell them what to look for, and give them bearings. Incidentally," he added, "we'll probably find the fleet some distance from Cadiz: the admiral won't want to frighten the enemy into staying in port..."

"Aye, and young Orsini, you'll know the shoreline of Cadiz well enough soon," Southwick said. "His Lordship will have a frigate or two close up to Rota and Cadiz – a mile or two off – and a line of repeating frigates to within sight of the fleet. Tack, tack, wear, wear...and where do you go if there's a westerly gale, eh? Not up on the beach, I trust."

Orsini knew enough not to answer, and he watched as Aitken picked up the speaking trumpet and hailed the foremast and mainmast lookouts.

It has been a long chase, Ramage thought, and we did not catch up with the *Victory*. Well, Lord Nelson was in a hurry but he could not have made Captain Hardy drive the big three-decker any harder than the *Calypso* had been sailed. But a bigger ship with a much longer waterline length would always be faster if there was any weight in the wind and it had been just the right wind for the *Victory*...

Half an hour later the foremast lookout hailed that he could just see clouds that seemed to come off the lee of a mountain; fifteen minutes later he confirmed one mountain and reported more cloud to the south of it.

Ramage looked at Orsini. "You know what to look for now, so take a bring-'em-near and aloft with you!"

Orsini seized a telescope and made for the ratlines of the mainmast shrouds, climbing at the run.

"I wasn't fair to him," Southwick commented. "He's a good lad. And just look at him, he's going up like a topman!"

"So he should," Ramage said drily. "When I was a midshipman his age, my captain expected midshipmen to go aloft *faster* than topmen."

The master chuckled. "Yes, but topmen don't have to remember places with these outlandish foreign names."

"They're not foreign to Orsini: remember, he speaks fluent Spanish. Cabezo del Moro means 'The Moor's Head' to him – which I'm sure it doesn't to you: and although he doesn't know it, I expect he's distantly related to the Medina Sidonia family anyway – these Spanish and Italian families were always marrying each other."

"Certainly these place names'd be easier to remember if I knew what they meant," Southwick admitted. He took off his hat and scratched his head. "I'm surprised we haven't come across other frigates or 74s joining the fleet."

"I think most of 'em are already out here," Ramage said. "Those two 74s in Chatham won't be ready for sea for another couple of months. We're probably the last to join His Lordship – except perhaps for the two frigates we saw off the Isle of Wight."

By now Orsini, a tiny figure perched at the masthead, was shouting down to the quarterdeck with his hail being repeated by the lookout. Southwick held the mouthpiece of the speaking trumpet to his ear.

He nodded to himself, gave a satisfied smile and then, turning the trumpet so he could talk into the mouthpiece, shouted back: "Very well, keep a sharp lookout for Medina Sidonia!"

The master turned to Ramage. "He's certain about 'The Moor' and Aljibe, and thinks he's sighted a sail in line with where Cadiz should be."

He thought a moment and then asked Ramage: "What's 'Aljibe' mean, then?"

" 'Aljibe' is a cistern or water catchment, and 'Pico' means 'Peak'."

"Your Spanish must be good sir; I keep forgetting that. I remember that time you were in Cartagena, pretending to be a Spaniard."

"Yes, I can pass myself off as a Castilian, but some of the local accents are hard to understand. A fast-talking Galician from the north, or an excited yokel from Murcia – the province of Cartagena – can leave me baffled."

The two men talked for half an hour, reminiscing over past actions ranging from Italy to southern France and on to Spain before crossing the Atlantic to the West Indies and the coasts of the Spanish Main.

"India," Southwick said, "now there's a country I've never been to. Can't say I've any great wish in that direction," he admitted.

"My wife loved it – her father was Governor of Bengal, as you know. She says the variety is fantastic: plains wider than you could ever imagine; great mountains: the cool hill stations to which everyone retreats in the hot season... Imagine a country so large you could drop in England and lose it!"

At that moment Orsini hailed again. Southwick listened with the makeshift ear trumpet and reported to Ramage: "He says it's definitely Medina Sidonia fine on the starboard bow and he can make out land below it. We must be about fifteen miles off."

"Near enough to Cadiz to sight some of the fleet soon. Tell him to watch for any sail. What happened to that ship he sighted?"

"He can't see her any longer: reckons she must have been steering south."

"Very well, tell him to instruct the lookout and then come down. There are a score of ships of the line off Cadiz: just our luck not to sight one. Still, our frigates will be off Cadiz..."

As the *Calypso* bore up for the fleet, pendant numbers flying, Ramage had the feeling he was walking into a forest. More than twenty ships of the line meant more than sixty great masts, and in the middle of them was the *Victory*. Then, with almost startling suddenness, he was tacking through the fleet – under the *Revenge's* stern, across the *Colossus'* bow, watch out for the *Ajax* because she's fore-reaching on you... What the devil is the *Orion* doing, is no one keeping a lookout?... Why the devil does the *Bellerophon* have to choose this minute to tack – no wonder she's always known as the "Billy Ruffian" – and now the blasted *Polyphemus* ("Polly Infamous" to the sailors) is heaving-to just as I was intending to go under her transom...now the damned *Mars* looks as though she is determined on a collision... Oh, the devil take it, who but a madman would prefer serving with a fleet to being independent?

"Are you watching for flagship signals?" Ramage snapped at Orsini, and a moment later bellowed to Kenton to stand by to rig the staytackle ready to hoist out a boat.

"Is the gunner standing by ready with the salute?" Ramage asked.

This was not the time to hazard a guess, Southwick knew; ships were flashing by like the pictures on those new magic lanterns, and Aitken's voice was already hoarse from shouting helm and sail orders.

Jackson, acting quartermaster and with four men at the wheel so there should be no delay, had long since given up watching the ships as the *Calypso* weaved among them. He thought momentarily of the jinking snipe they had seen coming down the Medway, and then returned to watching the luffs of sails, making sure that the *Calypso* kept moving fast: all would be lost, he knew only too well, if she was caught in stays and dropped on board one of the 74s.

Ramage was thinking the same thing: for a moment he imagined a snatch of gossip at the Green Room in Plymouth, with one post-captain asking another: "Hear how that fellow Ramage joined Lord Nelson off Cadiz? Why, drifted into the *Victory* and boarded her in the smoke, haw, haw!"

And with nine 74s passed, one or two by the thickness of a coat of paint (or so it appeared from the *Calypso*: the ships were apparently unworried), the *Victory* still seemed to be as far away through the mass of hulls and masts.

"Bear up," he snapped at Aitken: "We can just scrape across the bow of the *Belleisle* without carrying away her jib-boom."

"If you say so, sir," Aitken said doubtfully, bellowing into his speaking trumpet and snapping a helm order to Jackson. Topsail sheets and yards braced sharp up, men hauled at the headsail sheets to flatten the curve of jibs and staysails; the *Calypso* seemed to stagger for a few moments and then pointed even higher into the wind: just enough, Aitken realized, to get clear: but beyond the jib-boom loomed yet another 74, black-hulled with white strakes – the *Conqueror*? Aitken was guessing, but there seemed no way the *Calypso* could turn to larboard or starboard, luff up or bear away to avoid ramming her amidships.

Aitken glanced at the captain. He was startled to see that Ramage seemed to be enjoying himself: his teeth were bared in a wide grin; his hands were clasped behind his back. For a moment Aitken imagined a confident gambler watching the dice roll the way he wanted.

"Back the maintopsail, Mr Aitken!"

And stop the ship? Aitken shouted the orders which brought the men sweating and cursing at the braces, hauling the topsail yard round, and then the sheets were trimmed. The *Calypso* suddenly stopped, the pitching and rolling ceased; instead she just heeled slightly under the press of the backed sail.

And an unbelieving Aitken watched the *Conqueror* draw ahead: instead of the *Calypso*'s jib-boom lancing the 74s foremast shrouds, Aitken saw the *Conqueror* slide to larboard until her mainshrouds were ahead, then her mizen and finally her transom slid across the frigate's bow leaving – Aitken almost whooped with relief and joy – an empty space, then one three-decker beyond her, the centre of a spacious area, the *Victory*, her three yellow strakes glistening, with another three-decker, the *Dreadnought*, in her wake.

Aitken glanced again at Ramage and saw the satisfied grin on his face – the captain had calculated that manoeuvre down to the last few feet – and the first lieutenant was ready with the speaking trumpet when Ramage said: "Very well, let it draw!"

It took only moments to brace the yard and trim the sheets so that the maintopsail filled with wind and the *Calypso* began hissing through the water again with an easy pitch and roll like, Aitken thought, a young man strolling carefree through the park on a spring morning.

Still no signal from the *Victory*. But the three-decker ahead was Admiral Collingwood's temporary flagship, the *Dreadnought* (the *Royal Sovereign* had yet to arrive from England), and admirals did not like frigates bolting across their bow.

"Bear away and pass under the *Dreadnought*'s stern," Ramage said, "and then bear up on the *Victory*'s larboard side."

It was a long way from Clarges Street, Ramage thought, and Lord Nelson was probably missing Lady Hamilton as much as he was missing Sarah. Supposing one was bound for India, two years from home and probably more than that: did the pain lessen? It could not get worse; he was damned sure of that.

Now they were past the *Dreadnought* and running up on the *Victory*'s quarter. She was towing a single cutter. Quickly Ramage lifted his telescope and swept the *Dreadnought*'s deck. Yes, her cutter was missing. Lord Nelson's second-in-command was on board the *Victory*.

What was Admiral Collingwood really like? Ramage had never met him but had heard many stories. For a start, Collingwood was rarely separated from his dog Bunce. He was a Northumberland man who loved the country and was so worried about the rate at which England was using up her oak trees to build ships of war that when he was out walking in the country he had a pocketful of acorns, which he planted in likely places, to ensure that in a hundred years' time, in 1905, England would not lack for oaks. What else about him? He was a strict but very fair disciplinarian who hated flogging – he was reputed to have said that flogging made a good man bad, and a bad man worse. A quiet and reserved man, the complete opposite of Lord Nelson, who by contrast was like a bowl of quicksilver. But apparently both men knew each other well, and worked together.

"Start the salute," Ramage told Aitken.

A minute later number one gun on the larboard side gave a snuffling thud, and Ramage pictured the gunner timing the five-second firing intervals with the time-honoured phrase, "If I wasn't a gunner I wouldn't be here, number two gun fire... If I wasn't a gunner I wouldn't be here, number three gun fire..." He found himself repeating it, and the gunner seemed to be timing it correctly. A captain joining the fleet, to his commander-in-chief, seventeen guns. If the gunner had any sense he had seventeen musket or pistol balls in a pocket, transferring one to another pocket every time a gun fired, until the first pocket was empty: that was the only safe way of not firing sixteen or eighteen.

Fifteen, sixteen, seventeen: that was the end of the salute. And a flutter of flags from the *Victory*. Ramage read the *Calypso*'s three pendant numbers, followed by numbers 103.

"Signal from the flagship, sir," Orsini called excitedly. "Our pendant and then 103, *'Keep in the Admiral's wake'*. "

Which, given the limitations of the four hundred orders in the *Signal Book*, was the only way to order the *Calypso* to take up a position astern of the *Victory*. (There was no signal which could order the *Calypso* to take up a position ahead or on either beam...)

"See to it, Mr Aitken," Ramage said, knowing the first lieutenant had heard Orsini's report. "One cable astern of the *Dreadnought*."

A simple enough manoeuvre, but this time executed within yards of Admiral Collingwood's flagship, and several telescopes would be scanning the new arrival, eager to spot poor or dilatory seamanship. Thus, Ramage reflected ruefully, could a captain's reputation be sported away, no matter how many successful actions he had fought. Flag lieutenants and all the rest of the people serving an admiral (from clerks to a chaplain and a host of midshipmen) were like a medieval king's courtiers: they had little else to do but scratch each other's backs and gossip…

Ramage made a point of standing four-square on the quarterdeck, obviously leaving the handling of the ship to his first lieutenant – not to avoid responsibility but to show any prying eyes that the *Calypso*'s captain had complete faith in his officers. Obviously Lord Nelson (and almost certainly Admiral Collingwood) were above all the gossip, but the other ships in the fleet liked to hear it, especially if about a well-known captain making a fool of himself. And, Ramage reflected, he was just well enough known by now to be a target.

An hour later Martin, as officer of the deck, reported to Ramage that the *Victory* and the *Dreadnought* had backed their maintopsails.

"If we don't do something, we'll be aboard the *Dreadnought*," Ramage said. "Admiral Collingwood may well be put out if Lieutenant Martin puts the *Calypso*'s jib-boom through the sternlights of his great cabin…"

Martin grinned because the lieutenants enjoyed being teased by the captain. He lifted the speaking trumpet, which he had picked up the moment he saw the *Victory*'s maintopsail start to shiver, and bellowed the orders for the *Calypso* to follow suit.

Southwick lumbered on deck, saw what was happening and asked Ramage: "What's His Lordship doing?"

"Letting Admiral Collingwood return to his ship, from the look of it." He steadied the telescope. "Yes, I can see men hauling round the painter of that cutter. And there are two admirals walking the quarterdeck."

"That's our excitement for the day," Martin muttered. "Unless the cutter capsizes and we can rescue the admiral from drowning."

When Orsini laughed, Ramage said: "That reminds me: why was there such a delay in answering the *Victory's* signal to us?"

"The answering pendant wasn't bent on the halyard, sir," Orsini admitted lamely.

"If you want to live long enough to go up to Somerset House and take your examination for lieutenant, let me give you some advice," Ramage said. "When you're near a senior officer's ship, *always* keep an answering pendant bent on the halyard ready. And remember – in most fleets it matters less that a ship's gunnery is poor than that she answers signals quickly. Not with Lord Nelson, but with most senior officers."

"Yes, sir," Orsini said apologetically. "I had realized that – too late – but we have the pendant bent on now."

Ramage nodded. "Good – that's the first lesson you've learned about joining a fleet. There'll be more. Just remember that when you're in company with a flagship, you're standing at the wrong end of someone's telescope..."

CHAPTER NINE

Ramage was in his cabin, his sword, best frock coat and hat on the settee, when Aitken hailed through the skylight: "Sir, signal from the flagship...two...one...three. Orsini is looking it up... Yes, *The captains of the fleet, or of the ships pointed out, are to come to the Admiral*'. Shall I hoist out the cutter, sir?"

"Yes, and tell Jackson to assemble my boat's crew. And have 'em tidy themselves up: some of those captains of 74s dress up their boats' crews like puppets."

The captain of the *Harlequin* frigate, for instance: he was a wealthy man and dressed his men as harlequins. Ramage thought of some of the more unusual names in the list of the Navy: the *Alligator*, a 28-gun frigate, the *Beaver, Bittern* and *Badger, Bouncer, Boxer, Biter* and *Bruiser*.

He imagined men in shirts with stripes down their backs.

"What ship?"

"The *Badger*, sir."

He stood up and looked down at himself. Yes, shoes polished and the gold buckles fitted; silk stockings unmarked – he had remembered not to cross his feet: Silkin never managed to get all the polish off his boots or shoes, so the back of his stockings usually suffered. Breeches – not creased. He was just going to pick up his frock coat when Silkin hurried in.

"Thank goodness I fitted those gold buckles, sir," the man said. "The silver ones would *never* have done for seeing the admiral."

"Rubbish," Ramage said curtly, "admirals wouldn't notice if their captains arrived barefoot!"

"Oh sir!" Silkin exclaimed, as if he knew that Ramage was quite capable of arriving on board a flagship like that, to the eternal shame of his servant.

He held up the frock coat and Ramage eased himself into it. The price of a good tailor was being uncomfortable: he wanted your frock coat to fit like a glove, and breeches were so tight that sitting down suddenly was dangerous.

"You're not taking the presentation sword, sir?"

"No."

"It's a fine sword, sir."

"And it has 'Lloyd's' written all over it."

Silkin shook his head, puzzled.

It will be interesting, Ramage thought sourly, to see which of those captains with presentation swords actually wear them to meet Lord Nelson. It was like wearing a label, he thought, saying "I'm brave, sir."

Ramage looked at his watch. In half an hour there would be so many boats with impatient captains milling about at the foot of the *Victory's* entryport that a wise man either arrived very early or very late, thus avoiding the scramble. The *Calypso* was the nearest vessel now the *Dreadnought* had returned to her station. Arrive early, Ramage decided.

Just fifteen minutes later Jackson laid the *Calypso's* cutter below the *Victory's* entryport and, after a quick hitch at his sword belt, Ramage seized the sideropes being held out clear of the hull by the sideboys and began the long scramble up the battens to reach the port itself.

Conscious that the whole port was neatly painted, the scroll work picked out in gold leaf, Ramage entered, to be met by a large man wearing epaulets on both shoulders – a captain with more than three years' seniority.

The man held out his right hand. "I'm Hardy – you must be Ramage. His Lordship hoped you'd take advantage of your nearness and get here first."

"I've been chasing you for days," Ramage said. "I was hoping we'd get to St Helens before you sailed."

Hardy grinned amiably. "I'll let you into a secret: we only just beat you: we joined the fleet last night – you probably saw Admiral Collingwood reporting on board. Oh yes, by the way, today's His Lordship's birthday. He's forty-seven."

Ramage nodded gratefully and followed Hardy's directions up to the great cabin. That entryport, Ramage thought, told him a good deal about Hardy: only one lieutenant, the master at arms and two seamen were waiting there; the sideropes were scrubbed white, even though the *Victory* had been at sea for days, and every bit of brasswork in sight was gleaming. Nor was Hardy a scrub-and-polish captain; by reputation he was a fighter.

Ramage was met at the door of the main cabin by a man dressed in a dark-green suit, with spectacles and a slight stoop. "I'm Scott, His Lordship's chaplain. Allow me to announce you – the name?"

"Ramage."

"Ah," the man exclaimed, "you just joined the fleet in the *Calypso*. One of our famous young frigate captains! His Lordship was telling me that he saw you in London. Well, please follow me."

Nelson was sitting in a curiously shaped armchair close by the sternlights, reading a document. As soon as he heard Scott and looked up he gave an exclamation of pleasure, folded the document with one hand and slid it into a wide pocket sewn into the side of the chair like a large poacher's pocket. As he stood up, Ramage saw that the chair was very narrow and deep, obviously specially made for the admiral: dark-green leather, high back, and the curious pockets on each side.

"My dear Ramage, I'm glad you caught up with us: we just beat you from St Helens. You probably lost time taking on powder at Black Stakes – but you must have made good time across the Bay of Biscay: we joined the fleet only last night."

"I must wish you a happy birthday, sir," Ramage said.

Nelson gave a boyish grin, belying his forty-seven years. "Thank-you. I've now reached the age where I'll be held responsible for my actions! Tell me, you left the beautiful Lady Sarah well?"

"Very well, sir – though, to be honest, not delighted at my departure."

"Oh dear," Nelson gave a mock groan, "she'll hold it against me. Lady Hamilton and my dear god-daughter Horatia are convinced I go to sea only to avoid them. Twenty-four days, dinner to dinner – that was all the time I was in England, after two years all but a few days on board this ship without setting foot on land."

"You seem to keep remarkably fit, sir."

Nelson shook his head and Ramage remembered too late that the admiral, although far from fit, was a man who enjoyed bad health. "Ah, no, my health is ruined. After I've settled with the Combined Fleet I shall retire to Merton and cultivate my roses. Can you picture me as a country gentleman?"

"I'm afraid not, sir," Ramage said candidly. "It's hard to imagine you as anything but what you are."

"I know you mean that as a compliment. Well, my dear Ramage, we are not so far from Cape St Vincent, and I remember very well your very brave action in taking that little cutter of yours across the bows of those Spanish ships of the line, delaying them long enough to allow another insubordinate captain called Nelson in the *Captain* to come to your help.

Now you're a post-captain with a lot more experience of life, I trust you realize that Commodore Nelson and Lieutenant Ramage were lucky not to be court-martialled for that day's work?"

"Yes, sir – had we failed. But unless my memory betrays me, it resulted in the capture of four Spanish line-of-battle ships, two of which you took yourself."

"Two line-of-battle ships and a baronetcy, and all thanks to you, Ramage, which is why I hope one day to render you a service in return."

"You are not in my debt, sir," Ramage said hastily.

"I'll be judge of that," Nelson said briskly. "Now," and his face became sterner, and he gestured with his left hand to emphasize his words, "Mr Scott here tells me he understands you speak passable Spanish."

Ramage nodded, waiting for what was to come. Speak Spanish? What on earth had that to do with commanding a frigate in His Lordship's fleet?

"Just how 'passable'? Don't be modest and don't boast: it might lead to you getting your throat cut."

"It's fluent," Ramage admitted. "A Castilian accent."

"And if you were caught and questioned you could tell a convincing story, eh?"

Ramage nodded. "A story it'd take them three or four weeks to check."

Nelson looked up at Scott who, Ramage realized, had been watching him closely. "What do you think?"

"I agree with you," the chaplain said enigmatically.

"Very well, Ramage, I have a special job for you, but there's no time to tell you about it before the rest of my captains arrive on board, so wait behind when they go. I'm shifting the fleet further out tonight – fifty miles to the west – and I want to give you your orders before then. Ah, I hear the first of the rest of the captains. Scott, will you take up your duties by the door –

and speak the names *clearly*, man: I don't know at least half these fellows!"

Ramage stood back as two captains were announced: Blackwood of the *Euryalus*, whom he had met briefly in London, and a burly, fleshy-faced man with fair hair and red cheeks whom Scott introduced as Captain George Duff of the *Mars*.

Ramage heard Duff greet the admiral and realized he was a Scot.

After thanking him for birthday greetings, Nelson said: "And how is the family ship? Hardy tells me you have most of the Duff clan on board. Are there any Duffs left behind in Banffshire?"

Duff gave a delighted laugh. "Aye, sir, just a few!"

"How many are on board the *Mars*?"

"Well, m'son Norwich – he's just turned thirteen – joined the ship a few days ago and brought his young cousin Thomas with him. Thomas' elder brother Alexander is an acting lieutenant. Both are sons of my brother Lachlan."

"Why 'acting'?" Nelson asked.

"Too young, sir. He's passed his examination but has to bide a few months for his twentieth birthday."

Nelson nodded. "So your wife will he waiting for news of you all, eh? Where is she?"

"Ah, Sophie is living in Edinburgh. It's probably an anxious time in Castle Street until the letter arrives!"

The next captain to arrive was Thomas Fremantle of the *Neptune*, and at the sound of his name Nelson gave a delighted laugh.

"Ah, Fremantle – which would you have, a boy or a girl?"

Fremantle, who Ramage knew already had two sons and two daughters, said quickly: "A girl, sir."

"Be satisfied," Nelson said, smiling broadly, "and here is a letter for you from Betsy's sister Harriet."

A flush-faced Fremantle, who Ramage remembered had helped Nelson when he was badly wounded and lost an arm at Tenerife, withdrew to read his letter.

Several more captains arrived, among them Captain Edward Codrington of the *Orion*, who was immediately greeted by Nelson, who took something from the pocket of his armchair.

He turned to Codrington and gave him a letter. "I was entrusted with this by a lady, so I make a point of delivering it myself."

Codrington glanced down at the writing and grinned. "I haven't heard from Jane for a long time."

Finally Scott told the admiral that all the captains were present. The great cabin was now crowded with happy and chattering men, and Ramage took the opportunity to cross over to the larboard side to examine a small portrait in a gilt frame which was screwed to the bulkhead near the sternlight. It showed a smiling, curly-haired young child. It was a good portrait of Horatia.

The cabin sole, covered in the usual canvas as a carpet, had been painted in black and white squares so that the captains stood on it like so many chessmen. The most important piece, also by far the smallest, was of course Lord Nelson. The second was Vice-Admiral Collingwood, the second-in-command who had been handling the fleet off Cadiz in Nelson's absence. Tall, going bald, and with a cleft chin, although Collingwood talked with several of the captains clearly he was a withdrawn man.

The third piece on this giant chessboard was the third-in-command, Rear-Admiral the Earl of Northesk. Ramage remembered as a young lieutenant meeting him. Northesk was another Scot, one of the Carnegies and a Scottish peer, one of the older creations.

After a while Nelson's chaplain came up to him. "You don't know many of the other captains, Ramage?"

"No – don't forget I've never served with His Lordship, and I'm sure most of these men were with him in the Mediterranean."

"Oh, goodness me, no: most of them have never even spoken to His Lordship before! Let me see – " he looked round, counting.

"Yes, only five of these captains served with His Lordship in our famous chase round the Mediterranean and across to the West Indies. One joined us over there. And the rest – " he counted, " – the other twenty-one have all joined recently from the Channel Fleet, many of them while Lord Nelson was in England."

He looked over the captains, counting yet again. "My dear Ramage, you started me off on a train of thought. Would you believe it, but of the twenty-seven captains here in this cabin (excluding you), only *eight* of them have ever before served with Lord Nelson!"

Scott paused a moment, thinking and looking round the cabin. "What's more, only two of them have served with His Lordship since the year before last, and one of those is Captain Hardy! So, believe it or not, nineteen of the captains in this cabin have never before served with His Lordship!"

"You'd never believe it, to watch them all talking together! Well, I don't know when the Combined Fleet is going to come out and fight, but His Lordship hasn't much time to train *his* fleet."

Ramage looked round him and sensed the camaraderie that already existed. "I don't know how or why," he admitted to Scott, "but I think most of them share his spirit!"

"Well, that's the extraordinary effect His Lordship has on men," Scott said confidentially. "You should have seen him at Copenhagen. Wonderful with Sir Hyde Parker – they were both in a very difficult situation – and wonderful with the Danes after the battle."

At that minute they heard Nelson's high-pitched nasal voice. "Gentlemen, let me have your attention. Gather round. I want to explain how I propose – intend, rather – to beat the Combined Fleet, providing we can lure it out of Cadiz. My plan is simple: it will so surprise the French Admiral Villeneuve that his advantage in number of ships will be lost. I count on taking or destroying at least twenty of the enemy: I trust you won't disappoint me. And this is how we are going to do it."

Ramage, like every other man in the cabin, listened spellbound. Nelson did not hesitate once or use any of the "umms", "ers" or other hesitancies one might have expected. Nor had he exaggerated when he said his plan was simple. Ramage realized he might equally well have called it revolutionary. One thing was certain – if he succeeded with this plan he would be a hero; if he failed, he would be lucky to escape Their Lordships bringing him to a court martial, and (whatever the verdict) he would never be employed again by the Admiralty, even as a rat-catcher in a sail loft.

Up to now, opposing fleets fought by each getting into a line, one ship astern of the other, follow-my-leader fashion, and approaching obliquely until they were side by side. Then each ship had to try to drive its opponent out of the line. St Vincent had used these tactics against the French and Spanish at Cape St Vincent and (but for Nelson) they would have been as useless as they always were. At the Nile and Copenhagen, Nelson had successfully attacked the enemy at anchor. Now he could expect to be attacking an enemy at sea and, as he described it to the listening captains, the Combined Fleets of France and Spain would probably comprise a long line of thirty-four ships (unless more broke *into* Cadiz from Brest, or some such place, and reinforced them).

He lost no time in describing how he was going to surprise (and overwhelm) the enemy. The long line of thirty-four ships would probably be sailing with the wind on the quarter or on the beam. In other words, there would be a leeward end probably formed by the leading, or van, ships, and a windward end, the centre and rear ships.

If the leading ships wanted to turn back to reinforce the rear they would have to tack or wear and then beat to windward to get into position, zigzagging along the line.

We shall be outnumbered, Nelson said. He did not know how many ships of the line he would have on the day of the battle, but the British would be heavily outnumbered. So he would not even try to pit all his ships against the thirty-four of the enemy. No, he was going to attack and overwhelm one section of their line with two columns. Breaking through the enemy's line at right-angles, he would cut off the centre and rear divisions, leaving the leading ships sailing on to leeward and out of the fight until they could beat back to help the centre and rear – by which time the British should have captured several ships.

The two columns would in effect be two knives slicing a section out of a long snake. He would lead one column in the *Victory*, and Admiral Collingwood the other: two columns each of a dozen or so ships. But he wanted to lure the Combined Fleet out: that was his most difficult task. At the moment it was expected they would sail and head north to the Channel, to try to seize control of the Strait of Dover for long enough for Bonaparte to sail over the invasion flotillas he had waiting in Calais, Boulogne and all the other ports and anchorages) to land on the Kent and Sussex coasts. It is only in England, on English soil, that the French can finally beat us, Nelson said, and Bonaparte knows that well enough: he is camped on the hills at Boulogne; all he dreams about is his troops getting on shore in England.

My fleet here, blockading the Combined Fleet in Cadiz, is all that prevents Bonaparte from sailing his flotillas, Nelson said quietly. If we let them escape us, Bonaparte's flotillas will sail. Quite apart from that, we have a large British convoy of General Craig's troops sailing to the Mediterranean to join the Russians in Italy. Any French or Spanish ships at sea will threaten General Craig and his troops. Unfortunately, Nelson admitted, no one knew quite where the general and his convoy were at the moment.

But, Nelson emphasized, the Combined Fleet would not be lured out by the sight of a score of British ships of the line waiting on the horizon ready to attack. Therefore tonight – as soon as the captains had returned to their ships – the whole fleet would shift fifty miles to the westward, leaving a couple of frigates to watch Cadiz, and another frigate and three ships of the line (because he did not have enough frigates) would stretch out to the fleet, each within signalling distance of the other, and then they would wait.

Provisions, Nelson said abruptly. He did not know how long they would have to wait off Cadiz, but the men of the fleet must be kept fit. That meant fresh provisions. Yes, most of the ships had enough salt tack and water for three months but salt junk eventually meant scurvy, so for fresh meat he would be sending a few ships at a time the eighty-odd miles to get bullocks from Tetuan, watering at Gibraltar on the way.

And he intended introducing Sir Home Popham's new telegraphic code into the fleet, as a supplement to the *Signal Book*. "I brought out copies for each ship: make sure each of you collects a copy when you leave."

Nelson then asked if any of the captains had questions, or comments. It was already obvious that the captains were delighted with Nelson's two-column, cut-off-the-head attack.

Several indicated that they were in no rush to go down to Tetuan and so risk missing the battle.

And then it was over. Captains took their farewell of Nelson like excited schoolboys leaving for the holidays, and soon the great cabin was empty again except for Ramage, Scott and His Lordship.

"Ah, Ramage, now for your orders. First, I don't suppose you have anyone else on board who speaks Spanish?"

"Yes, a midshipman speaks it fluently."

"Is he Spanish?"

"No, sir: he is the nephew of the Marchesa di Volterra."

"Ah, the beautiful Marchesa you rescued on the Italian mainland." Nelson's face clouded. "But wait a moment, didn't I hear recently that Bonaparte seized her when she decided to go home during the Peace of Amiens?"

Ramage nodded. "Yes, sir. As far as we know she's still a prisoner – unless he had her assassinated. But three or four years ago her young nephew escaped from Italy, and she asked me to take him as a midshipman."

"And how has he turned out, eh?"

"As lively as the Marchesa. A fine seaman and one of the most popular people in the ship. Once he passes for lieutenant he'll be one of the best in the Navy."

"Well, 'uncle'," Nelson said with a grin, "the job I have for you doesn't require seamanship but you'll both need Spanish – and courage. You have good charts of Rota and Cadiz on board the *Calypso*?"

When Ramage shook his head, Nelson said to Scott: "Please go and tell the master to make copies of the ones we have. Mr Ramage must have them."

As the chaplain left the cabin, Nelson dived his left hand into the pocket of his armchair, obviously searching for a particular paper. Do I offer to help him? Ramage wondered. He decided against it: no one had fussed around the admiral while the captains were on board: Nelson seemed a man who overcame his own problems.

Finally he brought out a black folder held together by tapes. Holding the folder between his knees, he tugged at the tapes and then opened it on his lap.

"Ah, yes, here it is. Take this and read it."

Ramage walked over and took the single sheet of paper. In neat copperplate writing was a Spanish name and the name of a church.

"Now give it back," Nelson said and as soon as Ramage had handed it over he said, squinting his good eye and holding up the page to catch the light: "Now repeat the name and the church."

Ramage did so, and Nelson put the page back in the black folder.

"You can guess the rest," he said

Most of it, Ramage thought sourly. The clues were speaking Spanish and the name of a Spaniard in Cadiz, his address being somewhere near that church. Go and see him. Find out from him all you can about the enemy.

"I think so, sir," Ramage said. "Is he one of our agents?"

"I don't know about 'one of our'," Nelson said. "He's our *only* agent in Cadiz or Rota. A disaffected Spanish nobleman who hates the French. His name and – such as it is – address was written down for you by none other than the Secretary of State for the Foreign Department, which gives you some idea of the need for secrecy. This man's son-in-law is one of the Spanish captains commanding a ship in the Combined Fleet – with not much enthusiasm, I gather. Now, this nobleman has been passing his intelligence to Gibraltar, somehow or other, and he will not be expecting you. You will say you are a friend of the Secretary of State, who assures me that will be sufficient. Then you will ask him about the following."

Nelson reeled off several questions and then said sternly to Ramage: "Nothing in writing, mind you. This man, apart from being a friend of the Secretary of State's family since before the war, is a very important agent. So you report to me as soon as you have the information.

"You notice I am not giving you any instructions about *how* to carry out this task: you have more experience than most officers in landing on the enemy's shore, so I wish you good luck, Uncle Ramage and nephew...!"

CHAPTER TEN

The Spanish and the French must wonder what the devil is going on, Ramage thought. Last night they could see more than twenty ships of the line and some frigates, menacing sentries on the western horizon. When they woke this morning the horizon to the westward was clear of ships, except for a couple of frigates close in and another five or six miles out, and in the distance, its sails from time to time dipping below the curvature of the earth, perhaps another frigate: anyway, not a ship of the line.

So where had the English fleet gone? Ramage could imagine the puzzled faces and arguments on board the *Bucentaure*, which was apparently the flagship of Admiral Villeneuve, who commanded the Combined Fleet, and the *Argonaute*, the flagship of the Spanish admiral, Gravina.

As long as they argued, they would be less likely to concern themselves about Blackwood's *Euryalus*, now tacking back and forth just outside the El Diamante and La Galera shoals, a couple of miles into the bay beyond the entrance to Cadiz anchorage. From there he could see Rota on the north side of the bay and all the French and Spanish ships at anchor in Cadiz; a sharp-eyed man with a telescope could watch for any undue boat activity between the ships and, more important, see immediately when particular ships began bending on sails or swaying up yards. Both the *Bucentaure* and *Argonaute* were in sight from that position, Blackwood had told Ramage when they talked on board the *Victory*, so that by watching the boats coming and going it was almost possible to keep both admirals' visitors' books.

While the *Euryalus* kept watch on the north side of Cadiz city, by noon the *Calypso* was hove-to south of the small city, and Ramage was sitting astride a carronade, a telescope to his eye, Orsini on his left and Southwick, clutching a slate and drawing a rough chart, on his right.

Rota, Cadiz Bay and Cadiz harbour itself formed a huge sickle: Rota was at the tip; then the bay formed the curving blade with Cadiz itself at the end, at the top of the handle.

The handle itself represented the long anchorage with Cadiz on the seaward side, the anchorage itself getting very shallow and becoming marshes and salt-pans three miles from the entrance, with a narrow and deeper channel curving through it and allowing just enough room for ships of the line to anchor, though a sudden wind shift on the turn of the tide would give captains and first lieutenants a few anxious moments…

So there was Cadiz spread out before him at the end of a long sandspit. The spit stretched five miles northwards from the salt-ponds but was only a hundred feet wide for almost half its length before widening out into a bulge of land large enough for the city to be built.

Ramage started his detailed examination from the southern end. "Salt-ponds and marshes," he told Southwick. "There's a windmill down there that's probably the saltworks, pumping seawater into the pans, or grinding the salt itself: how the devil does one make salt?

"Then the spit starts, and it's not thirty yards wide. Runs along to the nor'nor'west and doesn't get any wider for…well, more than two miles. Ah, then there's a fort: that's the Fuerte de La Cortadura, the entrance to the city and which cuts off the spit.

"Have you got that, you two? Just over a couple of miles of spit and then the fort, and then the city – such as it is – begins. Oh yes, on the seaward side there are rocks with sand behind from the salt-ponds almost up to the fort, but then it is a wide sandy beach, a gentle slope up to it, just right for beaching a boat.

"Now…still going nor'nor'west from the fort, there's a castle and tower on the inshore side. Yes, that'll be the Castillo de Puntales, built to cover the entrance of the anchorage from the inside: it can't fire to seaward.

"Are you listening closely, Orsini? A mile along from the fort and almost in line from here with the Castillo, is a conspicuous church – and that's San José, the one we're interested in. Stands back three hundred yards from the beach, behind a long cemetery. A *very* long cemetery, with houses between it and the church. They must have a long walk to the grave after a funeral service in the church."

He handed the telescope to Orsini and pointed out the church. "Examine it: you're going to have to find your way round there in the dark. There's what looks like a bullring another three hundred yards along the shore north of the cemetery – so there's just a short journey for any bullfighter making a fatal mistake."

After five minutes Orsini said he had memorized the view and Ramage motioned to Southwick to look with the telescope. "Draw as good a chart as you can from the fort up to the bullring: show the castle, church, cemetery and some of the most conspicuous of those houses between the cemetery and the San José church."

While the master scratched away with his slate, Ramage continued looking north, towards the end of the spit. A mile along the shore was a tower and very close to it a dignified building with a dome which was obviously the cathedral: the weak sun reflected off the dome and, beyond it, on the other side of the spit, Ramage caught sight of masts and yards – part of the Combined Fleet, those ships anchored near the entrance on the other side of the spit.

The spit curved slightly to seaward where it widened, and Ramage counted three more churches in the last half a mile, the nearest being only three hundred yards from the cathedral. Towards the end of the spit, amid strong fortifications, was a big watch-tower – that must be the Torre de Taviras, with half a dozen towers close by. The Spanish always loved building towers: he remembered the dozens lining the coast all the way from the Portuguese border down to Gibraltar, and then along the Mediterranean coast, and as though they still had plenty of stone and energy, the scores built in Italy, to protect Spanish possessions in Tuscany.

"Not very promising, sir," Southwick said with a disapproving sniff, giving Ramage back the telescope. "Nice smooth sandy beach to land from a boat – with all the sentries in that fort watching you. Then you have to get through the gate attached to the fort, and the sentries will want passes. Probably a curfew, too, with all these ships in port. Dusk till dawn. So why're you out, eh? They'll pop you both in a cell and slap your hands."

"We could always wade through the marshes and avoid the fort."

"Then you'd stink so much a sentry would smell you a mile off, the dogs will follow barking in protest, and this Spanish gentleman will hold his nose and tell you to go away."

"Quite right, too," Ramage said gravely, "nothing worse on a hot night than the stink of a ripe marsh…"

"So what are we going to do, sir?" asked an alarmed Orsini.

"Avoid making a stink by landing on the city side of the fort, of course," Ramage said. "Now fetch Jackson and my boat's crew: they have a lot to do."

Nodding at Southwick's promise that he would go below at once and draw a fair copy of the chartlet, Ramage sat for a while on the carronade while the *Calypso*'s sails slatted as she sat hove to. From the shore it would seem natural enough for a frigate watching a place to be hove-to: watchers, whether soldiers or sailors, would imagine those English officers staring through telescopes, and could appreciate that this was more easily done from a stationary ship than one forging up and down the coast, pitching and rolling in the Atlantic swell which almost always thundered on the beach in a wind with any west in it.

Of course the west wind, he reflected, was the wind in which the French and Spanish seamen (even if not Villeneuve, who might well be impatient to carry out whatever orders he had received) could relax: they could not sail out in a west wind, and the English had to keep well out in case a sudden gale made the whole coast a dangerous lee shore.

An east wind...that was what Lord Nelson (and probably the French Admiral Villeneuve) dreamed about: an east wind (or, if they were determined enough, any wind with a bit of east in it) was the wind that would let the Combined Fleet of France and Spain, thirty-three ships of the line, sail from Cadiz.

At the same time, it put Lord Nelson and the English fleet fifty miles to leeward... The west wind that could bring Nelson to Cadiz at the rush was the very wind that prevented the enemy sailing: the east wind that let them out put the British fleet to leeward. English, British...it was difficult to be consistent when the French, Spanish and Italian always referred to "*les Anglais*", "*los Ingles*" and "*gli Inglesi*", and the English themselves (quite fairly, of course, because of the Scots, Welsh and Irish) referred to "the British".

Anyway, once having got out of Cadiz on an east wind, where would the Combined Fleet go? If north-westward for the English Channel, then (if they managed to evade Nelson) they had a soldier's wind and a calm sea. If they were bound for the Mediterranean, though, the Gut was only fifty miles down the coast to the south – five hours' sailing in a brisk breeze. But if the Combined Fleet was bound for the Mediterranean – for Malta, to try to intercept General Craig's convoy, or for some operation against Italy – as soon as they turned into the Strait that east wind would be foul for them...

Neither the cat (Lord Nelson) nor the mouse (Villeneuve) had an easy task – unless Villeneuve was bound for the English Channel. But there was usually some warning of an east wind, and sails had to be bent on... It would take the Combined Fleet many hours to get sails hoisted and anchors weighed, but using flag signals and Popham's new code, His Lordship should have the news in half an hour...

Cadiz and this coast, Ramage mused, was scattered with history: that mountain to the south-east, as Southwick had told Orsini, was named after the family one of whose dukes led the Spanish Armada; fifteen miles northwards from Cadiz was the mouth of the Guadalquivir and Sanlúcar de Barrameda, from where Magellan sailed in 1519 to go round the world. Thirty-five miles north of there, from Palos on the Rio Tinto, Columbus sailed in 1492 to discover the New World... Columbus' discovery, Magellan's circumnavigation and the Spanish Armada sailing from Cadiz just about covered all that mattered at sea in the last few centuries, and it all began along fifty or sixty miles of this coast...

The forthcoming battle (if it *was* forthcoming) might add a footnote, since if Nelson lost it (or the Combined Fleet evaded him) then there would be nothing to stop Bonaparte invading England (and Scotland and Wales!).

And whether or not the Combined Fleet evaded Lord Nelson or was brought to battle by him might well depend on the intelligence to be passed tonight by this Spaniard, who lived in the lee of the San José church.

His thoughts were interrupted by the arrival of Jackson and the boat's crew. Jackson was an American, Rossi an Italian, Louis, Albert, Auguste and Gilbert were French, Orsini was Italian, but could pass for Spanish, and he himself could pass for Spanish. A cosmopolitan crew.

So an inquisitive sentry answered in the dark in perfect Spanish or French might be satisfied...

Quickly Ramage explained to the men what their task for that night was to be. The thole pins of the cutter, as well as the looms of the oars, were to be bound with cloth to cut down the creaking and squeaking; the sail was to be painted black; they were to check that there were a couple of grapnels on board, each with at least ten fathoms of line; they were to have a cutlass each and tomahawks if they wished, but no pistols or muskets. They were to wear dark clothes – if any of them owned only light shirts, they were to draw dark cloth from the purser – there was plenty of time to stitch up another shirt.

"Might we ask where we're going sir?" Jackson asked.

Ramage pointed towards Cadiz city. "I have to meet a man over there, and I'll be taking Mr Orsini on shore with me."

"No chance of any of us having a run on shore to keep you company, sir?"

"Not this time," Ramage said. "And by the way, if anyone has to speak it must be in Spanish or French or Italian. That means you and Stafford keep your mouths shut. So you can all get busy and prepare the boat. Oh yes, Jackson: you'll need to keep a check on the time. Arrange to borrow a watch from one of the lieutenants, and keep a lanthorn under a piece of canvas. Make sure you pick a good candle and trim the wick..."

"Lentement, lentement," Louis hissed as Gilbert eased away on the halyard and the black-painted dipping lug of the cutter was lowered into the boat, the men stifling the thick canvas. As soon as it was bundled up with a couple of gaskets tied round it, the men at the oars resumed rowing.

Ramage, at the tiller, could distinguish the beach: a darker band of black with a thin white moustache where the small waves curled and broke on the sand. If they had sailed a good compass course from the ship and there had been no unexpected current running parallel with the shore, then the cemetery should be just at the back of the beach.

He listened, trying to cut out the muffled groan of the oars as the looms strained against the padded thole pins. There was the monotonous "quark" of a nightjar and now the buzzing of mosquitoes, showing just how close they were to the beach. No voices. In the distance he heard the thud of a galloping horse, but going away, down towards the fort and the town gate. Very few towns had a single gate, but being built on the end of a spit (like Port Royal, Jamaica, he realized) it was the only entrance by land.

And now came the smells as they approached the line of wavelets and he eased over the metal tiller under his right arm. Was that eucalyptus? Did cork oak have a smell, because he could not identify it. And the cemetery, the curious musty smell of stonework mottled with lichen. And of course rotting seaweed. Or seaweed, anyway, whether or not it was rotting; thrown up on the beach by the waves; it provided a home for flying and jumping insects, all of which seemed to bite with an irritating sting.

No challenge: no shout of alarm in Spanish or French. No shadowy figures running down the sloping beach towards them, shouting or shooting. Which meant that his gamble might work: he had guessed that the commander of the Cadiz garrison, or whoever was responsible for posting sentries, would never expect the English would dare send a party to land in the middle of the town. Beyond the fort or among the salt-pans, yes; but beside the cemetery, a short stroll from the cathedral, no!

"Stand by," Ramage whispered to Jackson, who hissed at the oarsmen. In a second the oars were tossed up, ready to be stowed flat along the thwarts, and Ramage had pushed the tiller hard over, turning the boat broadside-on to the small wavelets. While Jackson pulled up the rudder to avoid it being damaged, the boat grounded with a gentle scrubbing of the keel scraping on the sand. In a moment Ramage and Orsini had leapt over the gunwale, landed on the sand, and run forward to get their shoulders under the cutter's bow, to shove it seaward while the boat still had some buoyancy. As soon as the boat was clear of the beach, helped by oars pushing into the sand, Ramage and Orsini sat down and undid the laces securing their boots round their necks.

"The sand sticks to the skin like glue," Orsini commented in Spanish, brushing it off his feet. "And the mosquitoes!"

The high-pitched whining of the insects reminded Ramage that they had little time: trying to persuade an unsuspecting Spaniard of one's credentials while he had been in a room burning citronella candles and one's own face was puffy and gross-looking from stings, was making the job harder than necessary.

The two men walked to the back of the beach, stepped across a line of what Ramage knew only by their Italian name of *Fico dei Ottentotti*, and then found themselves walking on coarse grass. Almost immediately Ramage spotted the elaborate marble angels, Virgins and crucifixes surmounting the tombs of the cemetery about twenty yards away on their right.

Together they struck out for the far side, where they had to climb a low wall and almost immediately sighted a house.

Ramage touched Orsini as a warning and then said in a conversational tone, his accent rough Castilian: "San José should be just the other side."

A dog gave a disheartened bark and was promptly sworn at by someone in the house.

Ramage stopped. "Might as well ask here," he said. "There's the door."

As they walked along a short path the dog started barking despite the threats, and then yelped as it was obviously kicked. Ramage knocked on the door.

A man's querulous voice answered: "Who's there?"

"Visitors for Señor Perez."

"Not here," the voice said abruptly, without opening the door. "The house on the north side of the church."

"Thank-you," Ramage said politely.

"I wish I had a pistol," Orsini muttered as soon as they had gone on a few yards.

"Oh yes," Ramage said sarcastically. "We need a few pistol shots to rouse out all the dogs in the neighbourhood, not to mention soldiery. What about a set of handbells?"

Orsini was still trying to think of an answer which combined wit and brevity without being insubordinate when they reached the church.

Ramage groaned, because the main square was on the north side of the church, with half a dozen large houses built round it.

"Our fellow is probably one of the leading citizens of Cadiz if he owns one of those houses," Orsini muttered.

Ramage stepped out towards the square making no attempt to keep quiet. If there was a curfew – which he was beginning to doubt: the man in the house did not seem surprised, nor had he assumed that they were soldiers – then any patrol was probably on horseback.

Now there were town smells. Horse and donkey droppings ripened by hot sun, rotting cabbage, stale urine...a scurry told of rats interrupted at supper...and which house to choose first?

He picked the third of the five forming the north side of the square. The house itself stood back behind a high-walled garden, and when he paused to see if another would be more convenient, he saw in the darkness that they all had walls and gates.

He rattled the wrought iron a few times. A dog in the house started barking and a moment later a woman's voice demanded: "Who is that at the gate?"

"Visitors for Señor Perez."

"Who are you?"

Was this – by an extraordinary piece of luck – the right house?

"Is this the house of Señor Perez?" Orsini inquired.

"It is," a man's voice answered, and Ramage guessed from his accent that he was a manservant.

"Tell Señor Perez he has visitors."

"What name shall I give, señor?"

"Lieutenant Leblond," Ramage said on the spur of the moment, giving both words a pronounced French accent.

"Please wait, Lieutenant," the voice said politely, "I will inform Señor Perez."

Did custom demand that one stamped a foot and demanded the gate be opened at once, in the name of the Emperor, and was this the way to treat the representative of Spain's ally – or did one wait quietly?

Ramage decided to wait quietly: he wanted to be face to face with Perez as soon as possible.

He saw a lantern at the door and then in its light a man walked along the path towards the gate. In one hand he held the lantern, in the other a large key.

The man – yes, he was dressed as a manservant: that much was clear in the light of the lantern – turned the key and pushed back the gate with his shoulder. "This way, if you please."

Galicia? Yes, Ramage was sure of the accent: thick, as though spoken through cloth. He followed the man, with Orsini strolling along beside him.

What would the man be thinking? Neither visitor was wearing a uniform – which ruled out an official call. While both men were young, and spoke perfect Spanish, at least one of them was French, from the way he spoke his name. French officers out of uniform, obviously.

They reached the front door up half a dozen steps, and entered the house. Yes, the bittersweet smell of citronella, and Ramage felt his face beginning to itch: the mosquitoes had not wasted their time but with luck the swelling would be delayed.

Marble floors, plenty of furniture in the hall (unusual in a Latin house), a dog growling from the room in which he had been shut, two open doors…the room to which they were going was at the far end of the corridor, and the thump, thump of his and Orsini's boots contrasted with the shuffle of the manservant's slippers.

They reached a door which the manservant opened, standing back and saying in slightly more than a conversational tone: "Lieutenant Leblond and companion, sir." He gestured them to go into the room.

It was a large, high-ceilinged room with a tiled floor. On the far side a white-haired man sat at a table, a quill in his hand and obviously interrupted while writing, and a woman perhaps ten years younger but well dressed sat at a stool, embroidering. Two lamps in the room showed a man and wife spending a quiet evening, even if the harbour was filled with the ships of the Combined Fleet of France and Spain, and the British fleet was just over the horizon.

"Lieutenant Leblond?" the white-haired man inquired, and the woman looked up curiously.

Ramage bowed and said: "May I introduce my assistant, Lieutenant Poulain?"

Ramage listened for the door to close behind him as the white-haired man said politely, but obviously puzzled. "To what do I owe the pleasure of this visit, gentlemen? Do you come on the Emperor's business?"

Ramage heard the door shut behind him, and it was quite natural to continue walking into the room approaching the man sitting at the table.

"Not the Emperor's business." Ramage said in a quiet voice. "Can we talk alone?"

"I have no secrets from my wife," the man said calmly. "If not from the Emperor then, pray, from whom?"

Ramage gave him the message.

At the mention – with an unmistakable English accent – of the name of His Britannic Majesty's Principal Secretary of State for Foreign Affairs, the white-haired man sprang to his feet.

"Should I know that name?" he asked in Spanish. "What makes you think that, Lieutenant Leblond?"

"Forgive me," Ramage said in English. "In fact my name is Ramage, Captain Ramage, and I command a frigate in Lord Nelson's fleet. The Secretary of State saw Lord Nelson in London recently. As a result, Lord Nelson gave me orders to seek out a Señor Perez near the church of San José, and mention the name you know."

"Tell me more: mistakes could put the garotte round my neck," Perez said, speaking quietly and in good English.

"About the minister? I know little about him. His title is fairly new – a barony ten or fifteen years ago. A man of middle height – I've seen him a few times in the House of Lords. Hair grey now, bald on the top, does not wear a wig…that's about all."

"What were you doing in the House of Lords, Captain?"

"My father is Admiral the Earl of Blazey, and I bear one of his titles (although I do not use it in the service for obvious reasons)."

"Obvious? Not to me, my dear sir."

"When I was a midshipman – and even now – it is not very tactful to have a title when your senior officers have none! As it is, I have a title senior to and much older than that of the minister!"

The man held out his hand. "Yes, I think you are whom you claim to be." They shook hands, and Perez said gracefully: "Please introduce your assistant."

Ramage introduced Orsini, and then Perez sat down, giving a quiet laugh. "Captain Ramage, indeed. Yes, I know that name well. It would not be true to say you are a popular figure among the French: *Le Moniteur* frequently refers to you as a cross between a pirate and a sorcerer! You have had considerable success against the French Navy over the years."

Ramage shrugged. "Over the years one is bound to be in action many times…"

"True, but you are more successful than most. Well, tell me what Lord Nelson wishes to know – I think I can guess."

Ramage smiled and said: "I imagine you can. First, he wants to know the size and condition of the Combined Fleet in Cadiz."

Perez made a face as though tasting something very sour. "The French – the condition of their ships fairly good but there is no spare canvas, cordage or spars available for them. They could get no replacements either when they visited Ferrol or Coruña.

"The Spanish ships are in far worse condition. They have not been to sea for months (at least Villeneuve crossed the

Atlantic twice with the French fleet). Sails and cordage have rotted on the masts; those ships that put their sails below have had much of the canvas eaten by rats. Thanks to your blockade no replacements are available. Many have rotted spars."

Perez, now sitting down, sighed. "This is not easy for me, Captain Ramage. I am describing my country, even if those in control are my enemies."

He sighed again, and then continued. "So much for the ships. Far worse is the condition of the captains and officers, particularly the Spanish. As far as the French are concerned, the problem is mainly with Admiral Villeneuve. My informant – and he is in a position to know, although obviously I dare not reveal who he is – tells me that Admiral Villeneuve is out of favour with Bonaparte and will probably be replaced very soon by Admiral Decrès."

"But Admiral Decrès is the Minister of Marine!" Ramage exclaimed.

Perez nodded. "Yes, but presumably Bonaparte knows that everything depends on this fleet, and he must get it to sea. I don't think he believes Villeneuve is the man to do the job."

"When is this change expected?"

"I gather Villeneuve is afraid that Decrès will arrive any day, and he regards it as a dishonour."

"You mentioned the Spanish captains."

"Ah, yes. You are a practical man, Captain Ramage. Would you care to command a ship of the line and sail under the command of someone like this Villeneuve – and with your ship equipped with rotten rope, rotten sails, and short of provisions, those you have being rotten?"

Ramage grinned and shook his head. "Not even a rowing boat, let alone a ship of the line!"

"Exactly, so you can imagine in what a dreadful position the Spanish Admiral Gravina finds himself: his most senior captains come to him daily, begging for equipment he cannot supply; they beg him to tell the French it is suicide to sail with the English fleet waiting for them."

Perez shook his head, as though saddened by what he was going to say. "I'm afraid some of the captains are meeting among themselves and their talk is close to treason."

"But is the city of Cadiz so short of food and supplies?"

"The people are starving," Perez said frankly. "Every able-bodied man has been taken up for the ships, so women and children starve because they have lost the – how do you say, 'the breadwinner'.

"As you can see, this is not a fertile part of the country. No grain can get in because of your blockade – nor, of course, anything that can be used to fit out the ships."

Perez now looked haggard in the dim lamplight: telling such a tale of disaster seemed to be emphasizing it for him. Probably, Ramage thought, he thrusts it away at the back of his mind whenever he can, unless he can pass the word to the British in Gibraltar.

"Lord Nelson was concerned about the position of other French ships," Ramage said. "How many, in which ports, and so on."

"Well now, let me see. Brest – yes, Admiral Gantaume is there with twenty-one line-of-battle ships, and from what I hear you people are blockading him so that he can't get out.

"Then Admiral Allemand is at sea – I don't know where – with four ships of the line. Difficult for him to break in and join either Gantaume at Brest or Villeneuve here. He could make for Ferrol or Coruña, I suppose. That's all the ships I know about. And, of course, Villeneuve commands thirty-four French and Spanish ships here. A very large fleet – on paper."

"You have no hint when Villeneuve is likely to sail, I suppose?"

Perez shook his head, his white hair flowing. "No – but I'm sure he will sail as soon as he gets a fair wind. Not so much because he wants to fight your Nelson, but he feels deeply the dishonour there would be if he is replaced by Decrès."

"So we can expect the Combined Fleet to sail the minute there is an east wind. Heading for the English Channel?"

Perez held up a hand as though restraining Ramage. "I hear reports that Villeneuve has received new orders. Reports? Rumours, more likely, and you must emphasize that to Lord Nelson. You came to me for information, but I must ask you a question – and please feel free not to answer. Is there a big British convoy at sea somewhere carrying troops into the Mediterranean?"

Ramage thought for several moments, and then decided that the French knew it was at sea and its destination – that was hardly a secret even before General Craig's ships left England bound for Italy.

Ramage nodded. "Yes, I believe there is such a convoy at sea."

"Ah, that might explain it!" Perez exclaimed. "You see, I know that until very recently Admiral Villeneuve's orders from Bonaparte were to leave Cadiz and sail north to the English Channel, and guard his flotillas waiting at Calais and Boulogne as they crossed to invade England.

"But this rumour I heard – or, rather, my informant heard – was to the effect that Villeneuve had just received entirely new orders: he was to break out of Cadiz and sail into the Mediterranean, to find and destroy this English convoy or, if it had already gone through and landed its men in Italy to help the Russians, to land troops – this city is full of them, eating what little food is left – and drive the English into the sea."

Ramage felt himself tensing as he thought about the rumour. If it was true, then Bonaparte was no longer threatening England. Had he lost his nerve? Had the difficulties and dangers of getting his boats and barges across the Channel frightened him? Or (more likely) had he lost faith in Villeneuve's ability to get the fleet up to the Channel and therefore abandoned the invasion? But what about Decrès – did Bonaparte not trust him either?

And, of course, it was late in the year. Who would dare guarantee even a day and night's decent weather in the Channel (let alone an easterly wind, which the invasion fleet had to have) in October? – and it would be late October even if Villeneuve broke out now. Even if he escaped Lord Nelson and even if he had fair winds, and even if he could control his mixed fleet – more ifs than hopes – he could not be off Calais and Dover before the last week in October.

Ramage found himself feeling sorry for Villeneuve: the poor man's Emperor had, it seemed, given him the choice of defeat or dishonour…

Perez looked at Ramage. "Yes, I understand the importance of that rumour, because if Villeneuve sails for the Mediterranean there can be no invasion of England. But I beg you, Captain Ramage, do emphasize to Lord Nelson that it is only a rumour. My informant has tried to get more information but as you can imagine, even if he has received such orders, Admiral Villeneuve will guard them carefully. After all, his success will depend on surprising Lord Nelson by breaking out and turning south for the Strait rather than north for England…"

"Yes," Ramage said as casually as possible, trying to keep the excitement from his voice. "A rumour, I shall emphasize that. Now señor," he said, taking out his watch, "is there anything else? My boat will be waiting for me in about five minutes' time."

Perez shook his head. "No. I think that is all I have to offer. Is it of help?"

"Yes, His Lordship will be very grateful. Now, I suggest we leave by the front door, with you bidding us farewell, as though we have been paying you a normal visit. By the way, there is no curfew?"

Perez shook his head. "There was for a short while, but the people are too frightened to go out – because of the troops! So the garrison commander lifted the curfew."

As the gate shut behind them Ramage and Orsini, blinking to get accustomed to the darkness, began walking across the *plaza* to the cemetery. Both sighed at the same moment and laughed at the coincidence.

"What is troubling you?" Ramage asked in Spanish.

"A most interesting visit," Orsini said carefully, wary that he might be overheard.

"Yes," Ramage said, "we must pass the message to our master."

"He will be pleased!"

Will he? Ramage thought not. It was one thing to cover the Combined Fleet against the chance of escaping north to the English Channel, but it was quite something else (while staying out of sight, not risking deterring them from sailing) to guard against them escaping southwards to the Mediterranean. It was, indeed, a toss-up.

By now they were passing through the cemetery and they could hear the lazy slapping of wavelets on the beach. Ramage suddenly held Orsini's shoulder: "Listen!"

There were angry voices shouting in Spanish. Two voices. And equally vociferous replies in French. Ramage stared across the beach and gradually made out the shape of two horsemen at the water's edge and, just beyond them, the cutter. Spanish mounted guards, challenging the boat, and Gilbert and Louis shouting back in French, pretending to be indignant but not understanding whatever the Spanish sentries were asking.

Ramage crouched down and made his way across the sand, followed by Orsini. The Spaniards were getting more excited; they were clearly asking questions and demanding answers – why a boat full of men should be at this beach – but were not satisfied with the shouts in French.

Very soon Ramage could distinguish what the Spaniards were saying. They were very nervous, very jumpy and very angry at being answered in French: they reckoned that only Spanish boats should be out at night.

Ramage and Orsini were only five yards from the two horsemen when Ramage heard one of them bellow angrily: "Get out of the boat! Out! If you don't get out I shoot the nearest man!"

Surprise, thought Ramage. And noise. He whispered to Orsini. A moment later both men ran screaming and shouting at the horses, slapping each on the rump and starting them rearing. Without waiting to see what had happened to the equally startled horsemen, Ramage continued running, grabbed the side of the cutter and, making sure that Orsini was scrambling on board, snapped at Jackson: "Quick, shove off! Those two won't be able to aim pistols properly while their horses are dancing!"

The men on the beach side of the boat thrust down and away with their oars, levering the boat round, and the moment the bow was heading seaward all the oars dipped in the water and the men began rowing vigorously.

Ramage scrambled into the boat sprawling across a thwart. He twisted round to look at the horsemen and saw they were ten yards further along the beach, fighting the horses which were rearing and neighing: horses frightened by the screams and slaps of the two men approaching from the rear, and spurred and kicked by the startled riders they had nearly thrown. The yanking at the bits and the raking of the spurs had frightened the horses even more and they continued rearing and walking sideways along the beach, their riders concerned only with staying in the saddles, the boat for the time being forgotten.

Ten yards off the shore, twenty and increasing speed, thirty and Jackson cursing as he tried to fit the metal tiller on to the wooden rudderhead. Thirty yards and they were out of sight of the horsemen; fifty yards and they could no longer see the thin white ribbons of the wavelets breaking.

"Back to the *Calypso*, sir?" Jackson asked politely once he had the tiller fitted and tucked under his arm.

Ramage thought a moment. He had to sail at once for the *Victory*, but Blackwood commanded the little inshore squadron of which the *Calypso* was part.

"No, the *Euryalus*, first."

Blackwood would be patrolling between the El Diamante and La Galera shoals: a five-mile sail from here, and then another three miles or so to find the *Calypso*.

With the *Calypso* hove-to half a mile to windward of the flagship, Ramage boarded the *Victory* at exactly nine o'clock next morning, tired but shaven, wearing a frock coat that Silkin had insisted on pressing, and a neatly tied stock.

At the last moment a whimsical thought that the news he was taking to Lord Nelson could mean that England was safe from any invasion threat led Ramage to wear his Lloyd's sword. A puzzled Silkin had mumbled: "But you didn't wear it when all the other captains were there," and Ramage had laughed. "It's an old Spanish custom," he said.

Hardy greeted him at the entryport, anxious but trying to hide it. "His Lordship is worried – couldn't you carry out his orders?"

"His orders?" a puzzled Ramage repeated. "But he only gave me one set of orders."

"Yes, about landing in Cadiz."

"Ah yes," Ramage said, "that's why I'm here." And, he thought, you may be the admiral's flag captain, but if you think I'm going to make a report to you standing at the entryport with your first lieutenant and a couple of seamen, not to mention sideboys, all straining their ears, you are wrong.

With that he hurried to the great cabin, had the Marine sentry announce him after saluting in a cloud of pipeclay, and at Lord Nelson's call went in to find the admiral again sitting in his special armchair.

"Well, Ramage, what happened, eh? Problems?"

Ramage was almost alarmed at the admiral's concern – he had jumped up out of the chair, good eye glinting, the single arm clutching a handful of papers which he had been reading.

"No, sir: I carried out your orders and hurried out to make my report."

"What a stout fellow!" Nelson exclaimed, slapping him on the back with the handful of papers. "As soon as you hove in sight and were identified, Hardy and I decided you hadn't had time to land in Cadiz and get out here! I'm only too delighted to learn we were wrong! Well, what news have you got for me? Did you find our friend?"

Ramage nodded. "Yes, sir, we found his house in the lee of that church and paid him a call. We convinced him we were friends and he told us all he knew."

"You had no trouble with the Spanish getting on shore?"

"No, sir. We had to drive off a couple of mounted sentries to get back on board the cutter, but there was no difficulty."

"We? Who did you take with you?"

"Midshipman Orsini, sir, the nephew of the Marchesa di Volterra."

"Ah yes, you told me: he speaks fluent Spanish."

"As well as being a very resourceful young officer, sir."

"Yes. I'll keep an eye on him," the admiral said. "Has he passed for lieutenant yet?"

Ramage shook his head. "He won't be twenty for another couple of years."

"Well, we'll do something about him later. Now, what had Señor Perez to tell you?"

Ramage repeated the Spaniard's words as near verbatim as his memory allowed, so that he was near the end of his report when he came to the rumour – he carefully repeated Perez's warning about it – that Villeneuve might have new orders directing him to the Mediterranean.

The chance that his quarry might bolt either to the north or the south did not seem to bother Nelson. "Twenty ships, Ramage, I shan't be satisfied with less than twenty ships!"

"Leave one for me, sir," Ramage said jokingly.

"There'll be enough for everyone," Nelson said, sitting down in his armchair, "but no frigates in the line of battle, Ramage; one broadside from a 74 will turn your ship into floating wreckage...

"Signals – I want you frigates to repeat my signals quickly: if you do that, you'll have done your job. That's what frigates are for, when serving with a fleet. On detached service – which you are used to – well, that's a different matter. But with a fleet, keeping a sharp lookout and quick signals!"

"Yes, sir," Ramage said.

CHAPTER ELEVEN

Ramage sat at his desk, with the *Calypso* hove-to in a very light breeze five miles off the Fuerte de La Cortadura on the outskirts of Cadiz. The sun was occasionally breaking through high, watery clouds.

He pulled across his journal and dipped his quill in the ink. Blockading (or keeping a watch on an enemy port) must be the dullest job in the Service, apart from acting as guardship at somewhere like Plymouth or Portsmouth: for days you just stared at the same views. Days, weeks and perhaps months...

He flipped over some earlier pages. Sunday, 28th September: the day they joined the fleet, and next day was Nelson's birthday. On the next night he and Paolo had gone on shore to find Señor Perez, and on 1st October he had taken the *Calypso* out to find Nelson and report on what the Spaniard had to say...Since then the *Calypso* and *Euryalus* had kept a close watch on Cadiz and Rota (close enough to see what was happening on board the French and Spanish ships hiding in Cadiz), with Thomas Dundas' frigate *Naiad* and Thomas Bladen-Capel's *Phoebe* close in. Several miles out – close enough to distinguish flag signals – was William Prowse with the frigate *Sirius*, with William Parker in the *Amazon* frigate, the schooner *Pickle* and the *Weazle* lying further out, over the horizon. Then, making up the rest of the links out to the fleet, were three ships of the line, acting as frigates because of the shortage – the *Defence* with Captain George Hope in command, the 64-gun *Agamemnon* (the first ship of the line that Nelson had ever commanded as a young post-captain) with Captain Berry, one of the few who knew Lord Nelson well, and finally, in sight of the fleet, the *Mars* and the Duff clan.

The entries in the journal reflected the dullness of the task: "5th October – anchored in Cadiz Roads, no movement among ships of the Combined Fleet... 10 October – cruising between Castillo de San Sebastián (the western tip of Cadiz city) and the Fuerte de La Cortadura... 15th October – patrolling the *Canal Principal* off Cadiz harbour: 35 tons of water remaining... 18th October hove-to in light winds off Castillo de San Sebastian, opened one cask of salt beef, six pieces missing..."

And then frequent entries were: "Ship's company employed ATSR" (the abbreviation for "As The Service Required")... "Ship's company exercised at general quarters" (which meant at the guns)... "Topmen exercised at shifting foretopsail" ("shifting" meant sending down the topsail and then hoisting it up again and bending it back on to the yard, usually timing from "sail set to sail set again"). And painting...the gunner was given men to black the guns, painting them with a special mixture which included lamp-black and Stockholm tar (one drop of which, Aitken swore, would ruin his scrubbed decks). Aitken was perhaps the only man in the ship who favoured blockade and lookout duty – he had the men and the time to get all the jobs done that could not be undertaken in rough seas, when wet paint would be spoiled by spray or men having to move across it.

Jackson, Rossi and Stafford were busy at just such a job: Jackson had drawn a booklet of gold leaf from the first lieutenant which Captain Ramage had paid for (the Navy Board did not issue gold leaf: their nearest was white paint). From the boatswain he had drawn a bottle of special size (for sticking down the gilding), a fine brush, and a chamois leather pad. Stafford and Rossi had brushes and paint.

They had to gild and paint the capstan, which was the size of a large fat cask standing on end. On top, in the middle, was a crown, whose gilding was wearing off, attacked by the sun and chipped during normal use of the capstan.

The most fiddling of jobs, the first started by Rossi and Stafford, were the wedge-shaped drawers which fitted into the slots taking the bars when the capstan had to be turned. When the bars were not slotted in, breast-high, the slots themselves held small drawers in which were stowed pieces of cloth to be used as bandages when in action and short pieces of line, each with a monkey's fist knot the size of a walnut. They were the tourniquets that would be used to bind up a severed limb and stop the bleeding.

Jackson had already rubbed down the crown with shagreen: he was lucky to get a piece of dried shark skin from the carpenter, who hoarded his meagre supply.

The American scrambled up on top of the capstan and carefully pulled the cork from the bottle of size. He poured some into a shallow dish and recorked the bottle. He then painted size on to the part of the crown he intended gilding, found the pair of tweezers he had borrowed from the surgeon and, using his body to act as a shield should there be a puff of wind, opened the small book of gold leaf. The leaves were an inch wide by four inches long, and each leaf so thin that the gentlest breeze would blow it away.

He held a leaf in the tweezers and then gently tore it out. He transferred it to the part of the crown with size, blowing the leaf so that it settled on the carved wood. He then worked it in to the carver's indentations, using a piece of wood with a finely-curved end, leaving the odd edges of the leaf to be cleaned off when the size was dry. He then sized another section and repeated the transfer of gold leaf.

Meanwhile Rossi and Stafford had removed the drawers, emptied out their contents and placed them on a small sheet of old and paint-stained canvas.

"Mr Aitken's goin' ter want ter know 'xactly how many leaves Jacko's used," Stafford commented.

"Is not hard to see," Rossi grunted. He was putting on weight round his waist and bending over to work on the drawers was uncomfortable. Finally he sat down on the canvas, holding the first drawer to be painted.

"Gold leaf would be rare old stuff to steal," Jackson said. "You have to be careful when you puff it on to the size: if you breathe in you're likely to suck it into your lungs."

"Then you'll be the only sailor in the King's service with gilded lungs," Stafford said. "Every breff costs a guinea!"

"You know about the guinea?" Jackson asked.

"What guinea?" Stafford asked cautiously.

"That's what can be rolled to make enough gold leaf like this – " he held up the book, " – to stretch round the dome of St Paul's Cathedral."

"Don't sound right ter me," Stafford declared stoutly in the special tone he adopted to express extreme doubt.

"Can't help that: s'fact," Jackson said, in turn adopting the tone of voice that showed he was not prepared to argue the point.

"It would not go round St Peter's dome," Rossi said triumphantly.

"Is that the place in Rome?"

"Is the greatest church in the world," the Italian maintained.

"Not as big as St Paul's," Stafford declared, defending the city of London's superiority over anything foreign.

"*Mamma mia,*" Rossi said, knowing that it was an argument he could not win, since he had seen neither St Peter's nor St Paul's, and did not really care about their respective domes.

"Have you mixed the white?" he asked Stafford.

"Start off with the blue!" Stafford said crossly. "Where's yer brains, Rosey? Start off with white and then spill some blue on it and you 'ave an 'ell of a job getting rid of it. Starting orf with the blue, it don't matter if there's a splash of white: just dab on more blue."

"Better not to splash," Jackson said as he jumped off the capstan and gave it a half-turn so that his body would still shelter the other half of the crown from random puffs of wind. "You'd better get a move on – I'm half-way through the gilding, and if the bosun or the first lieutenant come along..."

"Why d'you always get the easy jobs?" Stafford demanded.

"I'm the only man in this ship that can gild proper, that's why!" Jackson said. "Needs skill and patience."

"An' don't take a deep breff," Stafford said.

After five minutes' silence, Stafford said: "Flat sort o' country, this Cadiz place. All sandspits and salt-pans. Wouldn't like to live 'ere!"

"Why not?" demanded Rossi, who tended to defend any person, place or thing criticized by Stafford.

"M'skeeters," Stafford said succinctly. "Must eat yer alive at night. All that whinin' and bitin'. Marshes and salt-pans, that's where they like to live, an' this place is all marshes and salt-pans."

"Maybe the Frogs and the Dons are relying on the mosquitoes to keep us away," Jackson commented. "Just trying to be irritating."

"Reckon they're going to sail out, Jacko?"

"Not if they've got any sense," Jackson said firmly. "Would you like to get across Lord Nelson's hawse? Damned if I would. I heard the captain telling Mr Aitken that Lord Nelson says he wants at least twenty of 'em."

"Twenty what?" Stafford asked.

Jackson groaned and said: "You know, Staff, sometimes you are so daft it's hard to understand you. Twenty French and Spanish ships of the line destroyed, sunk, burned, captured – His Lordship doesn't care about the details, but he's set his mind on at least twenty."

"Good fer 'im," Stafford said approvingly. "My mum always did things by the score. A score of candles, a score of eggs, an' so on: she 'ated dozens, but scores she was very partial to. Never did understand why."

"She should have met His Lordship," Jackson commented.

A footstep and then Aitken's soft voice said. "More talking than working, it seems to me. Who is scoring?"

"No, sir," Jackson said, leaning back to display how much of the crown he had so far gilded. "Not scoring, but a score. Twenty."

Aitken nodded. "So you heard the captain telling me, eh?"

"Couldn't help it, sir," Jackson said.

"We was just saying wot a good number a score is, sir," Stafford said. "My mum always bought things by the score."

"And you stole by the gross," Aitken commented, smiling as Rossi and Jackson began laughing.

"I'm glad to see you started with the blue and not the white," Aitken said and Rossi immediately began a long-winded explanation, repeating his own version of Stafford's earlier comment.

Aitken nodded and then said to Jackson: "There's some gilding to be done at the entryport, while you have the size and the gold leaf out."

"That gold leaf, sir," Stafford said. "You take a guinea and flatten it and you get enough gold leaf – "

"To go round the dome of St Paul's – yes, I know."

"So there!" Stafford said triumphantly to Rossi. "It'd probably go round St Peter's *twice*."

On Thursday the wind had occasionally fluked eastward, as though teasing; Friday – yesterday – had been fine, with the wind still occasionally whiffling to the east, and then back to the north and west. Then, at midnight, it had set in from the east and Ramage and Southwick, walking up and down in the darkness of the quarterdeck, the stars above bright and the black outline of Cadiz sharp, had agreed that it looked as if it was going to stay east for a few days.

Ramage had slept fitfully, fully dressed. Every hour or so he had gone up to the quarterdeck, talked with the officer of the deck and confirmed that the wind was staying east. The door to Cadiz was open; would the Combined Fleet make a bolt for it?

Certainly not in the darkness: more than thirty great ships (among them two which were the biggest in the world) would want time and daylight to get their anchors up and sails set; the channel out of Cadiz, opposite the city, was only about four hundred yards wide; not enough for a big ship (with an inexperienced crew, foul bottom, probably nervous captain and several other ships around) to tack in an emergency. And unless the ship held its wind it would go aground on a two-fathom bank on the larboard hand or hit the edge of a mud bank on the starboard hand which dried out at low water.

Ramage added a sentence to his night orders: "By dawn the *Calypso* must be passing south of the El Diamante bank steering for Cadiz Roads, and the captain is to be called."

As he tried to ward off the waves of excitement and sleep, Ramage reflected on the last few words of his night orders. Yes, the captain was to be called, and to set an example of imperturbability, he would have to pretend to be asleep. But sleep when the French commander-in-chief was probably working by candlelight giving orders for the Combined Fleet to weigh and sail at daylight? And the *Calypso* (by a stroke of luck) the frigate whose turn it was to be close up to Cadiz

Roads, so close at dawn that they would be able to see waves slapping on the breakwater and the beach at Punta de la Soledad.

What would daylight reveal? A straightforward situation where a single signal from the *Signal Book for Ships of War* would tell the *Euryalus* what was going on? Or would it need Popham's Code, allowing more details? Anyway, from the *Euryalus* the signal would be passed to the next frigate seaward and then on and on, like beacons being lit on a row of hills, until it reached the *Victory*.

For days now the first signal of the day, started on its way to the *Victory* from the *Euryalus* as soon as it was light enough to distinguish the colour of the flags, had been: "The enemy as before". The enemy, in other words, was still in Cadiz with a west wind (and perhaps no great eagerness to sail!).

The next thing Ramage knew was Orsini banging on his door: it was still dark in the cabin, but an excited Orsini reported that dawn was about to break. Ramage wiped his face with a wet cloth, pulled on his shoes and picked up his hat after dragging on his coat. He felt grubby and greasy, his chin rasping on his stock every time he looked down.

"Morning, sir," Hill said politely. "Wind due east; we're half a mile south of the El Diamante Bank in four fathoms, fore and main topsails set."

"Very well," Ramage said in reply to this routine report, "keep the lead going."

A long and wide sandbank thrust out into the *Canal Principal* from the actual sea wall protecting Cadiz harbour. As Southwick had commented, it was a deliberate trap for nosy frigates who did not keep to the north-east of it.

Yes, the sky was turning grey over to the east, above the sand dunes on the east side of the bay. No cloud was obscuring the stars which were beginning to fade. Yes, the outline of Cadiz was getting greyer and softer. He began to make out objects on the deck – the square box of the binnacle, the bulk of the mizenmast, the round-shouldered bulk of the 12-pounders and the carronades...

Yes, there was the breakwater protecting Cadiz harbour, the Muelle de San Felipe, jutting out to the north-east. The church of San Francisco was at the landward end and, further on, two towers and yet another church (Carmen, noted on Southwick's chart as "Conspicuous") and the whole city (really a small town) built round the Torre de Tavira, a watch-tower which could see all round the compass.

"General quarters, Mr Hill," Ramage said quietly and noticed that Aitken and Southwick had come on deck. The lieutenant gave the order which started bosun's mates hurrying through the ship, their calls twittering as they shouted vile threats to get the men out of their hammocks and standing to the guns. They would greet the dawn, as did every one of the King's ships in wartime, with guns loaded and run out, as ready to tackle an enemy as greet a friend. The deckwash pumps groaned asthmatically as they ran water over the decks, to be followed by men sprinkling sand. There were distant shouted orders and then the dull rumble as the guns were run out.

"Ship's company at general quarters, sir," Hill reported.

"Very well," Ramage said out of habit, and waited for the hail.

It came first from the lookout on the larboard bow. "See a grey goose at a mile," he bellowed in the traditional way of greeting daylight – or as much daylight as would allow that feat.

"A short mile," Ramage commented to Hill. The lookout was unlucky that instead of the usual (before the blockade) empty horizon there was the city of Cadiz, complete with cathedral, towers, castle and long stone mole, all less than a mile away.

"Send the lookouts aloft, but keep the men at general quarters," Ramage said. The wind was still east; he walked over to the binnacle box drawer and reassured himself that the copy of Popham's Code was there, along with the *Signal Book*.

Looking at the Mole of San Felipe, he took his telescope from the drawer and pulled the tube until the engraved ring was lined up. He scanned along the mole, shifting to one side so that the foremast was not in the way.

"Come round a point to larboard," he told Hill: the Mole was obscuring too much of the anchorage. He waited a couple of minutes and then lifted the telescope again. The nearest ships of the Combined Fleet of France and Spain were clearly visible.

He snapped the telescope shut and in a couple of paces, was at the binnacle box drawer, taking out Popham's Code and flicking over the pages, checking the words (in alphabetical order) and the numbers beside them.

"Orsini," he snapped, "make to the *Euryalus* the following.

"Telegraphic code flag; then 249 – 'enemy', 354 – 'have', 864 – 'their', 875 –, 'top', 756 – 'sails', 986 – 'yards', 1374 – 'hoisted'. Got that? Right, get it hoisted as quick as you can.

"Mr Hill, stand by to heave-to the ship. The enemy seem to have called in their gunboats."

"Yes, sir: I was going to report that as soon as you had finished with the signal."

The gunboats – boats from the ships of the Combined Fleet with a small gun mounted temporarily in the bow – had regularly patrolled the few hundred yards directly in front of the harbour, looking as threatening as water boatmen on a village pond.

Ramage opened the telescope and looked again. Yes, several of the ships were hoisting in boats, swigging away at staytackles and swinging the boats in to nest them on top of the spare

booms and spars. Topsail yards hoisted, along with boats…
today, October 19, was going to be the day the Combined
Fleet sailed from Cadiz, of that he was sure.

"The signal's sent and the *Euryalus* has acknowledged, sir,"
Orsini reported.

"Ship hove-to on the starboard tack, sir," Hill reported.

"I'm going below to wash and shave," Ramage said. "Keep
a sharp eye on the *Euryalus* for signals," he told Orsini. To Hill,
he said: "Pass the word the moment there's any sign of the
enemy ships weighing anchor."

Shaving in cold water – with the ship's company at general
quarters the galley fire had been doused – helped waken him
thoroughly: he was too impatient to strop the razor sufficiently,
and this morning the soap was reluctant to lather, so that each
stroke of the razor seemed as though he was wrenching out
each whisker by the roots. With his eyes watering he finally
rinsed his face and then combed his hair.

Silkin waited at the door with clean underwear, fresh
stockings and newly polished shoes, along with a clean stock.
Ramage dressed leisurely. Thus were legends started. The
captain had felt greasy and bristly and tired, in no shape to
think very clearly after an almost sleepless night, and as soon
as the morning's signal had been sent off he had shaved and
changed. But within a month (if they were all still alive by
then) the ship's company would have embroidered the tale so
that Captain Ramage was having a leisurely shave while thirty-
four ships of the line of the Combined Fleet prepared to sail
and give battle with the *Calypso*. Ramage grinned to himself.
He had heard many similar stories told about brother
captains, and guessed they had similar origins. Anyway, they
were a sign that a ship's company was proud of their captain
and the ship, and if it made them fight better, no harm was
done. Seamen had keen eyes, and if an officer was a braggart
they quickly ignored him, simply obeying orders.

The marine sentry was announcing Orsini.

"Mr Hill's compliments, sir, but the *Euryalus* has just repeated our signal to the *Sirius*, and one of the enemy has just let fall a topsail."

Ramage pulled on a stocking. So the signal was already on its way across the fifty miles to Lord Nelson's fleet, and the enemy were making the first (the first of thousands!) move towards sailing. The significant report would be when the first of them hove up her anchors.

Each ship would have at least a couple of anchors down – that was, apart from any other considerations, the only way of packing so many ships into such a confined anchorage without them swinging into each other. Heavy anchors and a muddy bottom: Ramage could picture the clunking of the pawls on the capstans – and the stench of the mud on the cable, with water similar to sewage being squeezed out of the strands of the rope as it came through the hawsehole...pity the poor fellows down in the cable-tier whose job it was to coil the cables as they passed below.

Finally Ramage was dressed and he went up to the quarterdeck. In the half-hour he had been below it had turned into a fine day: three miles away to the eastward there was the gentle slope of vineyards, and then the land trended southward to the village of Santa Maria at the entrance to a small river and became dunes. They continued on to the marshes and salt-ponds on the other side of Cadiz, separated from the spit by the channel in which most of the Combined Fleet were moored.

He examined Cadiz with the telescope. There was no flag on the Torre de Tavira, but that three-decker there, French (was she Villeneuve's flagship, the *Bucentaure*?), was making signals. One ship had just started catting her anchors. Another, Spanish, was at short stay and moving ahead slowly as the capstan hauled in the remaining anchor cable. He examined the ship's masts. There were men out along the fore and maintopsail yards – obviously throwing off gaskets.

Yes – there's the foretopsail let fall. The breeze is light, not enough to shake out the creases in the canvas. Now they're bracing the yards sharp up – the captain is anxious to get under way the moment the anchor is aweigh, so that the wind does not drift him sideways on to the mudbank only a few yards on his larboard side.

Ah, the other anchor is breaking the surface, and they've let fall the maintopsail. And there goes the maincourse and now the forecourse, and headsails are being hoisted. She's under way.

"Mr Orsini," Ramage said briskly, "to the *Euryalus*: make number 370."

Orsini, out of habit, said: "Number 370, sir, 'Enemy's ships are coming out of port, or getting under sail'. "

"Stand by to get under way," Ramage told Hill. A Spanish three-decker's broadside as she passed the *Calypso* at close range could reduce the frigate to so much firewood. There was plenty of shallow water on the east side of the bay, or northwards towards Rota, where the *Calypso* could sail but a 74 or bigger would go aground. The frigate's job was to watch and report to the *Euryalus*, not fight...

CHAPTER TWELVE

The big French ship of the line came out of Cadiz Roads with almost pathetic slowness. The wind soon dropped away to random zephyrs, so that her sails, in billowing curves when she got under way, flattened to hanging curtains of canvas by the time she was abreast of where the *Calypso* had been hove-to.

Ramage had seized the opportunity before the breeze went light to get out to seaward, deciding not to risk being trapped in the bay by the French and Spanish frigates he knew were anchored in Cadiz.

He watched as the Frenchman slowly steered northwards for Rota (at times turning round completely as she lost the wind and was at the mercy of the current) and then saw a second ship get under way and start struggling to get out of the Roads.

The first ship was the *Algésiras*, which his list showed him was the flagship of Rear-Admiral Charles de Magon. When the second ship finally cleared the entrance and then lost the wind for several minutes, turning like a languid dancer, Ramage saw that the name carved across her transom (and heavily gilded: enough to catch the eye at this distance as it glinted in the sun) was the *Achille*.

Although he was making for a position due north of the Castillo de San Sebastián, Ramage's last glimpse into Cadiz Roads showed him that a French frigate (the *Hermione*, he guessed) had managed to weigh and set sail, but almost immediately must have lost the wind because now her boats were towing her out, hard work against what was now a flood tide.

With the wind falling away and the young flood beginning to carry him out of position, Ramage ordered the *Calypso* to anchor, and the best bower splashed down into four fathoms just short of the El Banquete shoal, a mile north-west of the Castillo. The Spaniards had never opened fire from the castle, but if they started now the *Calypso* might be in trouble: with no wind and having to weigh anchor, the young flood might carry her on to Punta del Nao, a vicious-looking rocky peninsula just north-east of the castle.

But the castle guns remained quiet and the *Calypso* swung at anchor, watching the *Algésiras*, *Achille* and *Hermione* (eventually Orsini had read the name on her stern) struggle up towards Rota, revolving like sunflowers as they lost a puff.

As the men at alternate guns were allowed to go below for a meal and Southwick went through the daily ritual of taking a noon sight (although it was easy enough to take a bearing of the castle, and a vertical sextant angle would give the distance for those unable to estimate it) Ramage watched the *Euryalus* and *Sirius* drift, becalmed.

Well, Ramage commented to Southwick, today the wind was being neutral: it becalmed the Combined Fleet and it becalmed Lord Nelson – although, fifty miles out to the west, the weather might well be different.

But, Ramage wondered, what would Lord Nelson be doing: would he pay any attention to Perez's report about the Mediterranean and steer south, anticipating that (when he got out of Cadiz) Villeneuve would make for the Strait, or would he steer north to intercept the Combined Fleet on the assumption it was making for the English Channel?

"I'm glad I'm not His Lordship," Southwick said, apparently thinking on the same lines as Ramage. "Go north or go south...from fifty miles out he's got to rely on us frigates, but he's got to make a start now, and that means he has to guess. Like putting all your money on the turn of a card."

"Yes, betting on whether it'll turn up red or black."

"Yes, not odds for a sensible man."

"His Lordship has no choice," Ramage said.

Southwick pointed to the end of Punta del Nao. Another ship of the line, all sail set but with every inch of canvas hanging slackly, was being towed out by its boats. Curious, Ramage reflected, how a little wind made a ship graceful and lively, and yet a calm reduced her to a clumsy and sluggish hulk, at the mercy of sweating men in boats pulling on oars...

Soon they read her name, the *Neptune*. She was followed by another, the *Héros*.

"Four French ships of the line and a French frigate," Aitken commented. "Does that mean the Spanish are staying at home?"

"The first French out were probably the last to arrive," Ramage said. "Anyway, that French rear-admiral has set a good example."

The sun passed its zenith and began the slow dip towards the west. Southwick, filling in the master's log, started a new day at noon. Although the civil day began at midnight and by civil time it was still Saturday, by nautical time Sunday began at noon. Southwick filled in the *Calypso*'s position, the wind ("round the compass and frequent calms") and drew a line in the columns for "course" and "speed".

"Two more ships coming out, both 74s and both French," Orsini reported. "Having a race," he added sarcastically. "The boats are making half a knot, with double-banked oars."

Southwick took off his hat and with a characteristic gesture ran his hand through his flowing white hair. "They must be pulling against the full flood by now," he said. "Just needs two ships to get alongside each other and lock yards, and we'll see some fun."

Aitken gestured to the *Algésiras* and the *Achille*, still less than a couple of miles away in their tedious attempt to get up to Rota. "Not much of a day for sailing; better to anchor and give the men a 'make and mend' day."

"They've been 'making and mending' for months," Southwick growled. "No cloth for making and nothing left needing mending."

"The nearest is the *Argonaute*, sir," Orsini reported. "I'll have the name of the other one in a moment, as soon as the bearing changes… Ah yes, the…" he spelled out the name letter by letter, and then said: "Yes, the *Duguay-Trouin*, whoever he was."

"Another two for the log," Ramage said to Southwick. "Make sure you spell them right."

"Names are going to be a problem," Southwick growled. "We've got a *Neptune* and so have the French, while the Dons have a *Neptuno*. We have an *Achille*, so have the French. And there's a British and a French *Swiftsure*. And apart from the same names, the French have the *Berwick*, which sounds British, and we have the *Spartiate*, *Tonnant* and *Belleisle*, which sound French."

"The French captured the *Berwick*. But Lord Bridport took the *Belleisle* ten years ago. The *Tonnant* and the *Spartiate* were taken by Lord Nelson in '98," Ramage pointed out.

"That's what I mean," Southwick complained, "it's all very confusing."

Ramage smiled. "Don't forget the *Ville de Paris* was built at Chatham!"

"And there comes another, a *Spaniard!*" Orsini yelled excitedly. "That's six French ships of the line and a French frigate out before a Don gets his jib-boom past the Mole!"

"Hush," Ramage said in a sepulchral voice, "they are a peace-loving people and tomorrow is Sunday – for the people on shore, anyway."

For the remainder of the afternoon Ramage and the *Calypso* watched for the rest of the Combined Fleet to get out of Cadiz, but the easterly breeze did not freshen enough to give the big ships steerage way. Two more French frigates managed to get out, towing with boats. The *Themis* and the *Rhin* struggled to catch every whiffle of wind so that they could follow Rear Admiral Magon, trying to get across Cadiz Bay and reach the safety of Rota.

At nightfall, Ramage gave the order to weigh again and patrol close off the end of the Mole in case a breeze allowed more ships to sneak out. Rockets and portfires were brought out ready to signal to the *Euryalus* should enough wind spring up and the rest of the Combined Fleet decide to make a dash for it in the darkness.

Jackson stood up at the gun of which he was captain: the deck on which he had been lying seemed to be getting harder.

"My back," he grumbled to the rest of the gun's crew. "More than twelve hours at general quarters...and we'll be here the whole of tonight."

"And all tomorrow too," Stafford said. "Seven got out today, but there's thirty-four or so ships of the line. At this rate it'll take 'em five days to get out!"

"That's supposing they want to get out," Louis said. "If the Spanish have any sense they'll stay in port."

"One Spaniard did sail," Gilbert pointed out.

"Probably dragging his anchors!" Louis commented.

"Against a foul current?" Stafford asked. "Well," he announced, "I'm looking forward to seeing the *Santy Trinidaddy.*"

Jackson groaned at the Cockney's pronunciation. "You mean the *Santissima Trinidad*. Means the Holy Trinity."

"Does it?" Stafford said. "Well, they say she's the biggest ship in the world. Carries 130 guns, I heard Mr Ramage telling Mr Orsini."

"Too big for us to attack," Louis said jokingly.

"She could hoist us on board without strain," Jackson said.

"Just let her try!" Stafford said.

Jackson walked over to the low tub of water standing between his gun and the next and inspected the short lengths of burning slow match, fitted into notches round the lip of the tub, their glowing ends over the water.

"Have to change this match soon," he said. "May be needed for the rockets and portfires."

" 'Ere, Jacko, why're they called 'portfires'? – we never set 'em orf in port."

Jackson shrugged his shoulders. "Why call them 'fires'? All that matters is that they make a big glow when we light 'em! They last so much longer than rockets, so there's more chance of seeing them. A rocket's up, over and down in a minute: you could easily miss it. But a portfire – well, from a distance it looks just a glow but it lasts so much longer."

"They won't come out, anyway," Gilbert said.

The Italian seaman, Rossi, growled: "If you keep saying that, you give them the idea!"

"There are many admirals and captains in there – " Gilbert pointed at Cadiz, now over the starboard bow, " – only too content to stay at anchor. They're beaten already!"

"Beaten already?" exclaimed Stafford. "Wotcher mean, they ain't even gone to sea yet!"

"Nelson," Gilbert said. "Just the name. If they're Spanish they know what Commodore Nelson did at Cap St Vincent: if they're French they know what happened at the Nile. And whether they're Spanish or French they've heard all about Copenhagen. He's never been beaten in a big battle. Not only never been beaten, but he wins by destroying the enemy. How many ships of the line escaped at the Nile or Copenhagen?"

"Not many," a voice said out of the darkness, and the men sprang up as they recognized Captain Ramage's voice.

"Make yourselves comfortable," Ramage said. "Nothing so soft as a well-scrubbed deck or a gun carriage."

"Yus, sir," Stafford said cheerfully. "Trouble is I'm afraid I'll get so used to it I'll have trouble sleepin' in me 'ammick when all this is over!"

"If it's a problem," Ramage said with mock sympathy, "I'll tell the carpenter to give you half a dozen short planks to use in your hammock as a mattress."

"Do you think they'll come out tomorrow, sir?" Jackson asked.

Ramage shrugged his shoulders. "Depends on the wind. If the wind had held up today I'm sure most of them would have come out."

"What makes you sure they'll come out, sir?"

"Bonaparte," Ramage said grimly. "He's ordered them out. I think they might be more scared of him than Lord Nelson..."

"Silly fellows," Jackson commented.

"They've not much choice. Madame Guillotine or Lord Nelson's roundshot."

"Serves them right for siding with the Revolution," Gilbert commented bitterly.

"The Spanish haven't much choice either," Rossi pointed out.

"Bonaparte scared the Spanish government," Ramage said. "Eventually government decisions come down to seamen waiting in harbour."

With that Ramage moved on to talk to the next gun's crew, who were just as full of comments and questions. For everybody in the *Calypso* it was going to be a long and dreary wait for the dawn, but at ten o'clock Ramage intended to let the crews of alternate guns stand down. By doing watch and watch about they would all get some sleep before "see a grey goose at a mile".

CHAPTER **THIRTEEN**

Dawn on Sunday morning found Ramage pacing the quarterdeck in his boatcloak: during the night cloud had gradually hidden the stars, and the breeze, while freshening, had gradually veered to the south: now it was blowing straight out of Cadiz harbour, so that the *Calypso* had to beat (in an almost flat sea and a wind so light that the ship seemed reluctant to come round) to keep near the end of the Mole.

"All they've got to do now," Southwick said sourly, "is get their anchors on board: then they can't help *drifting* out to sea."

"Don't underestimate them," Aitken said. "Just imagine the *Santissima Trinidad* going ahead as they haul on their capstan and fouling the French flagship, the *Bucentaure*. Picture the shouting and cursing and running about. Jib-booms snapping like carrots, yards locked…"

"That's a fine imagination you've got," Southwick said. "They'll be so damned cautious it'll take 'em all day to get under way. You'll see, we'll have another night out here dodging the El Diamante shoal."

At that moment the starboard forward lookout gave the time-honoured cry of "See a grey goose at a mile" and two of the lookouts who had been stationed round the ship were sent aloft.

Almost at once they were hailing: at least five of the enemy ships of the line were weighing anchor in Cadiz Roads.

Ramage sent Orsini aloft with a telescope and orders to describe in detail how many ships had weighed and how many if any were actually under sail. "The flagships," Ramage emphasized. "What they're doing gives the clue to what the two fleets will do."

Very soon Orsini was hailing the quarterdeck. He had identified Villeneuve's flagship, the *Bucentaure*, and she had hoisted various flag signals. Seven ships of the line were actually weighing, two already at short stay, although the *Bucentaure* was lying to a single anchor. A brig was sailing through the anchored fleet – "Acting as whipper-in, I don't doubt," Orsini shouted in a hail which brought a smile to Ramage's face.

Several ships had let fall topsails, Orsini added, but none was under way. "The Mole, sir!" he called. "You should be able to see it from down there: thousands of people all along it, watching the fleet sail."

"Aye, weeping wives and sobbing strumpets," Aitken said unsympathetically.

"Listen," Ramage said.

Across the water came the tolling of church bells. The nearest were those of the Iglesia del Carmen, at the northern tip of the Cadiz peninsula and barely half a mile from the end of the Mole. Marked "Conspicuous" on Southwick's chart, it was the sailors' church. This morning, Ramage thought grimly, the sailors are out in the ships, weighing and catting the anchors, but their families are crowding the church and, judging from the deeper boom of its bells, the cathedral too.

Aitken said quietly: "They make the fleet's sailing a religious event, don't they. I can imagine dozens of candles burning, incense, monks chanting, priests droning away… Bit different from Portsmouth Point when our ships sail!"

"Aye, the Dons have bishops and mitres at the end of the Mole; we have bailiffs and mistresses!" Southwick said.

Orsini hailed from the masthead. "First of the ships of the line has let fall her courses."

"We'll go about, Mr Aitken," Ramage said. "Back to our original position a mile north of the Castillo de San Sebastián, only this time we won't anchor. And as soon as we're clear of the land and can get a sight of her, we'll make a signal to the *Euryalus*, telling Captain Blackwood that the Combined Fleet is at last sailing."

But...again Ramage decided he was thankful he was neither the French Admiral Villeneuve nor Lord Nelson. As far as the French admiral was concerned, yes, the south wind let him sail out of Cadiz, but supposing his orders were (as Señor Perez reported) to go to the Mediterranean and intercept General Craig's convoy...although the wind was fair for getting out of Cadiz, it was foul for the Strait... Lord Nelson would fall on him as he tried to get his Combined Fleet those fifty miles down to the Strait, the British ships savaging it (Ramage hoped) like wolves after so many spring lambs.

But...supposing you were Lord Nelson. Perez's report that Villeneuve might be sailing south after General Craig's convoy in the Mediterranean was (as Perez had been the first to emphasize) only a rumour. Villeneuve was just as likely to come out of Cadiz and, with this fair wind, head north-west for the English Channel...

Well, as soon as the Combined Fleet got out (and were joined by the seven ships which came out yesterday and were now lying up there to the north, hove-to off Rota if not actually at anchor) the line of British frigates and 74s could shadow the enemy, passing the signals to His Lordship, which would give him an early hint. Unless, of course, the French admiral sailed north and then cut south in the darkness – or headed south and changed to the north as soon as night fell.

The *Calypso*, sailing in a calm sea in the lee of Cadiz and with a clean bottom, reached fast across the end of the peninsula and as soon as she was north-west of the castle, with the *Euryalus* in sight further along the coast (obviously Blackwood was watching the enemy across the sandspit), Ramage gave Aitken the order to heave-to.

With the frigate heading south, the foretopsail backed, Ramage told Orsini, now down from the masthead, to get the slate and take down a signal for the *Euryalus*.

The signal was barely made before the first of the enemy 74s sailed out, followed five minutes later by a second and, close astern of her, a third.

"That's a total of ten of 'em out," Southwick said.

Orsini began reading off the names – the *Scipion*, *San Francisco de Asis* and the *Fougueux*. Then they came out almost as fast as he could make out the names. The *Montañes*, the Spanish Admiral Gravina's flagship the *Principe de Asturias*, *Pluton*, *Aigle*, Villeneuve's flagship the *Bucentaure*, the *San Justo*...and then, preceded by an excited shout from Orsini, they saw the *Santissima Trinidad* coming out under topsails and forecourse.

"Just look at her!" murmured Aitken. "Twice as big as a cathedral!"

"I wonder how she handles," Southwick said. "Probably needs a gale of wind to tack her..."

"Just think of her broadside," Orsini muttered. "Sixty-five guns a side... *Mamma mia!*"

How long would the French admiral allow a British frigate to sail back and forth in the lee of the Castillo de San Sebastián? But a moment later a hail from the masthead was drowned by a shout from Orsini: "One of them is turning towards us!"

Ramage looked across to the entrance to Cadiz and saw that a 74-gun ship was turning to larboard and either heading for the *Calypso* or making a bolt for the open sea. Which? Anyway it did not matter: she was a mile and a half away now and even if heading for the open sea (why? none of the others was) would pass within half a mile of the *Calypso*, which would be trapped against the land if she too did not make a bolt seaward.

"We'll get under way, go about and then steer west, if you please Mr Aitken," Ramage snapped. "Mr Orsini – go to the guns and make sure all the crews are ready; wet and sand the decks; make sure they're all loaded with roundshot."

He watched Aitken bellowing orders using the speaking trumpet and slowly, sails flapping, the thick rope of the sheets flogging like snakes held by the tail, the frigate turned, the yards were braced sharp up and the sails were sheeted home.

Ramage looked astern at the 74. French. Plum-coloured hull with two black strakes in way of the gunports. And in addition to topsails and courses she was now letting fall her topgallants...she was after the *Calypso*, not making a bolt for it: there was no one to stop her going off into the Atlantic; reaching out there, courses and topsails would be enough. But topgallants if you were in a hurry...

A 74 – and Villeneuve probably gave the order to a fast one. Eighteen- and 24-pounders. Thirty-seven of them on a broadside, quite apart from carronades, which were not counted. Against them, sixteen 12-pounders. Might as well pelt her with oranges, Ramage thought.

"She's moving fast," Southwick commented. "Just her wind, from the look of it, sir." He gave one of his gigantic sniffs. "She'll overhaul us."

Ramage turned to Aitken. "We'll have topgallants and royals, Mr Aitken. Then go below and change into silk stockings: those woollen ones are no good for going into action: more work for the surgeon with wool fluff if you get a leg wound."

He turned to Southwick, his eyes flickering to the *Calypso*'s wake. Already the frigate was heeling as she came clear of the lee formed by the headland on which stood the *castillo*.

"We can't outrun him, that's for sure, so we've got to outmanoeuvre him, Mr Southwick."

"We could turn north and try stunsails," Southwick offered.

"And so could the Frenchman," Ramage said. "We have only one advantage over him, and we'd better make the best of it."

Southwick took off his hat and scratched his head. "Blessed if I can see what it is," the master admitted.

"Tacking," Ramage said cryptically and since Aitken had hurried below he picked up the speaking trumpet and shouted: "I'll have another swig on those topsail sheets, and stand by headsail sheets: once we're abreast this headland we'll be hard on the wind."

Southwick sniffed again. "Once he's finished with us he'll go after the *Euryalus* and then the *Sirius*," Southwick said gloomily. "This damned French admiral wants to stop Lord Nelson finding out what's going on."

"He's left it too late," Ramage commented. "His Lordship already knows the Combined Fleet is putting to sea, and that's what really matters."

By now the *Calypso* was rolling and pitching her way round the headland, seeming excited at the idea of a hard flog to windward after days spent hove-to or just jogging along while officers and lookouts eyed the Combined Fleet at anchor. "Don't forget that isolated rock off this headland, sir," Southwick cautioned.

"Laja del Norte, you mean? It's a couple of hundred yards south-west of the end of the headland, isn't it?"

Southwick nodded. "Couple of fathoms of water over it. Enough to hole us but too deep for the sea to break on it."

Again Ramage looked astern: he could just see the trucks of the French ship's masts as she reached along the other side of the headland. She would be tacking in two or three minutes, just as the *Calypso* came into sight tacking southwards along the coast.

The idea was bold enough – maybe even stupid enough. He had thought of it several days ago while shaving, anticipating that the French admiral would try to drive the frigates off. The only mistake so far was that Villeneuve should have done it several days ago, before the Combined Fleet started to sail.

He had taken Southwick's chart (the one passed on by the *Victory's* master) and carefully taken off the bearings of the Fuerte de La Cortadura, and then measured the distances. There was a ten-foot rise of water at the top of the springs, so if the French admiral sent out a couple of frigates *and* the wind was south *and* it was the top of the tide *and* they were Spanish and knew this coast well, then the plan would fail. But a French ship of the line at low water (which it was now) and the wind south and her captain not knowing this stretch of the coast...well, it was all a gamble and he always reckoned he was not a gambling man. Not standing or sitting round a table watching the roll of a dice or turn of a card, anyway. But losing at dice or cards did not lead to the risk of a roundshot lopping off your head, which was what this particular gamble had as a stake...

"We're clear of the Laja del Norte now," he said to Southwick and then, seeing Aitken hurry back on deck, said to him: "I want you to get us due south of the point: I want to pass a point exactly two miles west of the fort at the end of the city."

He pointed to the slate "Write down this bearing and distance. I want you to tack exactly there."

Southwick was frowning and shaking his head, puzzled by Ramage's instructions.

"Bajos de León," Ramage said cryptically, and turned to look astern.

"Here she comes," he said, taking a telescope from the binnacle box drawer. "Pitching just nicely. Yes, fairly clean bottom. She's one of the ships that joined Villeneuve from Brest; that copper sheathing hasn't spent weeks in the Mediterranean and then crossed the Atlantic twice. Going to be a race, gentlemen."

"If she catches us, she'll slap our 'and," Stafford declared. He had been leaning out of the port, looking at the 74 astern. "Clean bottom – almost got a shine on the copper, she 'as. Everything set to the royals, and fairly 'urtling along."

"Well, we've got everything set to the royals and we're hurtling along, too," Jackson said.

Stafford spat through the port. "I ain't never," he said portentously, " 'eard of a frigate escaping a 74 with this wind and sea."

"The *Calypso* has never been chased by a 74 before," Rossi said.

"Na, only 'appens once," Stafford said. "Ain't nothin' left ter chase the second time!"

"Staff," Jackson said, "either cheer up or shut up; we don't need to hear you ticking away like a deathwatch beetle."

"Well, all I can say," Stafford said defiantly, "Mr Ramage is goin' to 'ave ter try somefing reely desperate this time."

"You sound as tho' you've never sailed with him before," Jackson said. "He's kept you alive so far."

"*Si*, and I don't know why," Rossi said. "Is a waste."

"You lot 'ave no 'magination," Stafford grumbled. " 'Ere, just look frew the port. We're being chased by a 74, not a porpoise. A plum-coloured 74," he added.

Jackson walked over and leaned out of the port. He inspected the French ship and then came and sat down on

the breech of the gun. "As close-winded as we are, I reckon,"
he said. "She's just about sailing in our wake."

"I just told you that!" Stafford exclaimed.

"Yes, so you did," Jackson said. "Well, there's one thing
about it, I don't reckon any judge'll be sending you to the
Bridewell or the Marshalsea now, and you've picked your last
lock. You're dragging your anchors for the next world, Staff; I
can't see you living to watch the sun set."

"Cheer up, Staff," Gilbert said. "If you go, probably we'll all
come with you, so you won't be lonely."

"I'm not ready to go yet!" Stafford said defiantly.

"Well, it was you who decided you were going," Jackson
said unsympathetically. "We were thinking of staying – with
Mr Ramage."

"We'll see," Stafford said darkly, and lapsed into a sulky
silence.

"What happens now, Jacko?" Gilbert asked.

The American shrugged his shoulders. "Damned if I know.
We're just heading south along a straight coast with a 74
chasing us, and if the *Euryalus* and the *Sirius* have any sense
they'll be making a dash for it. Frigates don't fight 74s – not
unless they're trapped."

At that moment Orsini arrived. "The captain wants you on
the quarterdeck, Jackson. So you, Stafford, become gun
captain and you, Rossi, are second captain. The rest of you
move up one. D'you know what you're supposed to be
doing?" he asked Gilbert.

"Yes, sir," he said confidently, kicking a handspike.

Orsini patted the breech of the gun. "A 12-pounder shot
may not go right through a 74," he said with a grin, "but the
bang is very heartening!"

As soon as he saw Jackson come on deck, Ramage said:
"You take over as quartermaster. When I say tack, you tack as
though the admiral's on board, and if you've thought you've

sailed this ship close to the wind before now, I can tell you it wasn't good enough..."

Jackson, recognizing the tone of Ramage's voice grinned and said: "Aye, aye, sir, we'll show those Frenchmen how to do it."

Now, as the *Calypso* plunged south, spray beginning to sweep across the deck (Ramage noticed gun captains fitting the canvas aprons over the flintlocks to protect them) the frigate on this tack was steering straight for the San José church, the wind now brisk on her starboard side as she heeled under the press of canvas.

Ramage stared ahead over the frigate's bow. Yes, she was steering straight for the church, a mile ahead. The water shallowed half a mile out from the beach, so they would tack *there*. He walked over to the binnacle. And as soon as they tacked they would be steering...well, just right.

Now he looked astern at the French 74. She too was shouldering up the spray – but was she catching up fast enough? Ramage thought not.

"Ease the topsail and t'gallant sheets a little – I want to lose a knot or two," Ramage told Aitken.

The Scotsman did not question the order but Ramage saw him give Southwick a puzzled glance.

The frigate slowed and Jackson had to let her pay off a little to keep the sails drawing. The best he could steer was slightly to the north of the San José church.

Ramage looked astern at the Frenchman and nodded. The 74 was now steering exactly in the *Calypso*'s wake. He would have to tack the *Calypso* along the four-fathom line, otherwise the Frenchman might lose his nerve and tack too soon.

"Have the leadsman start singing out the moment it starts shoaling from four fathoms," he told Aitken, "and we tack immediately."

Aitken was going to protest that they could go on to the three fathom line because the beach shoaled gently, but the look of concentration on Ramage's face made him stay silent.

The leadsman's chant was monotonous: five fathoms…five fathoms…five fathoms…four and a half…four and a half… four…

Ramage looked at Aitken, who snapped an order to Jackson and started shouting sail orders through his speaking trumpet.

As soon as the flapping of canvas stopped, Ramage reminded Aitken: "Sou'west by south, Mr Aitken, and make a note of the time."

Yes, a cast of the log would be useful, but he was dealing with a mile and a half, and by the time the log was reeled in…

He turned and watched the Frenchman. No, the luffs of his sails were not shivering yet. The Frenchman, too, was relying on his leadsman. On he went, until he was almost directly astern of the frigate and in line with the San José church. Then the 74 tacked – tacked smartly, Ramage had to admit. And now she was exactly in the *Calypso*'s wake and…yes, she was beginning to overhaul the frigate. Ramage imagined himself on the quarterdeck of the 74. Yes, overhaul her noticeably: they must be confident that in three or four more tacks they would be ranging up alongside the English frigate…yes, the French would reckon to finish the job in a couple of broadsides, although one should be enough.

"Hard to know on which side they'll overhaul us," Southwick said, his voice flat.

A criticism in his tone? Ramage thought so. The old master was expecting some miracle which would stop the 74 ranging alongside, guns squirting roundshot and smoke, and so far he could see no sign of the miracle happening. So he was getting testy. And the "which side" remark was intended to draw

Ramage into revealing what the miracle was and when it would happen.

Well, there is not going to be a miracle, thought Ramage, and it will not do any harm to let everyone on board think that a 74s broadside will soon be rattling round their ears. They have been lucky far too long: no frigate is going to sail through life (given the sea time that the *Calypso* has logged up to now) without running into a enemy 74 at some time or another, and for the *Calypso* the "some time" is now.

Again he looked astern: the 74 was a fine sight, even if a lethal one: guns run out on both sides, like stubby fingers, the open gunports spoiling the smoothness of the tumblehome. At each of the guns, he thought, excited Frenchmen are waiting, decks wetted and sanded, trigger lines secured to flintlocks, flintlocks firmly bolted to the breech of the guns, flints long since checked for the spark. Are the guns' crews singing patriotic songs like *Ça Ira* as they prepare to go into action against such incredible odds? Incredible, Ramage thought sourly, if you are French!

A dull, grey sky; a dull grey sea. Even the spray thrown up by the Frenchman's bow seems washed with grey. And a plum-coloured hull! This light makes it look bruised; even at this distance the salt drying on it makes it seem diseased, fruit that will be thrown away.

In line astern of the 74 is the San José church. The men at the wheel of the 74 are not doing a very good job: not just the surging of the seas, when one leaves the wheel alone, knowing that the ship will come back on course by herself. No, the Frenchmen are sawing the wheel from one side to the other so that she shoots off half a point one way, then swings back half the other. The 74s wake must look like a demented snake.

But for all that she is overhauling the *Calypso*, which is what matters. The French captain must be well satisfied: he has the

Englishman at his mercy. Whichever way he tries to escape (and he is cut off by the land from going east or north) the 74 has the advantage of speed: one needs patience, *mes braves*.

Ramage walked to the binnacle, glanced down at the weather-side compass, and then at the Cortadura fort. Yes, one and a half miles away. And the bearing was correct. But that damned 74 was making faster time than he anticipated. *A lot faster time.*

He felt the skin on his face and arms covered with goose pimples; there was a hollowness in his stomach. Yes, the 74 was going much faster in this wind (which was strengthening all the time: the royals would have to come in very soon before they blew themselves out). Yes, he had made a mistake. He thought the Frenchman would have a foul bottom and be badly sailed. In fact she had a relatively clean bottom and apart from sloppy steering she was being sailed well: even though her wake was wavy, she was being kept close to the wind.

They say a man is allowed one mistake. It was beginning to look, he thought grimly, as though his mistake was going to be his last.

"Harden in topsail and topgallant sheets," he snapped to Aitken. "A foot or two on the courses, too."

Southwick had his quadrant, taking vertical sextant angles on the 74s foremast.

"She's gaining fast," the master said. "She has two or three knots more than us."

Ramage nodded. "That's what I'd expect in this wind: she can stand up to her canvas – and look at that copper sheathing when she rolls."

"She's fast to windward: perhaps she doesn't reach or run so well," Southwick said hopefully.

"Going to windward is *our* fastest point of sailing," Ramage reminded him. "She's French-built, just like us..."

"True, true," Southwick admitted, lifting his quadrant again and balancing himself against the *Calypso*'s roll.

Ramage looked again at the compass and then at the Cortadura Fort. He caught Jackson's eye. "Steer small," he said sharply.

Jackson nodded obediently but thought to himself: steer small? One more tack (at the most!) and that Frenchman will be so close alongside they'll be able to pelt us with cloves of garlic. When he had first come on deck and relieved Kinnock as coxswain, he had thought the captain had (as usual) some unusual plan to let them escape. But ten minutes had been enough to convince himself there *could* be no plan: they were trapped, and that was that. When a frigate is caught by a 7-gun ship with a clean bottom and a good captain, that is that. Not Mr Ramage's fault: just that a well-sailed 74 is a good deal faster to windward than a frigate: you didn't have to be a master of tactics to know that.

Now Jackson saw Mr Ramage talking to Mr Southwick, who turned and stared at that fort on the edge of the town. Yes, he is staring at the fort as though any minute he expected a hoist of signal flags to go up its flagpole. Now he is looking at the French ship.

Jackson glanced astern and immediately wished he had not: five hundred yards away? No more. Close enough that they would soon fire a round or two from their bowchasers, trying the range. And it would be just their luck that a round from a bowchaser would bring down the mizen – or skitter across the quarterdeck and smash the wheel.

Jackson looked back at the binnacle and turned to the two men at the wheel. "Steer small, blast you!" he snarled, and felt better for it. The lubber line was precisely on the "SW x W" mark on the compass card, but Jackson thought, for the first time for many years, that he wanted to live. The point had not arisen with such urgency for a long time... Always Mr Ramage had a plan and it was easy to see what it was: easy to see, in other words, that one would live to fight another day. Not this time, though: there was no arguing that 74s were faster than frigates.

He glanced astern again. Three hundred yards, and already the blasted Frenchman was hauling out to starboard so that he could range alongside instead of poking his jib-boom through the *Calypso*'s sternlights.

Ramage looked at Aitken. The Scot was pale under his tan, but holding the speaking trumpet as casually as though he was going to give a routine order: a tweak on a sheet, maybe. And Southwick? The master was gripping his quadrant as though it was a charm that would protect him from the 74s roundshot.

Once again Ramage looked down at the compass, and then back at the Cortadura Fort. One and a half or two miles. Split the difference and that made it one and three quarters. And on course. Now he turned and looked astern. Feet apart to balance against the roll; hands clasped behind his back; a confident look on his face. So that the ship's company thought he was going to wave at the 74 as it came up alongside, each gun captain sighting, trigger line taut in his right hand, kneeling on the right knee, with the left leg flung out to one side to maintain balance... At least Ramage could not hear the bellow of *Ça Ira* against the moan of the wind!

A hundred yards? Less, perhaps. No, he had timed this wrong; there was no confused flurry of sea now, no rolling of the water, no darker patches, just that damned 74 slicing along. She did look rather splendid: he was prepared to admit that. And deadly and menacing, too; there was no denying that.

"If we tacked...?" Aitken said, as though talking to himself. Ramage shook his head: he had started them off on this dance and they had to complete all the steps: tacking now would mean the 74 would tack as well – and, if she was quick enough, get in a raking broadside, and just one raking broadside might be enough for the *Calypso*.

He watched as a spurt of smoke was quickly carried away by the wind from one of the enemy's bowchase guns. There was no thud of the shot hitting the *Calypso*. The 74 caught a strong puff of wind that missed the frigate and surged ahead, sails straining.

Fifty yards. Another lucky puff like that and she will be alongside and the *Calypso*'s decks will be swept by roundshot and grape; masts will collapse over the side as rigging parts; the wheel and binnacle will be smashed; there will not be a man left alive on deck. All because I underestimated a French 74, Ramage thought bitterly. He found he was not afraid. Deathly cold, but not actually afraid. Sarah would never know how it happened, and suddenly he wanted her to understand, understand that he had made a genuine mistake. Just one mistake that would leave Sarah a widow in – well, about a minute, and Aldington without a master. Still, Sarah would live there and she would –

He blinked: the 74 had suddenly stopped and slowly, as though they were tired, one mast after another toppled forward across the bow with yards and sails. She began to slew round as the heavy canvas fell over the side, acting as an anchor. Two guns went off, smoke spurting through the ports, as gun captains were sent sprawling by the shock. An anchor came adrift and fell into the sea with a splash, and the ship settled in the water like a broody hen on her nest.

"What happened?" Southwick gasped, "What caused all that?"

Ramage fought off a desire to giggle with relief. "The Bajos de León," he said. "Three scattered shoals. At this state of the tide they have just enough water for a frigate to get across, but not enough for a 74."

Jackson, the only man to spot a slight darkening of the water indicating one of the three shoals, heaved a sigh of relief. So the "steer small, blast you," *had* been important after all.

"Congratulations, sir," Aitken said lamely, his Scots accent broad. "No wonder you were so interested in the Cortadura Fort. South-west by west, one and three quarter miles! Do we go back and try to pick up any of those Frenchmen?"

Ramage looked astern at the wreck. She was perched on the shoal. More than perched: she was on there for good. Her gunports were out of the water – she was now just a hulk with her masts over the fo'c'sle; they had gone by the board as they always did when a fast-moving ship hit a shoal. And the sea was not too bad and the shore was – yes, one and three quarter miles away.

"No, they won't have lost all their boats and anyway they can make rafts. And the Cortadura Fort will be sending a horseman into town to tell them the glad news, so there'll soon be help. Wish we knew the name. Go about, Mr Aitken and cross her stern: we'll look silly reporting to His Lordship that we've polished off a ship of the line but don't know her name!"

CHAPTER FOURTEEN

The ship was *Le Brave* and Ramage was still looking at the hulk perched on the shoal (he reckoned it was the easternmost of the three) when Aitken reported that the *Euryalus* was closing from the south-west. A minute later, Orsini called that she was flying the *Calypso's* pendant numbers.

Ramage realized that Blackwood had been too far away to see what had happened: even now he would see through his bring-'em-near only the *Calypso* circling what would look at that distance like a large, flat rock roughly in the position of the shoals.

What, Blackwood asked using Popham's Code, had happened?

It was the time for a witty signal, but Ramage could think of nothing. Southwick had a chart spread over the top of the binnacle box, obviously checking up the Bajos de León and trying to recover from his embarrassment at firstly forgetting them and second not guessing that Ramage intended to lure the Frenchman on to them, and that was why he had wanted the Frenchman to chase as closely as possible...

Bajos de León...the Lion Shoals...something witty like "Lured enemy into lion's den..." Yes, but the nearest Popham's Code had to "lure" was "lurks-ed-ing", and the nearest to "lion" was "Lizard", the headland rather than the animal. To be witty a signal had to be crisp. He took the slate and the old *Signal Book*, and after he had finished writing he gave the slate to Orsini and told him to make the signal to the *Euryalus*.

The foremast lookout hailed and after listening with the speaking trumpet Aitken pointed northwards to the headland on which the Castillo de San Sebastián stood, four square and menacing in the grey day. Coming round the headland and heading out to sea was a 74, followed almost immediately by a second and then a third. Ramage took up a telescope. A fourth...now a three-decker...now a frigate...another 74... Villeneuve was (at last) taking the Combined Fleet to sea instead of letting them crowd in Cadiz Bay.

Orsini had finished making the signal to the *Euryalus* reporting *Le Brave*'s situation. "Is Captain Blackwood making any signal to the *Sirius*?" Ramage asked.

"A moment, sir." Orsini braced himself with his telescope. "Yes, sir, there go the *Sirius*' pendants." The young Italian read off the signal flags: yes, Blackwood was making a signal to Captain Prowse to repeat to the next frigate in sight: within twenty minutes, Lord Nelson would know that the Combined Fleet was actually sailing from Cadiz...

"Steer west," Ramage told Aitken. "We need to be seaward and to the north of the Combined Fleet before the French admiral gets it formed up."

As soon as he had spoken Ramage began to wonder. He had told Aitken to get the *Calypso* to the north of the Combined Fleet but, if the French admiral was making his way to the English Channel, then the *Calypso* would stand in his way – with more than a couple of dozen French and Spanish 74s to chase him, and no Bajos de León...

He had, without thinking, assumed that Admiral Villeneuve would steer south for the Strait of Gibraltar and the Mediterranean, going after General Craig's convoy. Which meant that he accepted Perez's rumour. But supposing Blackwood (who was commanding this little inshore squadron of frigates, a schooner and cutter) gave him orders to stay to the south?

Blackwood, he suddenly realized, knew nothing of Perez's rumour; he knew nothing of the chance that Villeneuve might be making for the Gut. There was no mention of it in the "memorandum" from Nelson delivered by the *Pickle*. That dealt only with His Lordship's intention of cutting the enemy's line in two places...

Blackwood had controlled his Inshore Squadron with a loose rein. The best thing for the *Calypso* to do, to avoid being run down by a swarm of 74s, was to get up to the northward without waiting for orders and hope that Villeneuve would steer south-west immediately he was clear of San Sebastián headland, so that Blackwood (while he might not guess that the French were heading for the Gut and the Mediterranean) would at least keep the frigates to the northwards.

Already the *Calypso* was turning north-westwards, sheets eased and yards trimmed to a wind on the larboard quarter. *Le Brave* was quickly being left on the starboard quarter, and through his glass Ramage could see French seamen (looking in the distance like a swarm of ants) cutting away the rigging and sails, obviously to get at the boats stowed on the booms. Well, *Le Brave* was sitting firmly on the shoal and there was no urgency because the ship could not sink.

The only urgency, Ramage thought grimly, concerns the *Calypso* herself: she has to pass ahead of the Combined Fleet which is at last getting out to sea: she has to pass ahead and get a safe distance to the north of them.

Orsini reported: "The *Euryalus* is making a signal to the *Phoebe* to move westwards to repeat signals to the *Defence*." A couple of minutes later he was reporting another of Blackwood's signals, this time to Captain Peter Parker in the *Weazle* cutter, telling him to sail south immediately to warn Rear-Admiral Louis that the Combined Fleet had sailed.

Southwick shook his head sadly. "Poor Admiral Louis. He's a fine man. He must have been upset when Admiral Nelson sent him off with those other ships to water at Gibraltar and get bullocks from Tetuan. There's no chance that the *Weazle* can warn him in time to get here for the battle."

"When is the battle?" Aitken inquired sarcastically. "Do you have the programme? If you have, you might give me a sight of it!"

"Tomorrow or the next day," Southwick said flatly. "Admiral Nelson will give 'em time enough to get well clear of Cadiz (he won't want to risk frightening them back in again or give them a bolt-hole once the fighting starts), so you can work it out yourself."

He took off his hat and scratched his head in a familiar gesture. "They don't get up very early, these French and Spaniards. So they'll spend most of the rest of the day manoeuvring. With a mixed fleet he's never taken to sea before, this Admiral Villeneuve will (if he's got any sense) spend a few hours making 'em back and fill and get into position. I can't see 'em doing much else than jogging along like sheep during the night – plenty of flares and a few collisions, I expect. Tomorrow – well, by then he'll be clear of here with them steering in the right direction, and I can't see Lord Nelson being far away."

Aitken slapped Southwick on the back, "Like to put a guinea on it being one day or the other, the 21st or the 22nd? I'll take whichever day you don't."

"No," Southwick said stubbornly. "Why should I bet against myself? I've already told you it'll be tomorrow or the next day, and that's all there is to it."

"That's the trouble with prize money," Aitken said, knowing that Southwick, like most of the men on board the *Calypso*, had grown rich from the money won under Captain Ramage's command, "it takes away the gambling instinct."

"Bet on the number of French and Spanish ships of the line captured or destroyed and you have a wager," Southwick growled.

"Very well. Twenty-one, and the 21st – tomorrow – will be the day of the battle."

"We're betting on the number of ships, not the date," Southwick said. "All right, my guinea says it'll be twenty-five. At least two more than twenty-one, anyway. How does that suit you?"

Aitken nodded, but added soberly: "Try and stay alive so you can pay up."

By now the *Calypso* was sailing fast to the north-west, passing three miles ahead of the leading enemy ships. More to the point, Ramage thought to himself, the *Euryalus* had not hoisted the *Calypso's* pendant numbers and ordered him to patrol to the south. The *Euryalus* herself, he noticed, was working her way out to the westward, along with the *Sirius*, the *Pickle* schooner and *Entreprenante* cutter.

The British frigates and the two smaller vessels would be like a small swarm of flies round the slow-moving ox of the Combined Fleet: always out of range of a lashing tail, but always watching – and signalling to Lord Nelson over the horizon.

It would be an interesting challenge to be commanding some thirty-four ships of the line – thirty-three now *Le Brave* has gone – Ramage decided, but he did not envy Admiral Villeneuve. If Señor Perez was to be believed, then most of the Spanish captains wanted nothing to do with the Combined Fleet: they preferred to stay at anchor, not go to sea to fight someone else's battle and ensure Bonaparte's schemes succeeded. Yet they were the captains in whom Villeneuve had put his trust. However, "better one volunteer than three pressed men": the old adage crossed Ramage's mind.

Yet, ship for ship (and in several cases size for size and gun for gun), Villeneuve had thirty-three ships against Lord Nelson's twenty-seven. French and Spanish ships were very well designed and always well built – the best ships in the Royal Navy, Ramage was ashamed to admit, were those captured from the enemy (the *Calypso* herself being a fine example). So it was going to be a question of men: of the skill and bravery of individual captains and their ships' companies. The British spirit was going to have to make up for Nelson's fleet being six ships weaker than the Combined Fleet...

Ramage noted to himself that *Le Brave* had stranded herself in the last of the good weather and the last of the south wind – which by noon had veered to the south-west. Rain squalls were whipping across to close down visibility for half an hour at a time and the seas were becoming heavy.

A south-west wind still meant it was foul for Villeneuve to get down to the Gut. And Ramage saw through his glass that Villeneuve had plenty of trouble. He had, according to Ramage's count, thirty-three ships of the line, five frigates and a couple of brigs. In the distance the ships of the line seemed great grey barns and their masts and yards looked like bare trees in winter because the wet sails blended with the low clouds hanging down to the horizon.

Many of the ships, it was obvious even at this distance, were being handled in a lubberly fashion. The most weatherly of them, Ramage estimated, were steering no closer to the wind than west-north-west and several (they looked like Spaniards) were sagging off to leeward as though in despair. All the ships had reefed at the same time, obviously on orders from Admiral Villeneuve. Some had tied in the reefs and hoisted the yards again while the rest were still struggling – Ramage pictured untrained and frightened, raw sailors up the yards, fighting stiff and flogging canvas, hands being torn, fingers getting caught in reef points, many of the men seasick and probably clutching yards and rigging, rigid with fear, misery and illness.

By noon it was obvious that Villeneuve was trying to form his fleet into three columns. It was an absurd formation, Ramage reckoned, given that the French admiral must know that Lord Nelson was waiting over the horizon, because only one column (the outermost on the engaged side) could fire on the enemy.

"They're like a lot o' wet hens with their legs tied together," Southwick commented, after studying them with his glass.

"Sheep," Aitken corrected him. "Like frightened sheep being chased by different dogs. Why they're not colliding I don't know. I think Villeneuve's got three French ships out ahead so the rest can form up on 'em, but just look – at least half a dozen are just sagging off to leeward as tho' they're embarrassed at the rest of them!"

Aitken had been right: thirty-three great sheep were milling round, all trying to head out to the west, as though yapping dogs to the east were nipping their ankles.

An hour later the confusion was even worse as the ships still tried to get into position, hidden from time to time in rain squalls and buffeted by gusts of near gale-force winds. After two hours, when the beginning of three columns was discernible, Aitken suddenly pointed to the wind-vane and the luffs of the *Calypso's* reefed topsails (the topgallants had long ago been handed), which were beginning to flutter.

The wind was going further round to the west: if Villeneuve stayed on this tack he would be forced up to the north and, from the look of it, some of the ships would be lucky to weather Rota; more likely they would end up on the Bajo de las Cabezuellas, looking like their unfortunate former shipmate, *Le Brave*.

Ramage felt almost sorry for Villeneuve – until he remembered that every French and Spanish ship disabled by collision or driven ashore by the gale would be one less to fight Nelson's ships: every casualty would lessen the odds.

"What are they going to do now?" Southwick asked incredulously.

"Getting a wind shift like that with the fleet not formed up – that's just bad luck," Aitken said.

"Bad for them, good for us," Southwick said grimly. Fifteen minutes later Orsini, who had been watching the Combined Fleet closely with his telescope as well as keeping an eye on the *Euryalus* when she appeared briefly between rain squalls, shouted excitedly: "The French flagship has hoisted another signal!"

"I wish we had a French signal book," Ramage grumbled. "Not that we can read the flags at this distance. Still, it's not too hard to guess."

"You think he is heaving-to the fleet, sir?"Aitken asked.

"No, with this west wind and Rota under his lee I think he is getting in a panic. I'm sure he wants to go south and he finds himself steering north. So he's ordering the fleet to tack."

"Tack!" exclaimed Aitken. "But half of them are just milling around, dodging each other. There aren't half a dozen of them formed up into columns."

"He's an unlucky admiral," Ramage said wryly. "There aren't many signals he *can* make at the moment. If he doesn't signal the fleet to tack and steer south, he's going to wave goodbye to several that won't weather the shoals off Rota..."

Within a few minutes they could see four or five ships emerging from the confusion and rain squalls to head south, forming into three columns.

"You were right, sir," Aitken said, "He did signal the fleet to tack. He's a braver man than I."

"Like most brave men, he has no choice," Ramage said

"You speak from experience, sir?" Southwick said teasingly.

"Very deep experience," Ramage said. "And I'd like a sight of the British fleet at this moment."

Southwick chuckled. "They won't be in this mess, I'll be bound. Snugly reefed, and probably in line of battle. Two lines, rather – His Lordship leading one and Admiral Collingwood the other, just as His Lordship describes in his memorandum."

"Give the masthead lookouts a hail," Ramage told Aitken. "Watch to the westward for a sight of our fleet."

It took Aitken several minutes, shouting at the top of his voice, to pass the order above the wind. "They've got their sou'westers pulled down over their ears," he grumbled to Ramage, who was becoming tired of wearing his thick oilskin coat: the smell of the tar that made it waterproof was giving him a headache; every move made the coat creak and crackle as the stiff material had to bend. It was easier to turn one's whole body than glance round – a movement of the head chafed the skin and also displaced the towel round the neck so that spray and rain soon trickled in and, slowly and coldly, snaked its way down the back.

By six o'clock the mass of ships of the Combined Fleet were at last steering south, but only a dozen leading them were in the three columns that Villeneuve had ordered hours earlier. From the *Calypso* they had, from time to time, sighted the *Euryalus*, *Pickle* and *Entreprenante*, as well as being reasonably certain that the *Naiad* and *Phoebe* were also hovering round the enemy fleet. Presumably the *Sirius* (well out to the west) was in sight of one of the ships of the line which formed the link with Nelson.

Although the *Calypso* was still at general quarters, Ramage continued the system of having every other gun's crew off watch, eating a meal or snatching some sleep. Every man could be back at his station for battle in less than five minutes, and a wet and windy night was in prospect.

A few minutes before seven, after a slashing rain squall and while the officers on the quarterdeck had taken off their sou'westers, they heard a hail from the mainmasthead lookout: he could see many masts to the westward.

"Ask him how many," Ramage told Aitken. "It's probably Lord Nelson, but it could be ships from Brest..."

The lookout soon reported again. Eighteen ships, in good order and on the same course as the *Calypso*.

"Very well," Ramage said, "we're steering south-east, and His Lordship intended sailing south-east once he had word that the Combined Fleet had sailed. No Brest ships bound for Cadiz would be that far out – and 'in good order'!"

Ramage burrowed into his pocket to get out his watch. There was very little daylight left, and the only way of keeping in touch with the enemy in the darkness was by getting much closer. There would be little risk: he was satisfied that, with the French and Spanish (the Spanish, anyway) in their present disorder, the *Calypso* could, if she wanted to, range up alongside a threedecker in the darkness and shower them with abuse without any risk.

"Pass the word to the gunner," he told Aitken. "Make sure he has a good supply of rockets and portfires ready: enough for one of each to be set off every ten minutes until dawn..."

The *Euryalus* and the other frigates would also be closing the circle as darkness fell, and if each of them lit a portfire or sent up a rocket from time to time Blackwood would know immediately if the enemy altered course. But unless Villeneuve was suicidal, Ramage knew he would not order any change while it was dark: instead, he would be praying that none of his ships collided and that (by chance if not by design) they managed to get into columns.

The ships of the Combined Fleet were becoming harder to see; objects on the *Calypso*'s deck – guns, binnacle, capstan, mizenmast – became blurred as night fell. Ramage gave night orders to Martin, who relieved Aitken as officer of the deck, but they were (apart from keeping a sight of the enemy) routine: Ramage knew that he himself would he spending most, if not all, of the night on the quarterdeck.

Silkin came up to tell him that a cold supper was waiting for him, and it was clear from the tone of the man's voice that he did not think that watching the enemy from this distance was a good enough reason to have the galley fire out. Ramage had thought about it several times, anxious that the men at the guns should have a hot drink and some hot food, but the regulations were very strict: with the ship at general quarters, the galley fire had to be extinguished. Lighting it now, "within sight of the enemy", made no sense.

No, with all that gunpowder around (and sparks would certainly fly aft from the chimney in this wind) it was not worth the risk: the men rarely spent hours at general quarters or went without hot food. And, he guessed, none of them, knowing they were watching such a large fleet of the enemy, would be grumbling.

And then it was dark: it happened slowly and almost imperceptibly. The candle in the binnacle had been lit half an hour before, and Ramage crouched over, looking at the compass and then sighting along the last bearing they had taken of the enemy. Nothing. Not blackness because it was rarely entirely dark at sea, but…but, yes, there was a darker mass there! Ramage gave an order to the quartermaster (Jackson had gone below to get his supper) and the *Calypso* edged closer. Within five minutes, without using the nightglass, both Ramage and Martin could distinguish a line of ships close on the port side, a faint black strip on the eastern horizon.

Ramage took the nightglass from the binnacle box drawer and put it to his eye. The nightglass inverted the image so that he could just see the bulk of the Combined Fleet apparently flying and going in the opposite direction. His eye caught a flicker of light on board one of the ships. And then another. Once he knew what to look for he could see many lights from lanterns being used carelessly in the ships or displayed to avoid collisions.

He gave the nightglass to Martin. "They're lighting up for us," he commented. "You'll have no trouble following…just keep on taking bearings in case you get a rain squall…"

So Sunday night passed: every fifteen minutes the gunner came up with a battle lantern and a rocket. He fussed about until he stood back smartly and the rocket crackled and then hissed its way into the night sky. From time to time Ramage saw other rockets from all round the outside of the enemy fleet. Blackwood's little inshore squadron was doing its job. And, if they were keeping a sharp lookout in Nelson's fleet, by now the nearest ships (and of course those forming the link) would be able to see the rockets too.

Two great fleets on similar courses sailing along in the darkness; rolling, pitching, whipping up sheets of spray, soaked by the same rain squalls – and, perhaps within hours, they would be battering each other, killing hundreds of men, with roundshot slicing through many inches of solid oak and grapeshot cutting men down in swathes and parting rigging like a cobbler's knife severing thread.

There was such a dreadful inevitability about it that Ramage shivered. Exactly sixty ships of the line, many of them three-deckers, had a grim rendezvous within a matter of hours, and at a guess half of them would be sunk, captured or so battered they would be scuttled before the sun set again. It was not often that he thought about death, but perhaps it was the sight of the Combined Fleet in such disorder at nightfall that brought it to mind.

Kenton relieved Martin as officer of the deck, and in turn Hill took over, and almost as soon as Kenton had reported the course, wind direction and strength, and that there were no unexecuted orders, Hill commented to Ramage. "I think the wind's eased a bit, sir."

Ramage, sleepy and dazed and wishing he had not rushed his cold supper because it kept repeating itself, had not noticed it. But yes, Hill was right: the ship was not heeled so much and the seas had eased slightly.

"Just as well," he commented. "Much more bad weather and I think the Combined Fleet would go back to Cadiz with torn sails and sprung masts. And once they're in there we'd never get them out again!"

"Half those Dons are seasick, I'll wager," Hill said. "If the story told by the man you saw in Cadiz is true, half the Spanish ships' companies were ploughing the fields or traipsing the streets of the city a month ago..."

"Yes," Ramage agreed, "but the fact that Villeneuve has stayed at sea this long instead of bolting back to Cadiz probably means he's determined to get down to the Gut, so there'll be a battle."

"I don't fancy spending the winter off Cadiz on blockade duty," Hill said. "There's no lee round here. We'd have to rush down to the Gut every time a storm comes up from the west..."

"The wind's now easing quickly," Ramage commented. "We'll probably be becalmed by dawn!"

"Aye, Southwick says this Gulf of Cadiz is famous as a strange place for sudden gales and calms, like the Texel. The seas are easing, certainly, sir, but there's the very devil of a swell."

Ramage watched the eerie blue glow of signals from the *Euryalus* as Blackwood passed the signal to the *Sirius* that the Combined Fleet was still steering south, and a minute or two later the *Sirius* repeated the signal for the next ship forming the link with Nelson's fleet.

Ramage felt very sleepy and his eyes seemed to have sand in them. The Combined Fleet was still jogging along to the south, probably much more concerned with avoiding collisions with each other than fighting the British. Now was the time to snatch some sleep: he would need to be wide awake during the coming day.

"Call me if there's any change concerning the enemy," Ramage told Hill. "And if we get becalmed!"

Three hours later, waking just before dawn, Ramage realized that the wind had dropped away, because the ship was rolling badly from the westerly swell left by the gale, the masts and yards were creaking wildly, with little weight on the sails.

By the light of the lanthorn left hung up in his bed place, Ramage hurriedly washed and shaved. He would be one of the few men shaved in the *Calypso*, but shaving was almost an obsession: he hated the rasp of stubble on his silk stock; unshaven, he always felt greasy and unclean and his brain never seemed sharp. The razor, it seemed, woke him up and cleared his head.

Aitken was officer of the deck and Southwick was with him. It was still dark but dawn was close, and the wind no longer howled across the quarterdeck. The guns gave impatient grunts as the frigate rolled heavily, allowing the carriages half an inch of movement, just enough to let the trucks turn a fraction.

"Bit o' a change in the weather, sir," Southwick said cheerfully as Ramage walked up to the quarterdeck rail. "I'll wager that Villeneuve fellow is thankful."

Ramage looked to the south-east. Yes, there was the long darker band representing the ships of the Combined fleet.

"Are we any closer?" he asked Aitken.

"No, sir – at least, I don't think so. They're steering a regular course and we're doing the same."

"I have the same feeling as you, sir," Southwick admitted. "They seem to be more stretched out…"

"They are, much more," Ramage said. "And it's not because the rear ships are straggling."

"What do you reckon is happening, then, sir?" Aitken asked. "They don't seem any different from when I came on watch."

"I think Villeneuve was in even more trouble last night than we thought. As night fell he seemed to be still trying to get his ships into three columns, which is the wrong formation for when he meets His Lordship.

"I think he realized that, and without us seeing it he signalled his fleet to form line of battle. That's why they seem to be more stretched out now – they're still trying…"

The poor devils, Ramage thought; they've spent the night trying to form up one ship astern of the other (in no particular sequence), a clumsy game of "After you" played in the dark with snapped jib-booms, locked yards and torn shrouds the penalty for misunderstandings or clumsiness.

Thirty-three ships trying to form the line of battle in the darkness… Much of the night there had been those slashing rain squalls…even now there was this miserable swell to knock the wind out of sails, catching the unwary in irons and sending them drifting into the next ship.

"Like tipsy one-legged seamen, playing blind man's buff," Southwick said, taking out his watch and looking at the time in the light of the candle in the binnacle. "Hmm, dawn is not far off."

Ramage could see stars here and there, fighting thin cloud and now fading slightly. It might even turn into a fine day... And just where was the British fleet?

Dawn came fast, or so it seemed to Ramage: as soon as there was enough light to see the ritual grey goose at a mile and lookouts went aloft, Ramage saw that the *Calypso* was about two miles to windward of the Combined Fleet which was still steering south. As he had guessed, the first dozen or so ships were in line of battle and regularly spaced, but astern of them the rest of the fleet was still lumped together. The leading ships seemed a row of leafless trees lining a road; the rest looked like a small forest, their masts and yards merging like trunks and branches bared after winter frosts.

And in the distance to the westwards, way up to windward, there were mastheads: the British fleet.

"His Lordship's got the weather gage all right," Southwick muttered admiringly. "Nicely tucked up to windward, ready to jump on Villeneuve whatever he does."

"How far are we from Cadiz?" Ramage asked.

"It's twenty-five miles to leeward of us," the master said. "Ah, now they're making more of an effort to form the line of battle," he added, lowering his telescope. "Fifteen in position ahead, as best I can count. Another hour, and they'll be ready!"

"They're still only jogging along," Aitken said. The first lieutenant had come up to the quarterdeck just before Ramage. He had relieved Hill as officer of the deck and sent him off to his division of guns. "Since we're staying in the same relative position, it's not hard to judge their speed."

"They won't be able to bolt from Lord Nelson now, that's for certain," Southwick said. "I reckon a third of them don't know how to get the best out of their ships, whether beating to windward or running, and Admiral Villeneuve won't be able to leave 'em behind."

For an hour, after having the ship's company stand down from general quarters to get their breakfasts, Ramage walked the quarterdeck with Southwick, neither man speaking but each watching the Combined Fleet on their larboard bow and the masts of Nelson's fleet approaching over the starboard quarter.

Suddenly Orsini shouted excitedly. "The French flagship's run up several hoists of flags, sir!" He was bracing himself against the frigate's roll as he watched the Combined Fleet with his telescope. "And yes, all the ships have hoisted what I suppose is the answering pendant."

"A signal to the fleet...hmm, I wonder what that is?" Southwick said.

"Well, it can't be ordering them to form line of battle," Ramage said. "Perhaps an alteration of course, though they're already on the right tack and they can't steer any closer to the wind."

He walked over to the binnacle box and took out his telescope. "I wonder..." he mused. "There's really only one other signal it could be..."

Even as he watched, the masts of the last ship in the line slowly diverged and then lined up again as she wore round and began steering back along her wake. Then the next followed, and the next.

"Cadiz!" Southwick bellowed excitedly. "Villeneuve's going back to Cadiz!"

Ramage ordered Orsini to hoist the signal to warn the *Euryalus*, although it was only a formality, since Blackwood could see what was happening. Within minutes the *Sirius* would be repeating the signal to the *Naiad*, and she to the *Phoebe*, and from her to the *Defence*, and so on until Lord Nelson was warned that his prey was making a bolt back to its lair.

By now the sun had come over the horizon, weak and watery, but the wind was falling away and through his glass Ramage could see that several of the Combined Fleet were having trouble wearing round, their ships hard to handle in a heavy swell and light breeze.

So now the Combined Fleet's line of battle was being led by what had been the last ship. Ah there was the massive *Santissima Trinidad*: she was wearing round slowly, and she would be the ninth or tenth ship in the line. And her next astern would be the French flagship, the *Bucentaure*.

Ramage could see several masts beyond the line: eight or more big ships were well away to leeward, though he was not sure if they had been out of position when Villeneuve gave the order to wear or had sagged off while trying to obey. From their ensigns (most of the ships had now hoisted their colours, having waited for sunrise) Ramage could see that half the ships out of position were French, so it was not all poor Spanish seamanship.

"They're making about five knots, and it's twenty-five miles to Cadiz eh?" he said to Southwick. "Well, with Lord Nelson up to windward, are you taking any wagers on this race?"

"Signal from the *Euryalus*, sir," Orsini said.

Blackwood was telling Ramage that he himself had been ordered to report on board the *Victory* and that the *Calypso*, along with the other frigates, should fall back on the fleet.

"I was hoping we'd be told to do that," Southwick said. "We're not doing any good out here now, and frigates caught between two fleets could get their toes stamped on! I see the French frigates are well to leeward of their line."

Ramage took one long look at the Combined Fleet before giving Aitken the order to tack to the westwards. He would never again see so many enemy ships drawn up in line of battle – at least, he hoped not. It was an awe-inspiring sight, although it was hard to believe so many ships could be so badly handled by a commander-in-chief. Indecision, nervousness, lack of experience, lack of faith in the ability of his captains... One could sympathize with Villeneuve. No, it was rather that one could understand his position; sympathy had to be withheld when one realized he commanded some 2,500 guns...

CHAPTER FIFTEEN

With the *Calypso* close to Nelson's column, Ramage stared at the scene, trying to fix it in his memory. If only he was an artist with an easel, canvas and paints set out in front of him. A pale, washed-out sky with wisps of high cloud had a weak and watery sun which seemed shy of lighting up such a dreadful, war-like scene.

Ahead of the *Calypso* (and the other four frigates, *Pickle* schooner and *Entreprenante* cutter) was the Combined Fleet of France and Spain: thirty-three big ships (and five frigates and a couple of brigs) sailing in line of battle from right to left, a line of ships stretching along half the eastern horizon, steering back to Cadiz.

Gaps in the line showed where ships were dropping astern and other spaces revealed ships sagging to leeward out of the line, forming another abbreviated and ragged line of battle, eight or so ships which mingled with the frigates. The ships had all their sails set – courses, topsails, topgallants and royals. They were stretching along on a reach but sailing just too high for studding sails to draw. Yet, Ramage thought, if anyone needs studding sails to hurry them along...

And Nelson's fleet: the two columns over on the starboard hand were steering to meet the centre of the Combined Fleet's line of battle like the points of two sabres intending to hack a section from the middle of a long snake.

Yet the grace: the French and Spanish ships were rolling heavily with the swell waves catching them on the beam, but they were big and all of them had fine sweeping sheers, masts buff-coloured with the mastbands picked out in black. Their ensigns drooped: the red and gold of Spain looked like twisted curtains; the French Tricolour hung so that the last colour, the red stripe in the fly, obscured the rest.

The *Victory* led the nearest British column: Nelson's proper place as commander-in-chief was somewhere in the middle of the windward column but, Ramage noticed, the *Victory* was just where one would expect her to be, leading the column – having a race with the *Téméraire*, which was rigging out studding sails. And as he watched, Ramage saw the booms also being slid out at the end of the *Victory*'s yards, as though Nelson was determined not to be overtaken.

Then came the *Neptune* – and Ramage remembered Nelson giving her captain, Thomas Fremantle, the letter which told him that his wife Betsy had just given him another daughter.

Then came the *Leviathan* and following her the *Conqueror* which (since she was commanded by Captain Israel Pellew) would be manned by Cornishmen. Astern of her was the *Britannia*, carrying Nelson's third-in-command, the Earl of Northesk.

Altogether there were twelve ships of the line in Nelson's column, but the last four, dull sailers, were beginning to straggle astern. Ramage could imagine the frustration of their captains as they tried every trick they knew to keep up.

And Admiral Collingwood's column: he too was leading it in the *Royal Sovereign*, followed by the *Belleisle* and then came Captain Duff's *Mars*: no doubt the Duff family were as excited as the Scot on board the *Calypso*, Aitken, who showed his excitement by not saying a word.

"What a sight! What a sight!" Southwick exclaimed for the tenth time.

"Let's hope the wind holds," Ramage said. "It might die any minute."

"Yes, His Lordship must be cursing this breeze," Southwick said, shaking his head. "His column isn't making more than a walking pace..."

"At least they're running before the wind and not spilling it as badly as the enemy," Aitken pointed out. "They're just pitching; Villeneuve's ships are rolling heavily."

The breeze was growing fitful: the *Calypso's* sails were going flat and then filling again with a bang which shook the ship. And Ramage saw with his glass that the same was happening to both the enemy ships and Nelson's.

As the enemy's line (forming, Ramage now realized, more of a gentle crescent round the edge of the eastern horizon than a straight line) slowed down, so did Nelson's two columns. And if this was in fact a dying breeze, every yard that Nelson sailed took him into greater danger.

When one ship attacked another on the beam the attacked ship's whole broadside could fire at the attacker, which was unable to reply because its guns could not be trained round. Nelson's plan for attacking the Combined Fleet's line was unique because every one of his ships would be attacking the enemy from the unfavourable bows-on position. It was, Nelson reckoned, the only way of smashing the enemy's line: it was the only way, he considered, that he could cut off the leeward ships from those to windward. But a ship's bow and stern were the weak spots: raking fire could send roundshot scything from one end of the ship to the other.

But – and it was a big but, getting bigger every moment – if the wind dropped as the leading ships of Nelson's column came in range of the enemy's broadsides they would be battered to pieces as they lay becalmed and helpless: scores of guns would be raking their unprotected bows with roundshot, grape and langridge while they could not reply – except from the laughable bowchasers.

For a moment Ramage pictured the *Victory*, *Téméraire*, *Leviathan*, *Conqueror* and *Britannia* in one column, and the *Royal Sovereign*, *Belleisle*, *Mars* and *Tonnant* in the other, wallowing becalmed, their bows exposed to the broadsides of a dozen or more French and Spanish ships. Imagine the *Victory* at the mercy of the raking broadsides of the *Bucentaure* and the enormous *Santissima Trinidad*...

And the same wind which was taking the *Calypso* along at the speed of a child dawdling to school was carrying Nelson's fleet down to fight what would be the greatest sea battle the world had ever known – if the wind kept up.

"It's going to be close," Southwick said gloomily. "If this wind dies on His Lordship..."

"It's a risk he's calculated," Ramage said, taking his copy of Nelson's memorandum from his pocket and unfolding it. "Listen, half-way through His Lordship says: 'Something must be left to chance, nothing is sure in a sea-fight beyond all others...' "

"Ah," Southwick said with a sniff, "*we* know what His Lordship is attempting and we agree with it, but what if he fails? The Board of Admiralty will sink him without a trace..."

"Perhaps that's what he meant when he wrote 'Something must be left to chance,' " Ramage said with a grin. "Just pray the wind holds for another hour...the *Victory* has only a mile to go... The French and the Dons will soon be opening fire..."

Orsini reported: "From the *Victory*, '*Prepare to anchor at the close of day.*' "

"Repeat it," Ramage said. So Lord Nelson recognized the weather warning in the sky: by tonight another gale would be blowing, judging from the clouds and watery sun.

Aitken said: "The *Victory* will be under fire for ten or fifteen minutes before she breaks through the line."

"A lot longer if this wind drops much more," Ramage said, "but don't forget all those enemy ships are rolling badly and their gunnery will suffer. And remember, providing he gets up to the enemy, the more the wind drops the more Lord Nelson's plan is likely to succeed: the leading enemy ships he's cut off from the main body will find it almost impossible to turn back to join the battle."

"What a gamble!" Southwick exclaimed. "It's all depending on a few puffs of wind. Dozens of ships, hundreds of lives..."

"And the safety of Britain," Ramage said. "That's why an admiral gets an earldom if he wins and disgrace if he loses. But a gamble? I think I'd call it a deliberate calculation."

Orsini called: "Signal to all ships from the *Victory*, sir. Telegraphic flag, then 253, 269, 863, 261, 471, 958, 220, 370 – and then, spelled out, 4, 20, 19, 24."

As soon as he had seen the answering pendant run up, Orsini took the slate on which Aitken had written the numbers, snatched up Home Popham's code book, and started writing in the words above the numbers, reading them out as he did so.

"The signal says, sir: *England expects that every man will do his duty* – they had to spell out the last word as it isn't in the book."

"Very well," Ramage said. "Repeat it." He then turned to Southwick: "You have the loudest voice: tell the ship's company what Lord Nelson says – not that they need reminding, but it's a good signal."

The master took up the speaking trumpet and with a bellowed "Now hear this!" told the men that the commander-in-chief, Lord Nelson, had just made them a signal which said – and he read from the slate as Orsini held it up for him.

Ramage was startled and then delighted as waves of cheering swept through the frigate: obviously Nelson had chosen just the right moment and just the right words. Both Aitken and Southwick were grinning.

At that moment, in a pause in the cheering, Ramage heard a snatch of "Heart of Oak" – the band on one of the ships of the line was striking up.

"Another signal, sir," Orsini exclaimed. "Numbers one and six." He opened the first page of the book. " '*Engage the enemy more closely*,' sir."

"Very well, Mr Orsini, repeat it," Ramage said. "Unfortunately that one doesn't concern us."

"No, sir," the youth said, and then repeated what he had heard said before: " 'Frigates do not stand in the line of battle.' "

"If they did, they'd stand about one broadside from a 74," Southwick growled. "Have you forgotten *Le Brave*?"

"No," Paolo said, "I really meant it's a pity we have to miss a good fight!"

Aitken suddenly pointed. "Look, the first shots!"

Winking red eyes followed by spurts of oily grey smoke started out of the side of one of the enemy ships along the line, close to the *Royal Sovereign*. Almost immediately another broadside followed from her next astern.

Southwick gave one of his contemptuous sniffs. "Those ships are rolling so much the gun captains will see blue sky one moment and green sea the next. Might as well try using a pistol to shoot a woodpecker from the back of a runaway horse!"

"Don't forget that if they fire late on the upward roll the broadsides can bring down masts and spars, or tear sails," Aitken said.

"Better than firing on the downward roll and hitting the hulls," Southwick growled. "Better a torn sail than twenty men dead from shot and splinters."

Aitken shrugged. "With this light wind, no one can afford to lose much canvas. Look, stunsails set on the *Victory, Téméraire, Neptune, Leviathan...*"

It was an interesting problem working out where the *Victory* and the *Royal Sovereign* would break the enemy line: because of the forward movement of the Combined Fleet's line, it would be four or five ships astern of the ones at present dead ahead of them. The *Victory* seemed at present to be heading for the second 74 ahead of the great *Santissima Trinidad*, which in turn was being followed by the French flagship, Villeneuve's *Bucentaure*.

And knowing Nelson, it was not hard to guess where the *Victory* was intended finally to arrive: Nelson's memorandum said that his column would try to cut through "two or three or four ships ahead of their centre", thus separating the enemy's van and centre squadrons, while Collingwood's column would cut through about the twelfth ship, separating the centre from the rear.

From the look of it, though, the *Royal Sovereign* would in fact (allowing for the enemy's forward movement) arrive at about the fifteenth ship from the rear while Lord Nelson would reach the twelfth from the van – attacking the *Bucentaure*, a happy coincidence: Nelson undoubtedly regarded it as his right to capture or destroy the French flagship!

But, Ramage cursed to himself, he was obliged to watch the battle from the deck of the *Calypso*, not firing a shot, with nothing to do but repeat any signals made by the *Victory* so that all the rest of the ships could see them. Yet, if he was honest, the brush with *Le Brave* had brought home to him that frigates getting into action with 74s were just asking to be blown out of the water.

It was a case of like against like. The *Africa* could be unlucky – she was one of the old 64-gun ships, most of which had now been replaced by 74s. In fact she was starting off the battle on the wrong foot: because she missed a signal during the night, she was only now catching up with the fleet and approaching the Combined Fleet's line of battle from the north-west.

Like against like: ship of the line against ship of the line; frigate against frigate – except that frigates did not get involved in a battle like this, even against enemy frigates…

But why not? Ramage asked himself. Tradition, he supposed, but the tradition that ships of the line only fought ships of the line was a little hard on the *Africa*: her sixty-four guns could be opposed to the one hundred and thirty guns of the *Santissima Trinidad*, which must be three times her size apart from carrying double the number of guns. In fact, Ramage reckoned, the difference between the *Africa* and the *Santissima Trinidad* was effectively greater than between the *Calypso* and *Le Brave*…

He looked across at the *Victory*: she seemed to be the sharp end of a thin wedge of ships aimed at the side of the enemy line of battle; but her sails flapped occasionally in the intermittent breeze as if hinting to Lord Nelson that Nature might not be on his side.

In the *Calypso*, Ramage knew everything was ready for battle, although they would not be firing a shot: the gunner was down in the magazine and the "fearnought" felt curtains were hanging down, doused with water and protecting the magazine and serving hatch from flashes; the decks were wetted and sanded; the guns were loaded, with flintlocks firmly bolted on, and their captains ready to grab the trigger lines which, until needed, stayed neatly coiled on the breeches of the guns. The second captains were ready with their prickers, which would be rammed into the vents to penetrate the cartridges, ensuring that the coarser powder ignited the moment the priming powder flashed into the vent. The men would have been issued with cutlasses, tomahawks, pikes or pistols, depending what was marked against their name in the general quarter, watch and station bill, which listed the name of every man in the ship and his task for every evolution, whether anchoring, tacking, wearing, furling, reefing or fighting the enemy.

Jackson had brought up Ramage's two pistols, loaded and ready to fire – a task the American had set himself years ago. And Ramage was, at Silkin's insistence, wearing his Lloyd's Patriotic Fund sword. Ramage preferred a seaman's cutlass for fighting, but today (of all days) he could be sure the *Calypso* would not be doing any fighting...

The *Victory* had half a mile to go. And there! the French 74 ahead of the *Santissima Trinidad* fired a broadside, red winking eyes giving way to smoke which, because the wind was too light to disperse it quickly, filled the ship and blurred her outline as it streamed out of the gunports.

Ramage looked at the *Victory* with his glass. The enemy's broadside must have fallen short. And then the great Spanish three-decker seemed to shiver as the guns on all her decks fired. Smoke curled up, wrapping itself round her tumblehome like fog and reaching up to her sails, following their shape. Again Ramage could see no effect on the *Victory* or the *Téméraire*, which seemed to be trying to race the *Victory*.

The range was now so short that it could only be bad gunnery, and while Ramage speculated whether he would see spurts of water from shot falling short, the French flagship fired a broadside, but wherever her shot fell she might as well have been pelting the *Victory* with snowballs for all the effect they had. By now the three enemy ships were sailing along in a bank of swirling smoke because the wind was so light that ships and smoke went along together.

But the range was closing fast and he saw that the *Victory* was passing through the line close under the stern of the *Bucentaure*. It was going to be a bad place, because another French 74 was very close astern of the *Bucentaure* while a third (she had sagged off to leeward) was just beyond the gap, ready with a broadside.

Suddenly the three enemy ships were firing at the *Victory* and the *Téméraire*; a moment later – or so it seemed – the *Victory* had steered under the *Bucentaure's* stern and, from smoke wreathing up from her bow and the clouds of dust now drifting across the French flagship's stern, had raked her with the great 68-pounder carronade on the larboard side of her fo'c'sle. Ramage could imagine dozens of grapeshot sweeping along the length of the *Bucentaure*, cutting men down in swathes,

Within five minutes the whole section of the enemy line of battle was hidden in clouds of twisting and swirling smoke as the *Leviathan* and *Neptune* broke through. Well beyond, the leading ships of Admiral Collingwood's column – the *Royal Sovereign, Belleisle, Mars* and *Tonnant* – smashed their way through and, like those in Nelson's column, immediately turned to larboard, to steer parallel with the enemy ships.

"What a sight! What a sight!" Southwick kept muttering. "Oh, why couldn't I be the master of the *Victory*!"

"It's worked, sir!" Aitken exclaimed. "The wind held up for His Lordship!"

"It needs to hold on a bit longer to bring up the rest of the ships," Ramage said grimly, "Otherwise the odds against Lord Nelson and Admiral Collingwood will be five to one…"

"Seems strange to be out here while all the fighting is going on over there, sir," Aitken said. "By the way, did you see that French frigate to leeward of their line?"

"Yes," Ramage said, "She's a sister ship of the *Calypso*, unless I'm much mistaken."

"It's hard to make out her sheer with all these ships of the line in the way, but that's the impression I get."

"Oh, she is, sir!" Orsini exclaimed "I saw her clearly through the gap between two ships!"

"You're not supposed to be listening," Aitken said sternly, and then demanded: "Are you absolutely sure?"

"Absolutely, sir," Orsini insisted, "The frigate to leeward of the *Santissima Trinidad*. She's just like us – except for our yellow strake, of course. The other four French frigates have flatter sheers, and the masts are differently spaced."

"Mr Aitken," Ramage said, his voice as casual as he could make it, "have grapnels rigged from the ends of the yards, and three or four ready here at deck level."

Southwick looked at him quizzically. "If you burn wet powder, you get plenty of smoke."

"Yes, I haven't forgotten." He turned and pointed to the tubs of water beside the aftermost carronades, round the edge of which slow match burned. "Have those tubs hauled over against the taffrail and send three seamen down to the magazine for cartridges."

CHAPTER SIXTEEN

"Orsini," Ramage said sternly, "you are far too busy to observe any signals. The *Victory* won't make any to us – she can't even see us with all the smoke – but the *Euryalus* can..."

"I understand, sir," Orsini said with a grin. "I'll give them a hand shifting those tubs."

"Stunsails, sir?" Aitken murmured questioningly.

Ramage looked aloft, where topmen were now busy at the ends of the yards, coils of rope over their shoulders, securing the grapnels. The stunsail booms would have to be run out and the stunsails themselves manhandled up from the sail room. He then looked across at the enemy's line of battle.

Ramage shook his head. "There's no time. We wouldn't have them drawing before we'd be cutting them away."

He looked across at Southwick. "I want all the leather buckets lined up along the taffrail, full of water. And give the deck an extra wetting."

He inspected the enemy line of battle. Even in the few minutes he had used giving orders, the situation had already changed: looking along the line from the van, the *Neptune* had broken through and rounded up almost alongside the *Santissima Trinidad*; the *Conqueror*, following her, had rounded up to leeward of the *Bucentaure*; the *Leviathan*, passing through the line, was about to run alongside the French 74 that had been well to leeward of the rest; the *Victory* was alongside the fourth French ship – he could just make out her name in the drifting smoke, the *Redoutable*, which was squeezed between her and the *Téméraire*.

There was not much space, but if one was fast enough...if the wind held... "Something must be left to chance..."

"Mr Aitken," he said, "as far as I can see the *Britannia* is going to pass through the line in the wake of the *Leviathan*. We'll pass through in the *Britannia*'s wake."

"Aye, aye, sir," Airken said, but added: "That means we shall pass the *Victory* fairly close on our starboard hand."

Ramage nodded. "I doubt if anyone will be looking out for us. Anyway, the smoke is so thick – " he gestured at the thick clouds now rolling like dirty fog along the line of ships, in places as high as their mastheads, " – we'd never be able to distinguish flag signals..."

By now the heavy drum-roll of broadsides was echoing across the water like thunder from an approaching summer storm. Occasionally there was the thud of a single gun as some gunner twitched his trigger line accidentally, but the broadsides were almost continuous.

"A point to starboard," Aitken told Jackson, who repeated the order to the four men at the wheel: four now not because there was any weight on the spokes with this light wind but because some of them might be cut down.

"Get Kenton, Hill and Martin up here," Ramage said. Lord Nelson's plan for breaking the line in two places, cutting off the van, seemed to have worked. Surprise: His Lordship had done the unexpected. Now Captain Ramage was going to try the same tactics. The scale would be vastly smaller but the principle was the same.

With the three lieutenants standing beside Aitken, all looking startled at having been suddenly called up to the quarterdeck from their division of guns, Ramage said: "There's hardly any time." Quickly he outlined his plan for the *Calypso* and then said: "So the three of you – " he indicated the junior lieutenants, " – will go back and assemble boarding parties.

"You, Kenton, will board and take the fo'c'sle. Cut all sheets and braces you can lay your axes to. Hill, you do the same amidships but you'll need to pick fifty men – you'll have all the French guns' crews to deal with. Take five extra men and give them axes: they *must* cut sheets and braces.

"Martin, you'll take fifty men and secure the quarterdeck. Detail five men to seize the wheel make sure they have pistols and cutlasses. And don't forget, sheets and braces. Right, off you all go!"

As the three lieutenants hurried away both Aitken and Southwick said in unison: "What about me, sir?"

"You remain in command of the *Calypso*," Ramage told Southwick, who groaned theatrically.

"Look here," Ramage said angrily, "I'm not having a debate about this every time we go into action. There'll be you and less than fifty men to beat off any attempt by the French to board *us*. Oh no, don't sneer at the idea. That's the best defence the French have, if they only realize it."

Aitken, watching the smoke rolling along the enemy line and keeping an eye on the *Britannia*, looked questioningly at Ramage. "You'll come with me," Ramage said. "The Frenchman's quarterdeck. Watch out for Martin's men and remember, we're interested in securing the wheel."

Ramage realized that Jackson was looking at him, pleadingly. "All right then, if you can get word to your relief, you can come with me!"

Jackson promptly shouted to a passing seaman, who then hurried down the quarterdeck ladder. Ramage turned to the Marine lieutenant. "Ah, Mr Rennick: a change in plans. There's a French frigate the other side of this smoke that interests us. You should put half your Marines under Sergeant Ferris and tell them to help secure the enemy's waist: Hill will be going across with fifty seamen, but most of the French guns' crews will be there. You take the other half yourself and make for the quarterdeck. You'll find Mr Aitken and myself strolling round somewhere up there, along with Martin and fifty seamen. Is all that clear?"

Rennick gave a wolfish grin and hitched round his sword. "Absolutely, sir: my men are getting bored just watching the battle."

Ramage thought of the boredom of twice daily parades when the Marines marched and countermarched, musket butts clattered amid showers of pipeclay and heels stamped. And they were bored watching the greatest sea battle – or rather the opening rounds of it. No, it wasn't possible. Then he realized that the men were bored not with the sight but the fact they could not join in: each of the Marines had the soul of a butcher imprisoned in a spectator...

At last he could look ahead again. Yes, the *Calypso* was tucked in nicely astern of the *Britannia*. The *Santissima Trinidad* had the *Conqueror* raking her stern and the little *Africa* raking her bow, while the *Neptune* was pouring in broadsides from leeward. The *Bucentaure* was firing broadsides into the approaching *Ajax* but any moment the *Britannia* would start raking her from astern. To leeward of the *Bucentaure* the French *Neptune*, heading east at right-angles to the line of battle, was exchanging broadsides with the *Leviathan* while the *Victory* was the first ship in a row – she too was heading east, almost alongside the *Redoutable*, which in turn was alongside the *Téméraire*, which was pouring broadsides into the *Fougueux*...

But all that really mattered to the *Calypso* was that the gap between the *Bucentaure* and the *Victory* was wide, and the *Leviathan* was on the French *Neptune's* larboard side. The *Calypso's* sister ship was a mile away on the *Leviathan's* larboard bow.

The *Calypso* caught a sudden puff of wind that did not reach the *Britannia* and she surged up on the three-decker. Ramage thought for a moment of Rear-Admiral the Earl of Northesk wondering why the *Calypso* frigate was following so close in his wake, but the Scotsman would probably assume she was acting under orders from the commander-in-chief.

That, he realized, was the advantage of doing the unexpected: everyone assumed you must have orders... And if he timed it right he would be able to stay on the *Britannia*'s larboard side as she passed the *Victory* to starboard so that no one would spot a little frigate apparently lost in the banks of smoke...

And there was so much smoke! He had expected the thundering roll of the broadsides but not all this smoke: there had not been nearly so much at the battle of Cape St Vincent (and thanks to the dilatory Earl St Vincent, or Sir John Jervis as he then was, not nearly so much action, either). But now he could understand Lord Nelson's foresight in ordering that all ships should fight under the white ensign (because the red or blue ensigns, hanging down in a light breeze, could be mistaken for a drooping Tricolour) and that another ship should paint her mastbands buff like the rest of the fleet – leaving them black (which was how the French and Spanish painted them) could lead to her being mistaken for the enemy when her hull and colours were obscured by smoke. Ramage realized that battles were won by this kind of foresight.

As the *Calypso* reached the line (now ragged, with many of the French and Spanish ships sagging or beaten to leeward by gunfire) it was as though the frigate was steering directly into a heavy thunderstorm: the thick banks of smoke hid the weak sun; the deep rumbling broadsides, like the growling of monsters, made even the calmest man feel uneasy.

Now the *Britannia* (notoriously a slow sailer) was on the *Calypso*'s starboard bow, and beyond her was the group of ships with the *Victory* the nearest. All the ships had the red winking eyes of gunfire on one side or the other; all were shrouded with smoke, like monks with cowls.

"Hot work," Southwick commented, raising his voice above the rumbling of the guns. "The *Victory*'s guns are firing as fast as they ever did at exercise against a watch!"

Ramage took his glass from his eye as Aitken stood in front of him. "I've just inspected the boarding parties, sir. Men are standing by at the grapnels. Will a dozen be enough aft?"

Ramage thought a moment and then nodded. "Southwick," he said, "you are in charge of the powder men. Use Rossi, Stafford and the Frenchmen. Make sure they know exactly what they have to do so that they don't blow us up. And," he added firmly, "make sure there's enough water..."

Then the bulk of the *Britannia* hid four ships that were alongside each other, guns blazing, masts and yards toppling, sails spotted with shot holes as though speckled with some vile mould: the *Victory*, *Redoutable*, *Téméraire* and *Fougueux* were locked together like wildcats fighting in a bag.

And then, with the rest of the enemy line and the British attackers over to larboard and the *Calypso* overtaking the *Britannia*, there were only two ships ahead – the *Leviathan* and French *Neptune*, with the frigate up to the north-east, well beyond the line. But the *Leviathan* was bracing up her yards: she was obviously going to leave the *Neptune* and join in the battle further towards the van... What would the Frenchmen in the *Neptune* do? She was well to leeward of the rest of the fleet: in fact she was so far to leeward she was almost among the frigates...

Anyway, the *Leviathan* had kept her out of the way for long enough: the *Calypso* had just to cross ahead of the *Leviathan* and then there would be a clear run.

"Two points to larboard," he told Aitken. "Give the *Leviathan* plenty of room. Then bear away."

They watched as the British ship came away from alongside the French *Neptune*, which still had her masts standing. Obviously Captain Henry Bayntun, who commanded the *Leviathan*, had his eye on the long row of enemy ships forming the van.

Boarders...Stafford and his shipmates handling the powder...the Marines have their orders...men are ready with the grapnels to hook the two ships together.

Ramage tried to make sure he had not forgotten anything... his pistols, tucked into the band of his breeches, nudged against his ribs (he would still prefer a seaman's cutlass to the Lloyd's Patriotic Fund sword). They were passing well ahead of the *Leviathan*, which was hardening in sheets to steer northwards, along the enemy line.

Stafford, Rossi and the Frenchmen hurried up on to the quarterdeck carrying the heavy cast-iron braziers used in cold climates to dry out damp between decks after the planking had been well scrubbed or there had been a long period of wet weather.

They had taken several handsful of twigs from the cook's supply of kindling, used for the galley stove, along with sawn wood, and quickly set up the braziers, watched by a fussy Southwick. The master looked ahead at the French frigate, now fine on the starboard bow, and then questioningly at Ramage, who said: "Get the kindling started, and then wait..."

Stafford found some small twigs which still had dried leaves attached, made them into a little nest in one of the braziers, and then went over to one of the tubs and took a length of glowing slow match from its notch.

He came back to the brazier, put the burning end of the slow match amid the leaves, and blew gently until first one and then two or three of the other leaves burst into flame. Soon, feeding the flames with larger twigs, he finally used sawn up pieces of wood that had obviously come from Chatham Dockyard.

"Pity it's not a cold day," Stafford commented.

"Be careful, Staff," Gilbert said, eyeing the flannel cartridge cases stacked up under the taffrail.

The Cockney, coughing from the wood-smoke, laughed. "Not used to the sight of flames, are you Gilbert? Don't be nervous – think what it must be like over there!" He gestured towards the flickering guns of the *Santissima Trinidad* and her attackers.

"She's not so near," Gilbert said, cautiously taking one of the burning pieces of wood and transferring it to another brazier and feeding it with wood. He was followed by Rossi and Auguste, and finally Louis lit the last of the braziers, until all five were flickering on the quarterdeck.

Southwick walked over to Ramage. "I was thinking, sir, if an unlucky roundshot knocks over those braziers..."

"We shall probably blow up," Ramage said matter-of-factly. "It's a risk I decided to take. You have plenty of buckets of water and the tubs, and you'll keep the deck well sluiced down."

Southwick nodded. "Thought I'd better mention it, sir."

"Oh, indeed," Ramage said. "No point in remembering as the ship blows up. Don't forget to wet the powder..."

Southwick laughed cheerfully. "You'll be the first to hear if I forget, sir," he said.

Jackson walked across the deck to join his shipmates. "Warm work," he commented.

"Yus," Stafford said, "but it'll soon be 'ot work! Is that the frigate we're after?" he gestured over the starboard bow.

The American nodded. "The one that looks like us. Like us without the yellow strake."

"Bit more our size," Stafford grunted. "I didn't fancy that 74 that was chasing us off Cadiz..."

"No shoals out here though; this has to be a guns, pikes, cutlasses and tomahawks job," Jackson said. "That's if you don't blow us all up with these braziers."

"If you hear a big bang, you'll know I did it wrong," Stafford said complacently.

"Not to joke," Auguste said anxiously. "Is bad luck to joke about such things."

"I'm not joking," Stafford assured him. "If Jacko hears a bang…"

Ramage was judging distances and giving Aitken helm orders. The French frigate was sailing along on a course parallel with the enemy's line of battle and roughly a mile to leeward. A mile or more ahead of her was another frigate, and well astern and scattered were three more, along with two brigs.

"She hasn't realized yet," Aitken commented.

"Her people are too taken up with what's happening to the *Redoutable* and the *Santissima Trinidad*." Ramage said. "Don't forget, 'frigates don't stand in the line of battle'!"

"Ah, yes, *I'd* forgotten, sir," Aitken said dryly.

Even though the wind was light the *Calypso*, with a clean bottom, was sailing too fast for the French frigate, which was jogging along under topsails only, obviously not trying to keep in any particular position with the line of battle.

"We'll clew up the courses, Mr Aitken," Ramage said briskly. The Scotsman picked up the speaking trumpet and gave the order that sent men running to the buntlines and clewlines. Quickly the corners of the big lower sails were drawn in diagonally towards the masts and then the middles of the sails were hauled upwards, until the great sails looked like bundled laundry.

Ramage walked to the side and peered down at the sea from a gunport, and then he looked ahead again. "We'll hand the topgallants, too, Mr Aitken," he said, and the moment the first lieutenant shouted the orders, topmen swarmed up the shrouds and out along the yards, folding the sails and securing them against the yards with gaskets. They were doing it as thoroughly, Ramage noted, as they would a "harbour furl", where a sharp-eyed port admiral would be ready with criticisms.

So now the *Calypso* was reduced to topsails – what was generally regarded as "fighting canvas", although none of Nelson's ships of the line, hurrying because of the falling wind, had reduced sail: like Nelson, they were content to let enemy shot do the furling for them.

Ramage watched the French frigate carefully. If the captain was awake, then the *Calypso*'s shortening sail should alert him. Frigates did not suddenly reduce sail in the middle of a battle without a reason. Come to that, frigates did not suddenly break through the line.

Yes, the French frigate was certainly at general quarters, with her guns run out, as of course they should be, and obviously loaded with roundshot or grape. But she seemed strangely uninterested in the *Calypso* – a sister ship, too, that a moment's thought should remind someone on board had been captured by the British...

At that moment a particularly large swell wave made the frigate yaw, and Ramage could at last read the name carved on her transom. *Le Hasard*. Green lettering – which had made it so hard to read – picked out with red. No gilt. The captain had obviously made do with what the dockyard had issued.

He told Aitken the name, but the Scotsman merely said: "She'll get a new name in the British service!"

Half a mile, and one point on the starboard bow.

At that moment Aitken pointed astern. The look on the first lieutenant's face made Ramage turn quickly.

The French *Neptune*, ship of the line, had turned to the north and was now getting into the *Calypso*'s wake, perhaps three quarters of a mile astern. Was it a coincidence or was she coming after the *Calypso*?

That did not matter much, Ramage realized immediately: the moment the *Calypso* opened fire on the frigate, the *Neptune* would come up on the other side and pour in broadsides: that was unavoidable. Something, as Nelson had written, must be left to chance – and he had left the ship of the line astern to chance…

Well, he could forget all about the attack and sneak back through the line of battle and take up the position he should never have left. He could, but having made all these preparations he was not going to.

Or he could try to race the *Neptune* and get alongside *Le Hasard*, perhaps overwhelming her before the *Neptune* could catch up. But even if he took the *Hasard*, the *Neptune* would be alongside moments later, and a ship of the line's broadside… He had avoided *Le Brave*'s broadsides by guile; there was no way of avoiding the *Neptune*'s.

He realized that he could keep the bluff he was going to use on the *Hasard* and try it on the *Neptune*. But it was only bluff; it was not a magic suit of armour that would keep out the *Neptune*'s roundshot. But, he shrugged his shoulders, it was the only trick he could play.

Five hundred yards to the *Hasard* "Stand by guns' crews and grapnel men," he said to Aitken, raising his voice against the rumbling broadsides. It was annoying to have to use the Scotsman to relay every order, but Ramage had long since realized that his voice did not carry.

The *Calypso*'s guns would fire once, then most of the men would snatch up weapons and board. Should he have ordered two broadsides? Even three? Damnation, he told himself crossly, the boarders are the ones who will carry the enemy; one broadside of the *Calypso*'s roundshot battering into planking will only make a lot of noise and smoke.

Four hundred yards...and the *Neptune* is closing up fast. Does her captain realize what is happening or is it just a coincidence? Might he not guess until the *Calypso*, guns firing, crashes alongside the *Hasard*? Or has he realized and is even now stalking the *Calypso*, waiting for the moment he can range alongside?

Three hundred yards. He could picture the *Calypso's* gun captains, down on their right knees, left legs flung out to the side, squinting along the sights of their guns, giving last-minute elevation orders to the handspike-men. The second captains would be waiting impatiently to cock the flintlocks and leap to one side, clear of the recoil; the gun captains would already be holding the trigger lines, ready to give the tug that would send the flint down to make the critical spark.

Two hundred yards – and yes, through his glass he could see that the French officers on the *Hasard's* quarterdeck were now alert. One was running towards the quarterdeck ladder; another was snatching up a speaking trumpet. A third was waving his arms, and a fourth was wrenching a pistol from his belt.

One hundred yards. He looked round at Southwick and raised his hand. Stafford and his shipmates began to bob and weave among the braziers.

Ramage looked across at the coxswain. There would be one more helm order – the one that would bring the *Calypso* crashing alongside the *Hasard* and, the rudder hard over, hold her there while the grapnels flew. If only Sarah could see this. And his father. Frigates did not stand in the line of battle – well, if only father would (in his splendid French) tell that to the *Neptune*.

Fifty yards – a frigate's length...now the first few guns of the *Calypso's* broadside are firing...a shout to the quartermaster... Aitken is bellowing at the grapnel men to throw high and hard... More guns firing...the officer on the *Hasard*'s quarterdeck is firing his pistol, obviously overexcited... Astern the *Neptune* is getting very close, the wineglass curve of her tumblehome and her masts nearly in line showing that she is almost in the *Calypso*'s wake.

"Mr Southwick!" Ramage shouted, and almost immediately there was a faint crackling and then smoke billowed up from braziers on the quarterdeck, to be carried by the breeze over the starboard side.

"It works!" bawled an excited Aitken. "Just look at it!"

At the root of the billowing smoke cloud Ramage could see Rossi and Stafford and the Frenchmen tossing handsful of what seemed like wet dust on to the flickering braziers.

Ramage hurried to the larboard side to look astern at the *Neptune*, which had been hidden by the tumbling smoke. How would the clouds of smoke appear to her?

Several sharp crashes showed that the *Hasard*'s gunners were firing. Thank goodness – fire from her would make it seem more likely from the deck of the *Neptune* that the British ship was ablaze...

"Most of the grapnels are secured, sir!" Aitken shouted. "We're right alongside!"

"Away boarders!" Ramage yelled over his shoulder, still trying to watch the *Neptune*. She had not altered course: she was steering to come close alongside the *Calypso*. In perhaps four minutes they'd all be blown to pieces.

But anyway, Southwick's trick certainly produced smoke: the breeze was blowing it right across the *Hasard*'s deck: Ramage could imagine the Frenchmen coughing and spluttering, gasping for breath. Thank God the breeze was from the west, from the *Calypso* to the *Hasard*.

And it was time he boarded the *Hasard* as he had planned: to lead the seamen and Marines. But should he continue with the wet powder to make a smokescreen? What would the *Neptune* conclude if the smoke suddenly stopped? At the moment she must think the whole after-part of the *Calypso* was on fire. Would that be enough to make her keep her distance, for fear the *Calypso*'s magazine would go up, hurling blazing wreckage all over her?

"Keep that smoke coming, Mr Southwick!" he called. And this was a splendid breeze, blowing in just the right direction, even if he could not see across the *Hasard*'s deck. If only the wind had bulk, so that it would be a shield between the *Calypso* and the *Neptune*; a shield that would ward off that broadside that the French gunners were preparing.

If only he had attacked the starboard side of the *Hasard*: then he would have the *Hasard* as a shield between him and the *Neptune*'s broadsides... The French 74 would never risk hitting the *Hasard*...

But the wind is west! he almost screamed at himself, snatching a quick glance astern at the *Neptune* before shouting at Aitken: "Let fall the courses! Quartermaster, keep the wheel hard over! Southwick, more smoke! Jackson, look quickly and tell me how our boarders are getting on!"

Would those grapnels hold, though? They were on comparatively light lines – light so that they could be thrown easily, but not particularly strong because it was always assumed there would be several – as indeed there were. But would they be strong enough to withstand the wrenching? Strong enough to hold the *Hasard* alongside while the *Calypso* swung her round?

The devil take it, there was just a chance!

"Courses, Mr Aitken, and let fall the topgallants! Watch those sheets and braces!"

Now there was a defiant shouting and the popping of muskets from the *Hasard*: more than a hundred of the *Calypso*'s seamen and all her Marines were swarming across the Frenchman's decks, fighting pike against cutlass, tomahawk against musket. Ramage could picture the bitter battle in the smoke drifting like banks of fog.

Overhead the great courses suddenly flopped down and as the yards were braced and the sheets hauled home the canvas took up the familiar curves. Then, higher up the masts, above the topsails, the topgallants spilled down and filled at once as men hauled on the halyards. The smoke seemed too thin as the sails bellied out, but Ramage realized it was a lucky fluke of wind.

For a few moments there was nothing for him to do, except look astern at the *Neptune* and wonder. Would the *Calypso's* sails draw in time so that, secured alongside the *Hasard* by the grapnels, she could pivot round, turning the *Hasard* and forcing the French frigate between her and the *Neptune* for long enough to act as a shield?

Would the grapnel lines hold the two ships close enough together? Anyway, at the moment the *Calypso's* hull was pressed hard against the *Hasard*: open gunports in both frigates would be jamming against each other as they rolled in the swell; the two ships' chainplates would probably lock; just long enough, Ramage prayed, for the *Calypso* to wrench the Frenchman round.

He stared ahead over the *Calypso's* bow. Yes, the horizon was beginning to shift. The *Santissima Trinidad* and her attackers, which had been on the beam, were gradually drawing round on to the quarter. The *Calypso's* sails *were* filling enough to lever round the *Hasard*.

But in time?

He looked astern at the *Neptune*. She was rolling heavily in a swell wave which shook the wind from her sails and then let them fill with a bang. Two hundred yards? Perhaps less.

But supposing this trick worked, what then? Would the *Neptune* heave-to and try to save the French frigate? Or (Ramage looked across the line of battle and through a gap saw more British ships coming into battle) would the *Neptune* make a bolt for the north, towards Cadiz and in the company of the van ships, which (so far, anyway) showed no sign of turning back to come to the help of the centre and rear?

Among thirty-three line-of-battle ships, one frigate more or less should make no difference – unless the captains were old friends: joined together by some revolutionary act in the past, or friends from the time that the *Neptune's* captain also commanded a frigate?

Now the *Calypso* was turning the *Hasard* fast: topgallants, topsails and courses against the Frenchman's topsails only: the two ships were fairly spinning! Now both frigates had their sterns pointing at the line of battle – and the *Neptune* was a ship's length away: Ramage could make out the planking of her hull, interrupted by the black stubby fingers of her guns, run out ready. Her sails were patched; they were old, pulled out of shape by too much use. And he could almost distinguish the lay of the rope of her rigging. The foretopsail yard curved so much it looked as if it was sprung. Dun-coloured hull, mast hoops black.

Would she risk a raking broadside into the *Calypso's* stern? Unless every gun was carefully aimed, there was a good chance that some of the shot would rake the *Hasard* too.

Ramage shook his head to clear his thoughts. There was nothing more to be done about the *Neptune*: the *Calypso* was doing her best to force round the *Hasard* as a shield, the smoke was now streaming forward over the *Calypso's* quarterdeck as she turned in the wind.

"Belay that smoke, Mr Southwick! Have the men heave those braziers over the side. You're now in command!"

With that Ramage unsheathed his Patriotic Fund sword with his right hand and hauled out a pistol with his left. "Come on!" he shouted at Jackson and made for the quarterdeck ladder, followed by Aitken.

The *Hasard*'s maindeck was crowded. The lines of the grapnels flung aboard the Frenchman from the *Calypso*'s deck were stretched tight, holding the two frigates together, and from the ends of the yards more grapnels were swung out and hooked into the *Hasard*'s rigging.

There were still pockets of smoke across the French ship's deck and Ramage ducked through a gunport, leapt across the gap to one of the *Hasard*'s open ports – noting that the lids just caught each other, despite the tumblehome – and a moment later he was racing for the *Hasard*'s quarterdeck, shouting "Calypsos, to me Calypsos!"

A Frenchman lunged at him with a half-pike and Ramage slashed it to one side with his sword. Blurred in the corner of his eye he saw the muzzle of a musket pointing at him, but from behind there was a sharp crack: presumably Jackson's pistol had taken care of it.

There were some of the *Calypso*'s Marines: Sergeant Ferris was holding the barrel of a musket and swinging the butt round his head like a flail as he ploughed through a group of Frenchmen, roaring curses and threats.

Ramage saw a screaming Frenchman running at him with a cutlass, flung his pistol left-handed into the man's face and sliced upwards with his sword. As the man collapsed he leapt over the body and made for the quarterdeck ladder.

He was conscious that Jackson was beside him and Aitken, shouting threats in broad Scottish, was just behind. Grinning faces blurred as he ran but he just had time to register they were Calypsos.

Suddenly someone was tugging his shoulder and shouting. Aitken. "There she goes! By God we did it! There she goes!"

An excited Aitken was pointing over the larboard quarter and, across the *Hasard*'s quarterdeck, Ramage saw the enormous bulk of the *Neptune* sliding past. He registered that she was a fine sight – and that her guns were not firing: the *Calypso* was completely shielded by the *Hasard* though, judging by the slatting of canvas, Southwick and his men must be doing some hasty sail trimming.

Now he was almost at the top of the quarterdeck ladder, slashing at a Frenchman's legs and hurriedly leaning to one side as the man fell. And there was the entire quarterdeck, a replica of the *Calypso's* but full of men fighting desperately, cutlasses slashing and pikes jabbing.

"The wheel!" Ramage shouted, and with Jackson and Aitken they slashed and parried their way towards it. A French officer, dead from a gaping head wound, hung over the wheel, his coat caught in a spoke. Ramage had just reached the binnacle when a cursing, sword-slashing Rennick reached it from the other side.

"Steady!" Ramage bellowed, recognizing the bloodlust in the Marine officer's face.

"Oh, it's you, sir!" Rennick exclaimed, as though startled in the midst of the frenzy. With that he turned and rushed aft, to where Marines were still fighting it out with a group of French seamen.

From forward the popping of pistols and muskets and the clashing of cutlass blades showed that neither the waist nor the fo'c'sle had been secured, and then Ramage realized that most of the fighting on the quarterdeck had suddenly stopped and a Frenchman – Ramage recognized him as an officer – was shouting at the top of his voice that the ship surrendered. At that moment for Ramage everything went black.

CHAPTER SEVENTEEN

Ramage came to knowing at first that he was lying on a hard deck, that his head rang as though inside a bell, and someone was pouring water over him from a bucket – salt water, which made his eyes sting.

As the red mist cleared from his eyes and with a great effort he managed to get them to focus, he found he was lying on the *Hasard's* quarterdeck with Jackson dousing him and Aitken kneeling beside him while Rennick, musket at the ready, stood at his feet.

There was still the smell of the *Calypso's* powder smoke and he could just distinguish a group of seamen – French seamen – being guarded by a party of the *Calypso's* Marines.

"Are you all right now, sir?" Aitken said anxiously.

No bones were broken; only his head throbbed as though an enthusiast was whacking it with a caulker's maul.

"Wha' happened?"

"As that French officer shouted that he surrendered the ship, you stopped to listen and one of the French seamen fetched you a crack across the head with the butt of a musket."

"Feels as though he dropped an 18-pounder on me," Ramage muttered. "Have we secured the ship?"

"Yes, sir," Aitken assured him. "The French officer," he added, "is waiting to surrender his sword to you – and apologize."

"The captain?"

"No, second lieutenant. The only surviving officer. Seems Rennick and his Marines did for the others."

"Too bad," Ramage growled, struggling to stand up. "Here, give me your shoulder."

Then, as though the noise had been blocked out for awhile, he heard the rolling thunder of the battle to windward. "What happened to the *Neptune*?" he asked

"Went on. Never fired a shot. Afraid of hitting this ship."

"I thought she might wear round on to our larboard side."

"She seemed to be in too much of a hurry to get up towards Cadiz," Aitken said. "And from what I can see of the battle, I don't blame her!"

By now Ramage was on his feet. There were twenty or thirty bodies sprawled in grotesque attitudes across the quarterdeck.

"What about the fo'c'sle and waist?"

"Hill, Kenton, Martin and Orsini are securing the prisoners."

Ramage fought off a wave of dizziness. "Casualties?"

Aitken shook his head regretfully. "Seems we've lost at least eight men dead and thirteen wounded, one badly," he said. "We're getting the wounded across to the *Calypso* so that Bowen can get to work. The Frenchmen, too."

Ramage, his vision still blurred, stared across at what had been the line of battle. Now it had become a ragged row of scattered groups of ships, many with masts gone by the board or topmasts canted like bent stalks. And every one of them coated with thick smoke: with some it was pouring from gunports as the breeze coming through the weather ports drove it out of the lee ones; with others, sails brought down on collapsed yards had caught fire, probably from the muzzle flash of the guns. Great ships now had less dignity than drunken men sprawled insensible in an alley outside a gin mill.

Ramage tried to put his thoughts together. Prisoners, wounded, and – he looked up at the wispy strands of clouds, mare's-tails coming in from the west and the distant outriders of bad weather – *now secure the prize.*

Well, he was going to get no help from the other ships: each one had enough emergencies of its own. So first, prisoners – how many? Probably a couple of hundred. Very well, leave a hundred on board the *Hasard* and shift the rest over to the *Calypso*. Sergeant Ferris and half the Marines can stay on board the *Hasard*, with fifty seamen: that should deal with the prisoners.

Wounded? Well, Bowen will have started his grisly work: he and his loblolly man will have all the help they need sent down to them by Southwick.

Colours! He glanced astern hurriedly, to see that the French colours had already been hauled down. Aitken saw where he was looking and said: "Jackson's gone back on board the *Calypso* to get British colours, sir – in fact, here he comes!"

They watched as the American hurried over to the seaman with the ensign halyard. The French Tricolour had already been taken off and was lying on the deck. Jackson tied a bowline on the hoist of the British colours and the other seaman (Ramage recognized him as Rossi) then secured the Tricolour. They shook out the flags to check that they were the right way up and then Rossi pulled down on the halyard while Jackson made sure the flags, British above French, were clear and then kept a strain on the other end of the halyard until the head of the British colours reached the block.

"Congratulations, sir," Aitken said. "You'll soon have a collection of this class o' frigate!"

Ramage, his head still wanting to spin, grinned feebly. "Find Rennick," he said. "Send word to Bowen how many wounded he can expect."

The Marine lieutenant, grinning happily, soon reported to Ramage.

"Prisoners," Ramage said, surprised how much effort it took him to concentrate his thoughts and enunciate the word, "what's happening?"

"All secured, sir. Kenton's men are guarding those on the fo'c'sle, Hill has them rounded up in the waist, and Martin has them under guard here on the quarterdeck."

"What about those below decks?"

"Sergeant Ferris and a dozen men are working their way through the ship, sir. The corporal has just reported to me that just about every Frenchman seems to have come on deck when we boarded: didn't want to be trapped below, I reckon."

"You can't repel boarders down below," Ramage said, and immediately regretted such a long speech as the caulker's maul battered his head.

"What about that French lieutenant?"

"He's waiting over there, sir," Aitken said. "Are you ready?" A Marine brought the French officer over. The man, in his twenties, was white-faced but unwounded.

"Captain Ramage," he said in French, "this gentleman – " he gestured at Aitken, " – told me it was you. My captain is dead, so I surrender my ship."

He proffered the sword which he was holding in front of him in its scabbard, closely watched by the Marine.

Ramage shook his head. "Keep it" he said, "you all fought bravely."

"Your head," the lieutenant said apologetically, "I am sorry that one of my seamen…"

"A mere cut," Ramage said, and gestured to the Marine to take the lieutenant away. By breathing deeply, Ramage managed to ward off another wave of dizziness.

He looked round the *Hasard's* decks. Yes, the French seamen were standing in groups, guarded by the *Calypso's* seamen and Marines. Wounded men were still being carried over to Bowen.

"Furl," he said to Aitken, pointing up to the *Hasard's* topsails. "Pass the word to Southwick. Furl, we'll just drift off to leeward."

Drifting off to leeward: that was what he was doing, too, and what he would continue doing until his head cleared.

"There's nothing more for you to do here if you'd like to get back to the *Calypso*, sir," Aitken said. "Perhaps you'd let Jackson put a bandage on your head. It's bleeding badly."

Bleeding? Ramage put his hand up to his head. The hair was wet – but they had doused him with a bucket of water. He looked at his hand, which was covered in blood. He put his hand back at the place where the caulker's maul seemed to be hammering hardest and felt the gash. Several inches long. Already the blood was clotting, drying in tangled hair.

"That Frenchman was really whirling that musket, sir," Aitken said. "You ought to get it cleaned up, sir: it's worrying the men."

"Worrying the men?" a puzzled Ramage repeated.

"The blood's running thick down the back of your neck and over your coat, sir. Some of the men think you've been badly wounded."

"Just a bit dizzy," Ramage mumbled. "But I'll leave you in command here. You're prizemaster."

"Thank-you, sir," Aitken said, standing more upright. "The French dead – we'll bury them here?"

"Have that French lieutenant read a service."

"Ours I'll send over to the *Calypso*?"

Ramage nodded and nearly fell as his head spun again. "I'll read the service for them. Now I'll…" He almost fainted and found himself held up by Stafford and Jackson. "Tell Southwick to furl everything: just lie a'hull."

"Yes, sir, but I'm sending you back to the *Calypso*," Aitken said firmly. "You're in no state to be on deck."

Jackson half-carried, half-dragged Ramage back on board the *Calypso*, and as they manoeuvred him through the gunport they were met by an agitated Southwick.

"Is that the captain?"

"Yes, sir, he's – "

"Wait, I'll get Bowen!"

"Sir," Jackson said firmly, "it's just a head wound. I don't think he'll approve of – "

"No Bowen," Ramage muttered, "my cabin."

Southwick bent down and inspected the wound. "Oh, not as bad as it looks. So much blood, though. Down the back, where he can't see it."

"Yes," Jackson said patiently, "now can we shift him, sir?"

They helped Ramage down the companionway, kicked open the door to the cabin – for once there was no Marine sentry – and finally lowered him on to the settee.

"I'll get a bowl of water and some cloth, sir," Jackson said. "Soon have you cleaned up."

Ramage fainted twice more before Jackson and Stafford had the wound washed clean. Stafford went up on deck to get a bandage from one of the drawers in the capstan head.

After he and Jackson argued how the bandage should be tied, Ramage ended up looking like a pale milkmaid with a scarf tied round her head.

Stafford took a small bottle from a pocket. "I asked Mr Bowen about the cut and he said to give you a drop of this, sir."

"What is it?"

"Brandy, sir."

"Hate brandy," Ramage said, a note of firmness coming back to his voice. "Give me a drink of water and then help me up on deck."

"I don't think – " Jackson started saying hastily.

"For God's sake, this is only a cut!" Ramage said crossly.

On the quarterdeck, in a refreshing breeze, Ramage began to feel better. Southwick had furled the courses, topsails and topgallants but now, with no sails to steady them, the heavy swell waves were making the two frigates grind together.

"Get Hill and Martin back over here, and pass the word to Aitken that as soon as all the wounded and prisoners are across, we are going to cast him off. Oh yes, you'll have about a hundred prisoners. You'll need guards. Tell Aitken to send back fifty men."

"Easier if I go across myself, sir," Southwick said, and bustled down the quarterdeck ladder.

The master was back in less than ten minutes. "I've told Orsini he can come back on board," he reported. "When the poor lad saw you being carried off dripping blood, he thought you were dying, if not dead."

"I'd come back to haunt him," Ramage growled. "Now, is Aitken ready? Right, unhitch those grapnels. Cut them adrift, if you have to; we won't be boarding anyone else today."

Ramage sat down on the breech of one of the carronades. Southwick gave him his telescope and he swept it along the former line of battle. Complete sections were still blotted out by banks of smoke, but British colours above French flew from several of the French 74s. All of Nelson's ships, even the slow sailers, had arrived in the battle, picked their opponents and gone into action. And so had Collingwood's column: there were no British ships to windward of the line.

God, what a battle! He could see that the French admiral's flagship, the *Bucentaure*, was dismasted and her hull badly damaged: masts and yards were spread across the deck as though thrown there by a wilful hand. The gigantic *Santissima Trinidad* was also dismasted, and so was the *Redoutable*, which with the *Bucentaure* had engaged the *Victory*. Nor had Nelson's flagship escaped: she had lost her mizenmast. Many other ships had lost masts, but it was impossible to identify them.

He looked to the northward. Yes, three or four of the leading French ships had turned back as though intending at last to help the centre and rear, but Ramage guessed their hearts were not in it: they were working their way out to windward of the line, while a dozen other ships, both French and Spanish, were making off to leeward, obviously bolting for Cadiz.

Twenty ships? He reckoned that by the time all the smoke had cleared and the gale of which the mare's-tails were warning actually arrived, twenty French and Spanish ships would have been captured or destroyed.

By now the *Hasard* had drifted clear; the heart-stopping grinding of the two hulls had ended, although, with no sails set to steady her, the *Calypso* was rolling so badly that Ramage was having to brace himself on the carronade.

Southwick lurched over, hard put to balance himself against the irregular movement.

"All the prisoners are now safely under guard: I've four men with musketoons watching 'em, too. Bowen says none of our wounded are in a dangerous condition. One o' those Frenchmen you brought out of Brest with Lady Sarah, the one called Louis, had a couple of nasty cutlass slashes, but Bowen's sewn him up. Bowen's starting on the Frenchmen now. Says he has time to put a few stitches in that cut o' yours, sir."

Ramage waved away the idea.

"Sir," Southwick said firmly, "it's a nasty cut and it'll scar badly if you don't have it stitched. It'll scare the life out of Lady Sarah if she sees it..."

Southwick turned away, having played his trump card, and a few minutes later a shaky Ramage came across to the quarterdeck rail. "All right, keep an eye on things while I go down and see Bowen. I'll only be a few minutes..."

Why were his knees so weak, more like the leather hinge on a flail? Nor was it easy to balance himself. He cursed as his sword scabbard caught between his legs. His sword? He remembered slashing at some Frenchman with it, and he was holding it when that fellow hit him with the musket. Well, Aitken or Jackson must have picked it up and put it back in the scabbard. It seemed silly going down to get your head sewn up with a sword slung round your waist.

Twenty minutes later, five painful stitches in his scalp and both stitches and gash hidden by a neatly tied bandage, Ramage sat in the chair at his desk and cursed the weather: already it was becoming gusty, the cloud thickening from the west. Just what Lord Nelson had anticipated in his signal that the fleet was to prepare to anchor at the close of day.

But all those prizes – could they be anchored? With the Spanish coast less than thirty miles to leeward, if the gale lasted more than a few hours most of the prizes would end up wrecked on the beaches...

Aitken had enough men to sail the *Hasard* thank goodness, although none of the admirals would care much about a prize frigate...not with the largest ship in the world, the *Santissima Trinidad*, drifting with no masts...

He listened carefully. The rumble of gunfire was dying down now. The previous summer thunder of massed broadsides had changed to occasional broadsides, like a dreaming dog fitfully growling in its sleep.

There was nothing more for him to do apart from making sure the *Calypso* and the *Hasard* were ready for the gale that would reach them at nightfall. He clasped his head before calling to the sentry: "Pass the word for Mr Southwick."

Before the master could be called, the sentry was announcing: "Mr Orsini, sir, says it's urgent."

The young midshipman was excited. "The commander-in-chiefs flag, sir: it's been hauled down!"

Ramage fingered the bandage round his head. "What do you mean by that?"

"Lord Nelson's flag, sir: it was flying from the mainmasthead of the *Victory* but it's been hauled down. There's just her ensign and the Union Flag that His Lordship ordered all the ships to fly during the battle."

Perhaps the *Victory* was so badly damaged that Lord Nelson had shifted his flag to another ship. He might have called a frigate alongside: Blackwood, for instance.

"Have you had a good look at all the other ships?"

Orsini nodded. "Yes, sir, including the frigates. Vice-Admiral Collingwood's blue ensign is still hoisted at the fore t'gallant masthead of the *Royal Sovereign*."

It could only mean one thing, but Ramage tried to avoid thinking about it. Had Lord Nelson had a premonition about his death? Could that flag halyard have been cut by a shot?

"How long ago did you first notice the flag wasn't flying?"

"About five minutes, sir. As soon as I noticed, I started examining all the other ships, in case he had shifted his flag."

Five minutes: time enough to reeve a new halyard or hoist the flag on another one. If not to the mainmasthead, then from a yard: from anywhere that it could be seen. But this had not been done.

The commander-in-chief's flag had been struck. It seemed that someone (presumably Captain Hardy) had waited until the fighting was finished, knowing the effect it would have on everyone in the British fleet.

Lord Nelson was dead; he must have been killed in the battle. He would never again hear that high-pitched voice with its Norfolk accent: he would never be able to listen to the stream of ideas, plans, orders: never again realize that he was in the company of the most brilliant man ever to wear a naval uniform.

Yet part of his mind rebelled. That little man who was like a coiled spring, who had played with his daughter in Clarges Street and been such a good host, who only a few days ago on board the *Victory* had kept more than thirty captains (and two admirals) spellbound as he had described how he was going to attack and destroy the Combined Fleet – no, that man could not be dead!

He could not be dead so that he never saw how his plan had succeeded brilliantly! He could not be dead before Britain could thank him for saving the country from Bonaparte's invasion. And Lady Hamilton and Horatia... Poor Lady Hamilton was only the great man's mistress, but Ramage had no doubt that Horatia was the daughter of Lord Nelson and Lady Hamilton, for all the admiral's careful references to "my god-daughter".

So Lady Hamilton – he began to accept it all now – had lost her lover and Horatia her father, and Britain her greatest admiral, and every captain in the fleet would mourn a friend, even though some of them had only just met him. And the ships' companies...they would mourn a father.

Orsini was watching him closely, tears in his eyes. "Does it mean...?"

Ramage nodded. "I think so," he said. "I can't think of any other explanation. But watch the *Royal Sovereign*: Admiral Collingwood may shift his flag to the main masthead...then we shall know for certain."

"What shall I say to Mr Hill? He's officer of the deck, and I reported to him: he sent me down to you, sir."

Rumours rushing through the ship… No, he did not want that. Better tell the men what he knew. The more he thought about it the more certain he became. Nelson's good luck had failed him: he was dead at the moment of his greatest victory. Hardy had hauled down the flag. And with the gale blowing up there would be no chance of Admiral Collingwood being able to tell each ship.

"Ask Mr Hill to muster all the ship's company aft – all except those guarding the French prisoners and the wounded."

As Orsini left the cabin, Ramage sighed. He had spoken scores of times to the ship's company: every Sunday at divisions, and often before some operation. But how was he to tell them news which made him want to burst into tears? Lord Nelson seemed to belong to everyone who met him or served under him, and now he had to tell the men (who had so proudly painted in the yellow strake along the *Calypso's* sides, "Nelson fashion") that he was dead. Killed while all around him his plan was succeeding so brilliantly; when his attack had cut off the van from the enemy's centre and rear, just as he had intended…

He buckled on his sword and carefully put on his hat, making sure he did not disturb the bandage. He would go up on deck a few minutes before the men could muster, to tell Hill, Southwick and the rest of the officers of his conclusion.

In this rising wind, would Orsini be able to distinguish if any of the ships had their colours at half-mast? No, they were too far away for that. What should he do with the *Calypso's* colours? Well, he was only *concluding* that His Lordship was dead, and that was all he could tell the men. Leave the colours as they are, until he could get sight of another ship, one nearer the centre of events.

As he prepared to go on deck he listened. The wind was beginning to howl and the ship pitch and roll. Already the *Calypso* had reduced to reefed topsails, having had them set only for a short while, and soon it would be time for storm staysails...

CHAPTER EIGHTEEN

The gale lasted five days: the wind blew from the west as though demented, sweeping dismasted prizes before it to their destruction on Spain's beaches and reefs, while other ships under storm canvas fought to ride out wild and mountainous seas racing in across the Atlantic.

Before the gale broke, Ramage had seen Vice-Admiral Collingwood's flag (the blue ensign, since he was a vice-admiral of the blue) struck on board the *Royal Sovereign* and hoisted in the *Euryalus*, while the mainmasthead of the *Victory* remained bare.

That could mean only one thing, and it was stupid to keep on hoping otherwise: Collingwood's move could only mean that he was now the new commander-in-chief.

But at least, after all these weary days, the storm was blowing itself out. The fleet had not anchored as Nelson had signalled because it was in deep water too far offshore, and whoever was in command (Ramage assumed Admiral Collingwood) had made no effort to get them close inshore, into shallower water. In normal circumstances, ships were better off riding out bad weather in the open sea under sail; but with so many lost masts and torn sails and rigging, not to mention the battered prizes...

Ramage went up on deck and found the wind had dropped considerably. The low clouds still scudded across but they had lost some of the menacing blackness: there was a hint that above the greyness there might be a blue sky.

Orsini suddenly pulled open the binnacle box drawer and snatched out a telescope.

"*Euryalus*, sir: our pendant numbers...213, for captain to come to the admiral..."

Ramage looked across the grey, wave-swept gap between the two frigates. "Hoist out the cutter," he told Martin, who was officer of the deck. "Double-bank the oars. I'm going below to put on my oilskins."

There were eight other ships in sight, apart from the *Hasard*, all rolling and pitching under storm canvas, little more than black clumps on the grey surface of the sea with masts scribing circles in the sky. There was no sign of the other French frigates; those ships in sight were all British, and all had either survived the battle without damage to masts or made jury rigs.

"Not much of a day to go visiting," Southwick commented. "I wonder what he wants?"

Ramage had a shrewd idea: the *Calypso* had attacked an enemy frigate without orders. He had not actually disobeyed any orders from Blackwood in the *Euryalus* but had ignored the possibility there might have been any and, more important, he had broken the tradition that frigates did not get involved in battles between ships of the line. Yes, one could argue that it was the sort of thing that Nelson might have done when he was a junior post-captain, but that was not the sort of argument with which Vice-Admiral Collingwood was likely to agree.

Why did you do it, Mr Ramage? He could hear Collingwood's chilly voice. Well, sir, I'm so pleased with the way the French shipbuilders designed the *Calypso* that I thought the Royal Navy should have another one like her, so I...

Collingwood would (quite reasonably) scoff at that, since it was not true. Very well, tell him the truth: I set out to capture her because my fellows wanted a fight, but the 74s were too big for me.

That way, Ramage knew, would lead straight to a court martial...

Up and down, the bow slicing off spray and sending it hissing across the open boat to run down his oilskins, the cutter rolling and pitching so badly that the men could not help catching a crab with the oars which, the next moment, would be caught in a rogue wave and snatched viciously so that the looms slammed them in the chest.

Every stroke seemed to hold the cutter midway between the *Calypso* and the *Euryalus*, even though the *Calypso* had hove-to to windward, so that the cutter would be rowing to leeward. Ramage held his hat on to stop the spray soaking the bandage round his head. Bowen had promised to take out the stitches later in the day. When he had inspected the wound this morning, as usual sniffing for smells of gangrene, he had declared that there was no sign of trouble: the wound was healing cleanly.

Ah, the *Euryalus* was at last getting closer. In fact he could see a small group of officers waiting at the entryport, and sideboys were waiting to scramble down and hold out the manropes...

It was all a lot of trouble, in this vile weather, just to administer a reprimand to a post-captain so junior that his name was still among the last twenty or thirty on the Post List. Nelson would have waited, but Collingwood was a colder sort of man.

Ramage began cursing to himself. He had left London full of enthusiasm and hope: he had said goodbye to Sarah and his parents thinking (he admitted it honestly) that with any luck he would be returning in something approaching triumph.

But now he would be going back in disgrace: when he arrived in Palace Street and they asked him what had happened (expecting a cheery reply) he would answer that he was due back in Chatham (or Portsmouth or Plymouth) to face a court martial. Perhaps, he thought idly, Admiral Collingwood would instead send him down to Gibraltar to face a trial: there it should not be difficult to muster the five post-captains necessary to convene a court martial.

And now Jackson was rounding up the cutter: the bowman hooked on and Ramage made a lunge for the manropes, jumping on to a batten as the cutter lifted on the top of a swell wave and paused a second. Many an officer arrived on the quarterdeck with his boots full of water because he jumped in the trough and was caught by the next crest.

Up, up, up...he climbed the battens, hauling on the manropes, and suddenly he was at the entryport, with a smiling Blackwood and another man, presumably his first lieutenant.

"My dear Ramage," Blackwood said, "a lot has happened since I last saw you! Congratulations on wrecking that 74!"

Ramage mustered a modest grin and thought: why mention *Le Brave* and ignore the frigate? A hint of what was in store?

"Yes," Ramage said, "he just followed us without looking at his chart. Forgot he drew several feet more!"

"You didn't, though," Blackwood said heartily and waited while the first lieutenant helped Ramage take off his oilskins. "Oh, what happened to you?" Blackwood asked, seeing the bandage.

"Just a cut; a bang on the head, in fact."

Blackwood asked sombrely: "Have you heard the news?"

"Not heard, but guessed. What happened?"

"A sharpshooter hit His Lordship as he walked the quarterdeck with Hardy. He died several hours later. Not in great pain, thank God." Blackwood looked down at the deck. "He *knew* he would be killed. His last words to me before I left the *Victory* were that he would never see me again. He wasn't sad; just a comment, as though he might have been remarking on the weather. Anyway, Admiral Collingwood is waiting..."

"How many?" Ramage asked.

"As far as we can make out, seventeen ships captured and the eighteenth blown up. Just two short of Lord Nelson's target. Not counting your frigate: just ships of the line."

Ramage nodded and followed Blackwood as he led the way to the couch, where Admiral Collingwood was now being accommodated.

The admiral, grey with tiredness, stood up and held out his hand. "Ah, Ramage, I'm sorry to have to bring you over in this weather, but I can't wait any longer. What have you done to your head?"

Ramage said briefly that he had a slight wound, but he felt chilly. Did the admiral regard the *Hasard* affair as *that* serious? With eighteen enemy ships captured or destroyed? What a victory – and, damnation take it, planned by Lord Nelson but with only Collingwood surviving to get the credit!

"By the way," Collingwood said tonelessly, "that frigate you captured. Under whose orders were you acting?"

"Er – well, sir, I had no orders actually to – "

"To break the line?" Collingwood asked.

"No sir. There was a gap, with the French frigate beyond, so I just followed the *Britannia*, and – "

"You just happened to run up alongside this other frigate and she surrendered?"

"Yes, sir," Ramage said, knowing it was hopeless to begin to explain (and not being quite sure even after five days, why he had done it).

"What's her name?"

"The *Hasard*, sir."

"How many men did you lose?"

"Eight dead and seventeen wounded."

"And the enemy?"

"Nineteen dead and thirty-three wounded, sir."

"Ah," Collingwood said enigmatically. He walked over to the desk and sat down. Blackwood, still in the cabin, was staring down at the deck planking, as though fascinated by the grain of the wood.

Collingwood opened a drawer, took out several sheets of paper and shuffled through them. Then he took the cap off the inkwell, wiped his quill on a piece of cloth, dipped into the ink, and wrote a few words.

He then took up the sand dredge, shook some on to the wet writing and, as soon as it was dry, tapped the paper. He then folded it again and gave it to Blackwood. "Have your clerk seal it carefully."

He looked at Ramage. His was not a face that hinted of a friendly nature, and his voice, still with the Northumberland burr, was remote.

"Well, Ramage, you disobeyed – flouted is perhaps the better word – orders: you flouted the custom that frigates do not get involved in the line of battle, going so far as to break through it. And Captain Blackwood tells me that off Cadiz you lured a French 74 on to a shoal where she was wrecked."

"Yes, sir," Ramage agreed.

"You were not acting upon Captain Blackwood's orders then either?"

"The *Euryalus* was too far away to see what was happening, and Captain Blackwood would not have known about the proximity of the shoal, sir."

By now Ramage had realized that the court martial would try him on two counts – both the *Hasard* and *Le Brave*. It seemed you couldn't do a damn thing in this man's Navy without having a senior officer in sight signalling orders...

"Your senior officer is always conveniently out of range, Ramage," Admiral Collingwood said.

But, damnation take it, senior officers in sight or out, I'll wager *Le Brave* and the *Hasard* will be included in the score you report to My Lords Commissioners of the Admiralty, Ramage thought angrily.

Collingwood suddenly smiled. "My congratulations over *Le Brave*. I'll make no comment for the time being over the *Hasard*. However, in my despatch to Their Lordships on the battle I have included your action against the 74, and you saw me write in the details of the *Hasard*."

A startled Ramage stared at Collingwood and then mumbled: "Thank-you, sir."

Collingwood gestured to Ramage to sit down, seating himself at the desk. "You realize that carrying the despatch concerning this battle back to Their Lordships is a great honour, and normally I would have chosen Captain Blackwood and this ship. But I cannot spare him, and when I look round for another frigate I find one commanded by a young junior captain who pays scant regard to orders or custom. However, I have the choice of sending you back with the despatch or court-martialling you, and I really cannot spare five captains for a trial, so you'd better make the best of your way to the Admiralty."

Ramage sighed. "Thank-you, sir," he said, and there seemed little else to say.

"There is one important point," Collingwood said. "The Admiralty must be the first to know – of the battle and the death of Lord Nelson. Wherever you land in England, you will anchor off and have yourself rowed on shore by a trustworthy boat's crew who will return to the ship immediately. Your first lieutenant will allow no one on board or on shore for a suitable number of days, depending where you land. You realize that anyone having this news before the government announces it could make several fortunes in the City of London?"

Ramage nodded. Yes, someone could buy up shares at a low price and sell them high when the market went up on the good news. Consols would leap up...

"And Ramage," Collingwood said, a smile on his face, "you can describe in detail how you stranded *Le Brave*, but I should add some embellishments to the tale of the *Hasard*: some admirals may not agree with the way I've dealt with the matter."

DUDLEY POPE

GOVERNOR RAMAGE RN

Lieutenant Lord Ramage, expert seafarer and adventurer, undertakes to escort a convoy across the Caribbean. This seemingly routine task leads him into a series of dramatic and terrifying encounters. Lord Ramage is quick to learn that the enemy attacks from all angles and he must keep his wits about him in order to survive. Fast and thrilling, this is another highly-charged adventure from the masterly Dudley Pope.

'All the verve and expertise of Forester'
– *Observer*

RAMAGE'S CHALLENGE

The Napoleonic Wars are raging and a group of eminent British citizens have been taken captive in the Mediterranean by French troops. The Admiralty traces their location and sends the valiant Lord Ramage to effect their release. As Ramage and his crew negotiate the hazardous waters off the Tuscan coast, they soon begin to doubt the accuracy of their instructions. Ramage comes to realize that in order for his mission to succeed he must embark upon a fearful and highly dangerous escapade where the stakes have never been higher.

Ramage's Challenge is another action-packed naval adventure from the masterful Dudley Pope.

DUDLEY POPE

RAMAGE AND THE GUILLOTINE

As France recovers from her bloody Revolution, Napoleon is amassing his armies for the Great Invasion. News in England is sketchy and the Navy must prepare to defend the land from foreign attack.

Lieutenant Ramage is chosen to travel to France and embark upon the perilous quest of spying on the great Napoleon. His mission is to determine the strength of the French troops – but his discovery will mean the guillotine!

'The first and still favourite rival to Hornblower'
– *Daily Mirror*

RAMAGE'S PRIZE

Lord Ramage returns for another highly-charged and thrilling adventure at sea. Instructed with the task of discovering why His Majesty's dispatches keep unaccountably disappearing, Ramage finds himself involved in a situation far beyond his expectations. Based on true events, *Ramage's Prize* is another gripping story from Dudley Pope.

'An author who really knows Nelson's Navy'
– *Observer*

Dudley Pope

Ramage's Signal

With Napoleon Bonaparte at the height of his powers, the Mediterranean can be safely considered exclusive French territory. So when Captain Ramage and his crew are sent alone into Mediterranean waters, they can expect to be outnumbered. But it is the French who discover they have an enemy they had not bargained for…

The Ramage Touch

The Ramage Touch finds the ever-popular Lord Ramage in the Mediterranean with another daring mission to undertake. He soon makes a shocking discovery which dramatically transforms the nature of the task at hand. With the nearest English vessel a thousand miles away, Ramage must embark upon a truly perilous and life-threatening course of action. With everything stacked against him, he has only one chance to succeed…